Before she could begin her plea for shelter, she was swept into the arms of a tall gentleman she caught only a glimpse of from beneath her wet hood, although she could not help noticing that his embrace was powerful and not unpleasant.

"At last, my dear! I feared you had changed your mind."

He pressed several poorly aimed kisses upon her snowy hood and endeavored to hold her even closer. Miranda managed to toss back her sheltering hood. The kiss meant for her lips went wild. A man she had never seen before stared at her in disbelief.

"I fear I am not the person you expected."

RENDEZVOUS WITH LOVE

Jane Hinchman

FAWCETT CREST • NEW YORK

CHAPTER 1

One iron-gray day in February, a large, old-fashioned traveling coach splashed along a rough country road in a downpour of cold rain. Inside were Miss Miranda Trafford, her companion Mrs. Shelburne, and her maid Harris.

Mrs. Shelburne lay across Miranda's lap. Her face was flushed and her eyes were closed. Anxiously Miranda applied a handkerchief saturated in cologne to the older woman's forehead.

"Shelly is burning with fever," Miranda murmured to the maid. "Signal them to stop. I must consult with Patrick."

By the time the cumbersome vehicle had slowed to a halt, Miranda had lowered the window and was leaning out, beckoning to her coachman.

"Is the going as bad as it appears, Patrick?"

The grizzled coachman nodded grimly. "Terrible bad and worse to come, Miss Miranda. Snow'll lay a foot by nightfall or I'm a liar. 'Less we get a move on, we'll find no place to bide twixt here and Wayland."

Ignoring the icy wind that blew back her hood and tossed her brown curls into a tangle, Miranda cast a countrywoman's eye up at the ceiling of gray clouds and shook her head.

"We dare not take a chance. Mrs. Shelburne has

1

fallen unconscious. We'll have to stop at the first inn we find and get her into a warm bed."

The old man shuffled his feet stubbornly in the wet mud alongside the road. "Wayland's where your papa always stays short of London, and Wayland it'll be."

"Nonsense! He couldn't know that Shelly would fall ill or that we would run into heavy weather. Just do as I ask and leave it to me to settle matters with Papa later."

With a gloomy shake of his thick white hair, Patrick ceased arguing. Mounting to the box, he gave his handsome team of grays the office to start.

Though where they were to wind up, only the good Lord knew, he ruminated, what with Miss Miranda issuing orders as high-handed as her papa, him who had gone away to Vienna on some business to do with a peace treaty after they finished off Boney and then on to Russia, when by rights he should have stayed home and found a proper husband for his only daughter.

Pretty as a picture and clever, too, Miss Miranda was, he thought as he wiped off drops of sleet from his forehead, but not getting any younger. Sir Henry should have married her off to one of her suitors long ago, whether she would or no. Sir Frederick had always been after her, or there was Squire Hamilton's son or that captain back from the Navy. But no, Sir Henry needed her to manage his household and care for her two young brothers, so nothing at all was done.

Miss Miranda might not have the airs of a London beauty, not with her pink cheeks and untamed curls and sun freckles across her small nose, but when it came to cases, Patrick would bet on her every time.

Full of common sense, he thought as he eased his grays across the rumbling planks of a narrow bridge, excepting times like yesterday. I shouldn't never have let her cozen me into going that far out of our way, never mind if she did want to visit old Nanny Green.

The wind was veering to the west. Patrick lifted his head as he felt the first flakes of snow on his cheeks. It grew thick so quickly that he could not be sure which one of the postillions it was who came trotting back with word that there was a tiny village up ahead.

A sense of foreboding lay as heavily on Patrick's spirit as the accumulation of wet snow on his mustache. Guiding his precious grays with the delicacy of a surgeon, he worried beyond their present trouble to whatever was to come when they finally reached London.

Miss Miranda was not the sort to bowl over a parcel of dandies, nor she would never be happy flitting about to routs and balls, her as had managed Templeton the same as a man and been a mother to those two young scamps of brothers after her mama died of the cold in Russia.

But her papa had sent word that she must finally have a London season. No good will come of it, Patrick thought. Miss Miranda will never make a London lady, nor I wouldn't love her the same if she was.

The village lay dim behind curtains of snow by the time they approached. Babb's Crossing, the postillion shouted. At the Happy Angler tavern, Patrick himself climbed down and beat on the door with his whip handle.

From inside the coach, Miranda listened in disbelief as a harried innkeeper made it plain that there were no rooms to be had. She let down the window and cried, "Sir, my companion is desperately ill! You *must* let us have a bed for her to-night!"

"There ain't so much as a corner to spare, miss. The stable's already full and others waiting to sleep on the tables once supper's cleared."

"Is there no house in the village to take us in? I will pay well."

"Not as I know of that would suit the gentry. If you're in a bad way, I advise you to drive on to the manor. Nobody lives there except a housekeeper and her girl and a nevvew that's not right in the head, but what with forty rooms in the place, might be there's beds left from the mice."

"Where is the owner?"

"Lord Wendover, he's soldiering abroad, miss."

Miranda made a quick decision. Any roof was better than none under the circumstances. With a plea to the innkeeper to get word to a doctor, she shook snow off her hood and said, "Follow his directions, Patrick. We've no time to spare."

The snow now fell as thick as pudding. Twice one of the rear wheels slid off the road, but Patrick managed to prevent his nervous team from panicking until, after thirty anxious minutes, they arrived at a pair of sagging gates which stood open and proceeded up an avenue that might once have been graveled but now deteriorated into a washboard of half-frozen mud.

As they rounded a curve, Miranda made out a large structure looming up darkly through the snow. When the coach came to a stop she saw that only one narrow window showed a light.

Harris, who reveled in gloom, whimpered that she was sure they would all be murdered if they dared go inside.

"We'll die of cold if we stay out here," Miranda reminded her, although she felt far from optimistic herself.

Patrick, climbing down from the box stiffly, came back to speak to his mistress. "I don't like the look of things, Miss Miranda. You stay inside and leave me to deal with this."

"I had best apply to the housekeeper myself. She won't turn away a woman on such a night, whereas you look as fearful as a highwayman with your mustache all frozen. Have Ebbets let down the steps, please."

The snow lay an inch deep already. Clutching her hood close against the wind, Miranda mounted two shallow stone steps and came to a halt before a forbiddingly massive oaken door. Her feet were soaked in her light traveling slippers and a dismal shiver ran down her spine as Patrick raised a clamor with his whip handle.

All went silent inside. What if the place was vacant after all? Miranda pulled her hood lower to keep the snow from sticking to her eyelashes and made up her mind that if no one answered, she would simply have to break a window and enter.

"Hark," Patrick growled.

Miranda, too, now heard the sound of footsteps approaching rapidly. She stationed herself close to the door. "If I put my foot inside the moment they open up, they can't very well turn me out," she whispered to Patrick.

He heard the smile in her voice. It was like Miss Miranda to find some humor in the worst situations, he thought.

The latch lifted with a screech, as if it needed greasing. Then, to Miranda's amazement, the door was flung wide so suddenly that she almost fell inside. Before she could begin her plea for shelter, she was swept into the arms of a tall gentleman she caught only a glimpse of from beneath her wet hood, although she could not help noticing that his embrace was powerful and not unpleasant.

5

"At last, my dear! I feared you had changed your mind."

He pressed several poorly aimed kisses upon her snowy hood and endeavored to hold her even closer. Growling like a watchdog, Patrick rushed to Miranda's aid just as she managed to toss back her sheltering hood. The kiss meant for her lips went wild. A man she had never seen before stared at her in disbelief.

"I fear I am not the person you expected," she apologized, suppressing a smile at his chagrin with some difficulty. "We are travelers in distress. My companion, outside in the coach, is gravely ill. I beg you to lend us a place to sleep this night."

A pair of candles stood on a table near the door. Not even their feeble light could dim the splendor of the gentleman's appearance. Miranda got an impression of hair and complexion of the same tawny color, and of strong, perfectly even features accented by surprising black eyebrows above the bluest eyes she had ever seen.

And the coldest. He retreated into the hall as if he meant to close the door in their faces.

"This is not an inn. The tavern at Babb's Crossing will serve your needs."

Miranda stiffened. Small and tired she might be, but she had a way of standing up to people that made Patrick proud.

"I never imagined it was an inn, sir! I believed it to be the residence of a gentleman. Since it is plainly not that, we will leave at once."

Her unwilling host appeared to hesitate. "There are no servants in the house except a caretaker and her family. I regret to seem inhospitable, but I am only passing through and will be gone by tomorrow."

"I have my own servants with me. I ask only that

you lend us rooms for the night. We can provide our own linens and food."

He looked beyond her into the white curtain of snow. "I am sorry. It is not convenient to admit strangers to the manor tonight."

Miranda's temper rose from simmer to boil. Ignoring Patrick's hand on her elbow, she blazed away at the spoiled town dandy in his exquisitely tailored blue superfine coat—which was now spotted with melting snow from her hood, she was happy to see—who was so ignorant of country ways that he would leave a party of travelers to freeze on a winter night in order to keep some sort of tryst.

"Sir, I do not ask, I *demand* that you allow us to hire such rooms as my party needs for the night, at any price you care to name. You cannot in decency turn away travelers in such a storm!"

He should have been insulted at being offered money. Instead the blue eyes regarded her in a speculative, half-amused fashion.

"You may hire the entire estate—after tonight."

"But we need rooms now!"

"Perhaps, if you give me your promise to remain above stairs, you can find beds in the west wing. I am expecting a guest, you understand."

Patrick drew Miranda aside urgently. "There's something havey-cavey about this, Miss Miranda. I don't like it, that I don't."

"Neither do I. Go out and see how Shelly does. If she is at all improved, we'll drive on to Wayland."

The coachman departed with a worried backward glance. The owner of the manor—if he was that person, which Miranda had begun to doubt—offered her a chair covered in threadbare tapestry near a deep hearth where no fire had burned for a long time. The great hall echoed eerily to their footsteps. Ancient beams bisected the vaulted roof. Trophies and bits of armament from past generations hung against dark, paneled walls. Miranda shivered.

"Permit me to introduce myself," the gentleman said with a slight bow. "I am Lord Wendover, owner of this crumbling pile of masonry."

"I am Miss Miranda Trafford, on my way to London to meet my father."

She saw him measure her from beneath his dark brows and judge her a country chit, quite beneath his touch.

"Do schoolgirls know anything of a code of honor? If so, I beg you to forget that you saw me here tonight."

"But word is bound to leak out in such a small village, is it not?"

"Not until we . . . until I am safely away to the Continent. After that you may lease the manor for as long as you wish. Forever, preferably. Do you happen to have five hundred pounds with you?"

"Good heavens, of course I don't! I can spare a hundred, but you will have to trust me if you require more."

"A hundred must suffice, I suppose." He got up and went toward the door as Miranda watched.

He is planning an elopement, she decided. If he had behaved with ordinary courtesy, she might have sympathized with him since he appeared to be deeply in love, but as he was a perfect stranger and abominably rude, she felt that he deserved whatever befell him.

Before he reached the door, it opened from the outside. Patrick and Tom Groom entered carrying the slack figure of Mrs. Shelburne. Lord Wendover took one look at her and ordered the men to follow him.

Traversing a long, dim corridor, the little procession came at last to a room lined with books, which, though shabby, was warmed by a bright fire. Several branches of candles lighted the room, and near the fireplace stood a table covered with a fine linen cloth and laid with silver for two.

The men lowered Mrs. Shelburne onto a sofa. Miranda knelt beside her, loosening her bonnet strings and endeavoring to make the unconscious woman comfortable.

The door opened soon after to admit a plump, gray-haired woman wearing a white apron. She dropped a curtsy to Lord Wendover with a sidelong look of curiosity toward Miranda's group.

"Mrs. Curry, these persons will be staying in the west wing tonight," Lord Wendover informed her tersely. "Please see to preparing rooms for them."

"The rooms'll have to wait till we set the dinner, my lord. The bird's done to a turn and Mag and Mudd waiting to serve, though we didn't expect as my lady was to bring other company with her and the bird only enough for two, my lord."

"This is *not* the guest I was expecting, Mrs. Curry." Her host's handsome face was a study in impatience. "I will dine later, after they are settled. Are there any decent beds available in the west wing?"

Mrs. Curry bristled, her crisp gray hair appearing to curl even more tightly. "Indeed there's aplenty, all aired regular the way your own mama liked, God rest her poor, sweet soul."

"Then go along and see to it, but first send Mudd with more wine."

Watching the little scene unfold from where she knelt beside Shelly, Miranda realized that her host was deep in his cups and oblivious to affairs other than his own. It was not until Patrick gave a rude snort that Lord Wendover roused from his unhappy reverie and spoke.

"I regret that I cannot invite you to share my supper, Miss Trafford. Mrs. Curry will send you a

9

tray after you are settled. Your servants will find something to eat in the kitchen. These are matters you will understand when you are older."

"I shall be four and twenty in June, Lord Wendover."

He stared at her as he poured the last of the wine out of a Venetian glass decanter with an unsteady hand. "Do not take me for a fool. You can't be a day past sixteen."

She and Patrick started to speak together but were interrupted by a knock at the door. Outside stood Harris, sniffling and twittering. Surrounding her were the footmen and the two postillions and a mountains of trunks and parcels and baskets, as if they meant to take up permanent residence in the manor.

Lord Wendover gave one incredulous look at the cavalcade and went for the bellpull, which came away in his hand. He threw it across the room with a violent gesture.

"Never mind," Miranda soothed automatically. "I'll have my servants put all in train if you do not object."

"Do what you must. Your first business must be to get your companion into a bed. She looks gravely ill."

Lord Wendover tossed down his wine and paced the length of a worn Turkish carpet, turning his tawny head from side to side for all the world like a captive lion, Miranda thought, aware of a stirring of pity. How sad that love should have brought him to such straits.

Mrs. Curry appeared and guided Miranda's party back along the dim passageway, across the great hall, and up a staircase to the west wing, where she opened doors upon a spacious suite which she said had once housed Queen Anne for a night.

Miranda had sent Patrick and Ebbets to make up

fires in both bedrooms. She settled Mrs. Shelburne inside a monumental bed hung with dusty patterned damask curtains that made her sneeze when she drew them close to prevent drafts from reaching her companion.

As she knelt by the fire to warm a soft bit of flannel to place on Shelly's chest, Miranda wondered whether the expected lady had arrived yet and thanked fortune that she herself was too sensible to suffer from the kind of unruly emotion that caused Lord Wendover to behave in such an irrational fashion.

It was not that she didn't know a great deal about love. Having mothered her two brothers for seven years had taught her that love could bring pain and sorrow as well as deep satisfaction, yet at no time had she been driven half out of her wits as Lord Wendover appeared to be.

While Harris was off in the adjoining room unpacking the needful for Miranda, a stout thump on the door announced the entrance of a young country girl who carried a tray in a pair of large, red hands.

"I'm Mag, miss. Ma says you're to have the remains of Lord Wendover's roast chicken, and only one leg ate by him, miss! Milord, he ain't in appetite." She put down the tray with a clatter of cutlery, her large face red with excitement. "Ma says as how she expected a real London lady 'stead of a little girl with her chaperone."

Miranda examined the tray closely to hide a smile. "Your mama is quite right. I am not the lady who was expected. I have never heard of Lord Wendover nor visited this part of England before tonight." And never will again, she vowed mentally, if I can avoid it!

"Ma was sure you was the wrong lady, seeing as how Lord Anthony looks to marry an heiress, and

11

none too soon, either. Lor', miss, I beg pardon. My tongue flaps like a loose shutter, Ma says."

"It's true I'm not the heiress Lord Wendover expected, Mag, but my pockets are not entirely to let. If you will take this and find some way to get word to a doctor, I shall be grateful."

Mag bobbed a curtsy as she stole an awed look at the gold piece Miranda gave her. "Lor', Miss, I never had one of my own afore! The doctor? He'll never come tonight. Snow's up to the scullery door and ice under. Is there anything more I can do, miss?"

"See that we have plenty of hot water, please. Have you food in your larder in case we're forced to stay here for another day or two?"

"Not much to speak of, miss. There's flour, and Ma's got her hens, and plenty of turnips."

"Have your mother unpack the baskets of provisions we brought and serve them as far as they will go. We'll buy whatever we need in the village if we stay."

"Yes, miss. If there's aught to buy, miss," Mag muttered mysteriously as she departed.

Aware of icy drafts flowing through the windows despite the heavy damask that draped them, Miranda wrapped her shawl tighter and settled close to the fire to eat her supper. The chicken leg scorned by Lord Wendover, although somewhat cold, tasted good. She sampled the white meat but prudently left most of it for the morrow, satisfying her appetite with the bread stuffing and a large helping of woody turnips.

Harris returned from below stairs complaining that she was coming down with a cold which was sure to turn into lung fever. Miranda sent the maid to bed, and after dosing the half-conscious Shelly with a tisane of the herbs she carried in her kit of remedies, she got into her bedgown and clambered

12

into the huge old four-poster beside her companion in order to be at hand if the fever worsened.

Outside, the wind alternately purred and screamed, and the cold intensified. A sense of foreboding kept Miranda from sleep.

Trust Papa to start home from the Continent in winter and demand that his daughter arrive in London ahead of time to prepare a house for him! She shouldn't have been surprised. Papa was handsome and charming, but there was no denying that he was selfish.

Of course she was fond of him and willing to assume the responsibilities he had put upon her, but this time it wasn't so easy. Here she lay in a strange house, miles from her destination, with a desperately ill companion to care for and no one to depend on but Patrick.

Unless one could count on Lord Wendover. However, he had said he would be gone by morning, so she dismissed him from her mind as another of Papa's sort, handsome, demanding and undependable.

CHAPTER 2

It was Harris, sniffling woefully as she brought in the breakfast tray, who wakened Miranda and her companion the next morning.

"Where are we, Miranda?" Mrs. Shelburne inquired faintly.

"Somewhere near Babb's Crossing, in a rather neglected old manor house." Miranda reached out unobtrusively to feel Shelly's pulse. "Are you more the thing this morning? No, don't try to sit up! It's cold and you have a fever. I'll help you to take a little warm broth."

"Later this morning, Miranda, when I feel stronger, please ask the lady of the manor to visit me so that I can thank her for her hospitality."

"I believe she is from home. The snowstorm, you know. However, there is a housekeeper who seems quite respectable." Under no circumstances must Shelly discover that there was a gentleman in residence with no sign of a wife or aged parent to mitigate matters.

"I am feeling too ill to make decisions, Miranda," Mrs. Shelburne gasped after a few sips of broth. "You will have to get word to your papa somehow."

Her voice trailed off and fever clouded her dark eyes again. Hearing her ever dependable companion begin to ramble incoherently, Miranda fell into an uncharacteristic panic.

"Harris, we must have a doctor for her now, at once!"

"Miss Miranda!" cried the scandalized maid. "You don't mean to go below stairs in your dressing gown, not with a strange gentleman in the house!"

"I only hope he is still here! Someone must fetch a doctor as soon as possible."

But after she had run down the two flights of stairs and reached the frigid great hall, Miranda hesitated, aware that she had no idea of the geography of the manor. Where would she find Lord Wendover's rooms?

As she stood undecided, a door opened down the corridor and that gentleman himself emerged clad in buckskins and boots beneath a caped greatcoat. His face was somber and he raised his eyebrows as he approached Miranda, as if he had forgotten who she was.

"Lord Wendover, I beg you to help me!"

He gave her a wary glance as he pulled on a pair of heavy gloves. "I am leaving for London at once. If you have a message, I shall be glad to carry it for you."

"Mrs. Shelburne must have a doctor. You saw for yourself that she is dangerously ill."

"Yes, I believe she is," he agreed, "but God alone knows where Rob Purvis may be at the moment— sitting with a sick cow or delivering a set of twins. However, as I have to stop at the vicarage, I'll leave a message with his father." He sketched a slight bow and made for the door.

As he pulled it open, a cloud of wind-driven snow-flakes flew in and engulfed him. After a second of hesitation, he plunged down the steps through heaped drifts toward a pair of dim figures standing by his horse. Miranda ran to the door and watched him go.

"If it was me, my lord," she heard Patrick say in his most wheedling tone, "I wouldn't be risking a fine bay like this here fellow, not on a day like this. There's a sheet of ice under the snow, my lord, and no footing at all."

"Omar will get me through. Mudd, give me a hand up. I've business in town that won't wait."

The snow fell like paste. Miranda, straining her eyes, lost sight of Wendover's dim figure almost at once after he mounted.

"Patrick," she called. "Come inside before you catch a chill. I need to talk to you."

The old coachman stomped up the shallow steps and came to a stand before her, shaking off the snow like a sheepdog.

"That's a brave 'un, but foolhardy. I doubt he'll reach Wayland, leave alone London town."

Either brave or too besotted to care what becomes of him, Miranda thought before she dismissed Lord Wendover from her mind.

Shivering in the drafty great hall, which was not much cozier than a hilltop on the moors, she poured out her worries to Patrick. He soothed her with a promise to make up, himself, a wee small poultice, about the size for a foal, which he was sure would help to draw the humors from Mrs. Shelburne's lungs.

"As soon as possible, please, Patrick. But there is more. If we have to stay on here because of the storm and her fever, we are bound to run out of food quite soon."

Patrick cogitated, rubbing his long nose.

"There's wood aplenty, so we won't freeze, and still some provisions left in the hampers we brought from Templeton. We can hold out for another day or two. By that time things may be better."

"I hope so." Miranda was about to inquire whether the grays had suffered from their hard pull through the storm when the door burst open to admit, Mudd, Mrs. Curry's nephew. He was shaking, and his speech, which was almost unintelligible normally, came out in so garbled a fashion that Patrick had to ask him twice what the trouble was.

"Him. G-gone down . . . by the gates . . . bad hurt . . ."

Patrick shed half his years in a second.

"Go fetch a hurdle of some sort, and be sharp, lad. Miss Miranda, you set Mrs. Curry to find blankets to wrap up the master. Send Ebbets to help carry the litter. I only hope that fine bay ain't broke a leg."

Miranda found Mrs. Curry and Mag placidly peeling turnips in the kitchen. Under her direction, they soon got a bed made up afresh in a large, shabby suite of rooms where the remnants of a fire had only to be built up and an empty wine bottle carried away to make it ready for Lord Wendover.

Mag put a pair of bricks to warm. Mrs. Curry hastened back to her kitchen to prepare a hot drink. Panting heavily, Patrick, Mudd and the footman carried in a shutter upon which lay Lord Wendover in an unconscious state.

While they transferred him to his bed, Miranda sent Mag running for spirits of ammonia. It was she who was bent over him administering the restorative when he came to a dazed wakefulness and stared at the odd company assembled around his bed.

"Am I dying?"

Mrs. Curry spilled the mulled wine she was carrying. Mag began to sob.

"Of course you're not dying," Miranda said sensibly. "You've had a fall, that's all. Omar slipped on the ice."

"What are *you* doing here? Who are you?"

Considering that she had paid him a hundred pounds and got nothing in return save the loan of some cold beds and a chicken leg, Miranda had to force herself to be charitable.

"You . . . er . . . took us in during the storm. I am leasing your west wing. My coachman and my footman carried you inside."

Comprehension flickered across his handsome face. He made a move to rise. Miranda saw him go white, though he stifled the groan that rose to his lips.

"I've damaged my right leg."

"Patrick is of the opinion that it is broken," Miranda said bluntly. There was no time to waste. "He is a genius with broken bones, better than most physicians. Let him examine you and then we'll know how to go on."

"If I must. Ladies, kindly leave the room."

Mag giggled her way out after Miranda. "Called us ladies, Lord Anthony did. What do you want we should do now, Miss?"

"Find a bottle of your best brandy and bring it here. Lord Wendover will need it soon."

Miranda paced up and down the corridor after the housekeeper and her daughter departed. She wished for a shawl to wrap around her shoulders over her dressing gown but did not dare to desert her post until Patrick emerged finally from the sickroom.

"Broke, just as we thought, Miss Randa."

"Can you set it? It may be another day or two before the doctor comes."

"I could but I dassent, not with him a stranger and a lord."

"What will happen if it is not set soon?"

"He could be crippled. Or if it swells up more and putrifies, he could lose the leg and maybe his life."

18

"Come along with me and tell him what you think. He should be rational enough to make a decision, but if he isn't, I will assume the responsibility."

Upon being applied to with a bald version of the situation, Wendover fell silent. After a moment, he directed a searching look from beneath his thick dark brows, first at Miranda and then at Patrick.

"Let me have you opinions, and be frank."

"To wait very long will put you in danger," Miranda said, "but if you think Mudd can find your doctor and bring him back by nightfall, the choice is yours to make."

"Patrick?"

"You were jolted bad, my lord. The leg is already swelled up. If 'twere a horse, I'd shoot him, but you being human, I'd put the bone back in place as quick as I could."

The black eyebrows rose higher and the ghost of a smile touched Wendover's lips.

"I honor your judgment, Patrick. Do what you must. Quickly."

"I'd better send Tom Groom along to help," Miranda planned rapidly, "and you'll need Ebbets as well. Mag is bringing brandy, and I have linen for bandages and remedies for pain in my kit as usual, Patrick. Better send Mudd to fetch wood for a splint."

Patrick drew Miranda away from the bedside and shuffled his feet uncomfortably. "I don't like this, Miss Randa. Your papa—"

"Isn't here to help, as usual. I don't like it either, but we must do what we can for him."

With a vast sigh the coachman returned to his patient. Miranda hastened up to the west wing in search of such remedies as would be needed. She found Mrs. Shelburne awake, her cheeks stained red with the fever. The older woman tried to raise

19

her head off the pillows when she caught sight of Miranda.

"We must leave this place at once," she declared. "Harris tells me that Lord Wendover is in residence. To stay under this roof for even a night is to jeopardize your reputation beyond hope!"

"Harris?" Miranda accused sharply.

"She kept asking, Miss Miranda," the elderly maid whined. "I couldn't quiet her without telling."

Miranda had to take a deep breath to control her temper.

"Mrs. Curry needs you in the kitchen, Harris. There has been an accident. No, nobody is dead, although I find the notion very appealing at the moment. Go along now, quickly."

After the door closed behind Harris, Miranda perched on the side of the big bed and endeavored to soothe her companion.

"First you must lie back, Shelly. Then I promise to tell all. There, that's better."

She went on to explain about the snowstorm and how she had paid to lease one wing of the manor, doing her best to make an amusing tale of their plight, but Mrs. Shelburne appeared to grasp only the dangers of their predicament.

"Tomorrow," she repeated over and over. "We must leave here tomorrow somehow."

"The roads will not be open, Shelly. We really have no choice. With luck, perhaps the day after tomorrow," she coaxed.

Mrs. Shelburne seized Miranda's hand painfully. "Tell me the truth, dear. Has Lord Wendover made advances?"

Miranda could not contain her laughter. "He kissed me. Unfortunately, his aim was poor and it landed on my hood. He mistook me for someone else and dropped me like a hot chestnut when he had a good look at me. He is convinced I am no more than sixteen."

This news appeared to relieve her companion. "That is fortunate, but while I am less feverish, it is my duty to warn you that the Wendovers are notorious for their vices."

"Are they? Which vices?" Miranda inquired with interest.

"I am not sure, only that I have heard Wendover House in London spoken of as a gambling hell frequented by disreputable people."

"Lord Wendover does indeed seem reckless. However, you needn't worry about him at present. He will be imprisoned in his room for a considerable period with a broken leg."

Mrs. Shelburne, normally a kind person, leaned back with a happy smile on hearing of the accident to their host. She even consented to have her face bathed in tepid water and to drink all of the concoction Miranda had made up for fevers.

"But you must promise me to have no dealings with that evil man," Shelly insisted as her eyelids began to droop.

"Do you think me so foolish as to be taken in by him?"

"Since you have not gone about yet in fashionable society, you know nothing of the subtle tactics gentlemen of his sort are skilled at using to ruin innocent females. How glad I am that he is tied to his bed!"

Miranda sat beside her companion until she fell into a deep sleep before going to her room next door to wash and put on a warm woolen gown over a flannel petticoat.

She found it easy to dress without Harris' help since the day she had been forced to cut short her thick brown hair, although she had wept and worn a cap for weeks after a fall from her mare caused her to have several stitches set above her left ear.

While he stitched, old Dr. Williams had scolded her roundly for taking a fence not even her brothers had dared try. Tears had run down her cheeks, but she clenched her fists and endured in silence, taking care to keep her eyes shut until he finished.

"Lucky you're still alive!" the good man had declared gruffly. She peeked up at him from under thick, wet lashes and was astonished to see his eyes suspiciously shiny. "You're needed here at Templeton, Miranda. I don't want to think what would have become of Charles and Edgar without you."

She was touched and at the same time annoyed. "Am I valued only because I am useful?"

The doctor blew his nose and started to repack his kit.

"You are recognized throughout the county as an excellent sort of female. What more do you want?"

It was true she had a host of friends among both her neighbors and the tenants on the estate. Of course it was gratifying to know that one carried one's share of burdens with grace and fortitude, and she did love her brothers and was loved in return.

Still, observing Lady Minshall at the local assemblies, she had often thought it must be a happier fate to be born a beauty. With only a smile or an occasional insipid remark, Lady Minshall somehow managed to command the attention of all the gentlemen in her orbit.

She herself was not downright plain, Miranda decided as she smoothed the folds of her travel-creased gown. And she didn't care what the wicked Lord Wendover thought of her. Yet she did wish that she had brought along in her travel luggage at least one of her newer gowns.

Not that it mattered, now in this time of crisis. Tense with worry, she tried to busy herself with the arrangement of her medicine kit until Patrick knocked on her door at last to let her know that the job was done. Finger to her lips, Miranda tiptoed down the corridor, out of Shelly's earshot, to confer with him.

"Poor Patrick: you look so tired! Was it bad?"

"Bad enough, but a clean break. We got it straight and splinted. It'd already swelled up something fierce, so I made a pack of snow for it. Lord Wendover said as it helped. He's a gentleman, that I'll allow. Never so much as groaned, only asked for a towel to wipe off the sweat and give me a proper thank you when it were done."

"Then I suppose there is still a grain of decency left in him in spite of his vices."

"Vices?"

"Shelly tells me that the Wendovers are famous, or infamous, for a variety of sins she refused to name for me. I am forbidden to have any dealings with him."

"Well now, that won't do. He asked to talk to you later, after his man gets him cleaned up and ready for visitors."

"His man?"

"Wibberly, my lord's valet. A little shriveled-up, yellow-faced fellow what was supposed to get here last night with a lady and her maid, from what I overheard. Wibberly won't say more than that the lady never came to the meeting place."

"How did Wibberly manage to get here through the storm?"

"On foot from somewhere south of Wayland, where a farmer set him down. Said as how he'd walk through H ... the hot place if his lordship needed him. Nigh froze when he came in and no wonder, dressed in town clothes like he were. I made him take a tot of brandy, but I don't doubt he'll come down with a cold."

Miranda sighed, and leaned for support against the smoky wood paneling. "Counting Wibberly, there are now thirteen of us marooned here. Three need a physician, and Mrs. Curry tells me her supplies of flour and sugar are already running low. If you can find Mudd, you had best send him to the village to buy whatever there is for sale."

"He'll never get through today. Mebbe tomorrow." Patrick began to shuffle, always a sign of perturbation. "You've no need to worry yourself, not with me here, Miss Miranda."

"I'm not afraid of anything except illness. Why should I be?"

"If I had known about Lord Wendover being a rake—"

Miranda's comfortable chuckle bubbled up. "Oh, Patrick, I'm as safe as the Tower what with you and Wibberly and Ebbets and Tom Groom to protect me. Especially as Lord Wendover has shown nothing but distaste for my presence!"

Patrick lingered, glowering. "That's 'cos he don't know you yet, nor ever will if I have my say. Handsome he is and a gentleman, but he's not for the likes of you."

"I've been pursued by gentlemen before now, Patrick."

"Maybe, but you take a soldier has fought on the Continent, and what he don't know about making up to females hasn't been writ. I wouldn't trust him an inch around a pretty girl like you."

"Thank you for the compliment. You're usually sparing of them. But you needn't fear. While you may not trust Lord Wendover, you can be sure of *me*."

"I hope so, Miss Miranda," the coachman replied gloomily. "Excuse me now whilst I see to my grays."

Miranda watched him walk away toward the

24

stairs with his familiar rolling stride and thought it was like him to attend to his beloved horses before he allowed himself to rest.

Since childhood she had felt a deep affection for him. It was Patrick who had put her up on her first pony. He had shown more concern over her childish scrapes and ailments than Sir Henry had ever displayed when he was at home briefly between diplomatic assignments.

In return, Miranda had taught Patrick his letters, which he had been forbidden to learn in his native Ireland. Patrick had never married. Perhaps he had spent so much love on her and her brothers that he had nothing left to give a family of his own. Miranda sighed, thinking how unevenly love was parceled out between human beings.

She had just returned to her own room when Mag, pink with all the excitement, brought a summons from Lord Wendover.

"Wibberly says within the half hour, if you will be so kind, miss. Ma and me, we wonder what become of the lady he were to bring with him."

"It's not surprising that she feared to travel through this storm," Miranda pointed out kindly. "Was Mudd able to get through to the village?"

"He only just got as far as the gates, Miss, and he were half-froze when he came back."

Miranda straightened her collar. "Ah, well, the snow is sure to stop soon and we can send off to Wayland for supplies."

"Yes, miss. Snow don't go on forever. Only, when wind's out o' the west it do come down and down till we're near buried. After maybe another Sunday it'll melt away."

Miranda stopped short at the door. Two more weeks of snow? Impossible! Like Harris, Mag probably enjoyed making dire forecasts.

Wibberly was waiting to admit her to the shabby

apartment of his master. The valet, not much taller than Miranda, bore himself like a soldier. He had dark, patient eyes in a long face topped off with thinning, mouse-colored hair, not at all a man to notice in a crowd, yet Miranda felt an instant liking for him.

"I do hope you haven't taken cold, Wibberly," she said with her friendly smile. "I've brought along a kit with my old nurse's remedies, so if you feel unwell, don't hesitate to call on me."

She noticed that he had done his best to make the rooms comfortable for his master. The curtains were partially drawn and he had placed a table convenient to the bed on which sat a decanter of wine along with a dish of biscuits, a pile of books, and a stack of mail that looked like tradesmen's bills.

Lord Wendover lay against a heap of pillows looking exhausted, though scrupulously barbered and wearing neat bandages over the gash on his forehead and the cut on his left hand, his splinted leg propped on a pillow beneath a light coverlet.

Wibberly went out with a bow. Wendover's dark blue eyes were bleak as he watched Miranda approach, not with resignation but with a kind of angry hopelessness, she saw with surprise.

"I understand you wished to see me, Lord Wendover."

"It seems that I owe you and your coachman a debt of gratitude. I regret deeply that I am now become a burden on you. Please accept my thanks."

"Pray do not let it weigh on your spirits, my lord. Patrick and I did no more than we would have done out of charity for any creature in distress."

The dark eyebrows flew up. "Were you expecting tears of thankfulness? If so, I shall try to oblige!"

"Not at all, sir. I was surprised at your expression. I have seen the like only once before, when I dressed the paw of a fox I freed from a trap."

He scorched her with a bitter glance. "You are very sure of yourself for a girl still in the school-room, Miss Trafford."

"I have been out of the schoolroom these seven years, since I was sixteen. My mother died during a visit to Moscow with my papa. As he could not come home, it fell on me to supervise our estate and to rear my two younger brothers."

"Was there no one to help you?"

"Mrs. Shelburne. Without my companion I would have been lost. And I have an elderly steward and a solicitor whose advice I take sometimes."

"There should have been a male relative to lend you a hand."

"There was my Uncle Bracebridge. He informed me that he was too nervous of constitution to endure a week, much less a season, in a country house with two rampaging boys."

"Bracebridge?" Wendover smiled. "I know him. Separated from his clubs and his tailor, he would perish. Your mother's brother?"

Miranda nodded. "Her only one, and he never married. There is an aunt living. Aunt Louisa married a Russian prince and has come home to England only once. Now, if you have finished interrogating me, sir, I must return to Mrs. Shelburne."

She saw his fist clench on the coverlet. "If you were in my command, I would teach you manners in a hurry."

"I am generally known as a pretty-behaved young lady, but of course, everything depends on the company I keep. It is only when I am insulted that I allow myself to give back as good as I get!"

"Which you do amazingly well. I owe you an apology if I sounded brusque. A soldier falls into the habit of command."

"*Sounded* brusque?" Miranda had been sitting in

27

the large, deep-cushioned armchair Wibberly had placed for her. She started to rise but discovered to her chagrin that she had to push herself upright with her hands on the arms of the chair, like a small child. "Lord Wendover," she said, her face hot, "you have been downright rude. Let us both pray for an early end to the snow so that we may be released from a thoroughly unhappy situation."

Wendover had watched her maneuvering herself out of the chair with interest. Now he gave her a disarming grin. "It was your own idea to lease the manor. With your spirit I'm surprised you didn't drive on to Wayland."

"I wish I had. There I could now be happily scolding the landlord for indifferent lodgings instead of being scolded by you."

She turned in a sweep of blue skirt and made for the door.

"It is hardly Christian to rub salt into my wounds, Miss Trafford. I did at least share my supper with you last night. Does a roast chicken leg count for nothing?"

Miranda hesitated, secure in her righteousness and yet unable to help smiling over the chicken leg, for it had been more like a whole chicken, and thoughtful of him. Later she knew it had been a mistake to turn back, for she happened to see him grimace with pain as he lay back against his pillows.

"I am sorry to sound like a virago, Lord Wendover. I *did* enjoy the leg and even a slice of the white meat. I thank you for your kindness."

"Since you have paid for your lodgings, you need not elaborate. No point in tossing pearls before a swine."

Miranda could not repress a ripple of laughter. When she saw her host smile in return, she said impulsively, "We are idiots to quarrel when we are

28

marooned here together. If you will stop behaving so swinishly, I promise not to be shrewish—if I can help myself."

"Agreed. Your charity puts me to shame."

"So it should," Miranda responded smartly, and left the room without looking back so that she did not see him smile as he watched the small young woman depart in a whirl of blue skirts.

CHAPTER 3

Miranda finished an indifferent midday meal of boiled egg, a slice of the ham she had brought from Templeton, and turnips, and went across to her window. There she scratched away at the ice to make a peephole and gazed with awe at the increasing blizzard outside. A wild wind whipped up fast-falling snow into curving, frothy ridges for all the world like waves so that the manor appeared becalmed in a vast ocean of white.

Harris entered at her back, sniffling and complaining of indigestion.

"For I never could abide turnips, Miss Miranda, as you well know. If we don't freeze to death, we may well die of wind in the stomach. The doctor has come at last and is busy attending Lord Wendover as if he's the only one ill in this unhappy place."

"I had better go and talk to the doctor while you waken Shelly and prepare her for his visit."

Miranda ran lightly down the stairs and came to a halt at the closed door to Wendover's rooms. Having no desire to intrude, she went back to the great hall and sat down to wait, hugging her shawl around her shoulders, until the doctor should emerge.

She had been sitting there long enough to notice

that her feet were numb with cold when she saw Wibberly come and out and walk a few steps in the direction of the kitchen. Suddenly he staggered and leaned against the wall. His shoulders quivered as if he might be weeping.

"Wibberly, what has happened?" she cried, running to his side. "Has the leg begun to putrify?"

"No, miss." Under the hand she had placed on his arm urgently, she could feel him shaking. "It's the ague has come on me again. I'll be better with something hot to drink. I must be better. Lord Wendover needs me now."

"Take my arm and let me help you. I've seen these fevers in men back from the war. It will be a few days before it runs its course, but you're not to worry about Lord Wendover. I have four menservants with me who will assume his care."

The kitchen, around a bend in the passage, was the friendliest room in Wendover Manor. A pot emitting delicious aromas hung over a hearty fire in the vast fireplace. In the center of the long, low room stood a table with benches along both sides, and a pair of cupboards held bright pottery plates and an assortment of pewter pieces. Mudd, Mrs. Curry's nephew, sat hunched over a basin of soup. At sight of Miranda and Wibberly, he stumbled to his feet and bobbed a stammering welcome. "M-m-miss . . ."

"Mudd, will you help Wibberly to a seat by the fire? Where is your aunt?"

Before Mudd could articulate any words, Mrs. Curry came hurrying in from the scullery, followed by Mag. Both of their hands and arms were covered with feathers.

Miranda stared in dismay. "Oh, I do hope you haven't slaughtered your hens! How will we manage without a breakfast egg!"

"It's not hens was killed exactly," Mrs. Curry re-

31

plied. "That's to say, not chicken hens. As there has been far too many pheasant in the fields, what with Master Anthony off at the war all these years, I says to Mudd, look at them birds strutting around like they own the place and people going hungry inside! So Mudd, he catched us dinner, and there's a plenty more out there waiting to be served up."

"Well done, Mrs. Curry! See here: poor Wibberly has fallen ill and we'll want the doctor to see him as soon as he has finished with Mrs. Shelburne. Meanwhile you might give him a cup of soup, as hot as he will drink it."

She left to keep her vigil outside Wendover's door. When the doctor emerged at least, Miranda, who had been expecting to deal with a country surgeon of doubtful skill, was startled to be faced with a stocky, firm-chinned man of perhaps thirty years who demanded to know where his other patient was to be found.

"There are two more patients, if you are Dr. Purvis."

He gave a short laugh. "Who else would come to the manor through a blizzard? Wendover informs me that you were forced to stop here when your companion fell ill. If you were in truth on your way to London, it is strange that you happened to be in this area," he remarked suspiciously as he followed Miranda up the angled staircase.

"Not so strange. We made a detour to visit my old nanny in Hopewell," Miranda replied coolly.

They found Shelly tossing about in her vast bed while Harris fussed helplessly with her pillows. Banishing the maid, the doctor ordered Miranda to help him partially disrobe the sick woman and proceeded to give her a painstaking examination.

"Her lungs are badly invaded," he pronounced at last. "She should not have tried to travel in her condition."

32

"She seemed perfectly well when we left Templeton four days ago."

The doctor threw Miranda a challenging look. "No doubt she feared to mention her indisposition to you."

Miranda returned his look steadily. "Mrs. Shelburne is not dependent on me for her livelihood. She companions me because she is fond of me, strange as that may seem to you."

The doctor, who had begun to measure out a liquid, paused, gave her a half smile, and had the grace to say, "You seem to be a very capable young woman."

It was annoying, Miranda thought, to be considered freakish simply because she didn't fall into spasms when trouble arose.

"You will find Wibberly in the kitchen," she said when the doctor finished giving her instructions for the care of her companion. "He appears to have the intermittent fever so many soldiers brought back from abroad."

"Leave your maid with this patient and come with me," Dr. Purvis ordered. "You'll need to know how I want Wibberly cared for. When did his fever develop?"

She explained the situation as they went down together to the kitchen, where they found poor Wibberly still sitting huddled in a settle close to the fire, shaking with chills. Dr. Purvis issued orders, made up a draft which the valet managed to swallow with Miranda holding it steady, and sent Mudd and Mag to prepare a bed with extra blankets and a hot brick.

Obeying the doctor's instructions, Miranda followed him back to the great hall. Her admiration for his skill had grown in proportion to her annoyance at his dictatorial manner. He gave her several packs of medicine with terse instructions for their uses.

"I do not like this at all," he said, folding up his bag. "Is there no older woman I may rely on to help with the nursing?"

"Only Mrs. Curry, and she has too much to do already. Like it or not, you will have to depend on me."

"Like it I do *not*. What was your family thinking of to let a young girl go jaunting around the countryside alone?"

"I am far from alone. There are seven in my party, and we would have gone to any lengths to avoid this county had we known that you are prone to snowfalls that would put Moscow to shame."

"Still you must realize that it is not at all the thing for a young, unmarried woman to stay in this house unchaperoned."

"Nothing would make me happier than to escape! Only tell me how soon I can travel with Mrs. Shelburne."

"It depends on the course of the fever. I had intended to leave for London myself tomorrow, but now I shall have to wait."

"Do you practice in London and have come here on a visit?"

"No, I am going to take further training. My work here has taught me how little I know about medicine."

"We have not really advanced very far beyond Galen, have we?" she murmured, ignoring his surprised glance. "Please tell me what more I can do, beyond your doses, to help my patients, Dr. Purvis."

"Give them as much hot, nourishing food as they will take. Above all, keep their spirits up."

Miranda's smile broke out. "It will require more than a pheasant poached in wine to lift Lord Wendover out of the doldrums. I fear he has suffered a romantic setback."

Dr. Purvis, by now muffled in a heavy coat, turned sharply at the threshold. "Has he confided in you?"

"Everyone in the household knows that a certain Lady Trent was to have arrived last night. Lord Wendover's disappointment when he found me on his doorstep, instead of the lady, threw him into such a temper that I have barely had a civil word from him."

The doctor laughed. "I know Anthony's temper from childhood. We studied together with my father at the parsonage. In his defense I should say that Anthony's life was never easy. His mother, after her first two children died, smothered him with affection. Then she succumbed to a crippling form of rheumatism while he was still a lad. As if that were not bad enough, his papa immediately wed an impossible female who drove the foolish old fellow into early senility before he was fortunate enough to die."

"I am sorry for Lord Wendover. However, the accident was his own fault. He would not listen to reason."

Dr. Purvis gave her a keen glance out of observant gray eyes.

"Still, I must ask you to try to keep his spirits up. He is more restless and feverish than I like."

"Of course I will do whatever is necessary."

He put his hand on the latch and hesitated. "I have never met a young lady quite like you, Miss Trafford."

"We are not all of a kind, even though you gentlemen like to categorize us in groups by age or beauty—or lack of it."

He shrugged as if he admitted himself bested.

35

"Good day, Miss Trafford. You convince me that I leave my patients in good hands. Your servant."

The bow he gave was creditable, Miranda reflected as she fastened the door after him. He was no simple country doctor. As she mounted the stairs to go back to Mrs. Shelburne, she could not help marveling at the odd company she had fallen among in this out-of-the-way place.

Some time later, Miranda was busy in the kitchen overseeing the preparation of an herbal broth for Shelly when Mudd erupted from the pantry, a grin on his square face, which normally looked as if carved out of a block of wood. Holding out the pink carcass of some small creature with a proud gesture, he indicated that it was a present for Miranda.

"What is it?" she asked, suppressing a shudder, for the thing looked almost human.

"It's pig, miss," Mrs. Curry informed her firmly. "He won't look the same when I get him roasted with apples, though it won't be till tomorrow that I can get him done proper."

Miranda sank down on a bench beside the long table. "I can wait. Do I smell bread baking? There's nothing I'd like better now than a hot slice with a bit of butter or jam."

Mag hurried away to unwrap a fresh loaf. Miranda ate two slices with the appetite of a healthy young woman and inquired when the pheasants would be done.

"Master Anthony says as how he'll dine at eight."

"Then you may cut me two more slices of bread. I'll take them to Lord Wendover while my herbs are brewing. Dr. Purvis says he'll need cosseting until he can move about again."

"Ladies shouldn't ought to carry trays," Mag reproved.

"But you're needed to baste the birds. Only hold the door for me, if you will."

Miranda knocked and was admitted by Patrick. She discovered Lord Wendover looking hot and furious in his confinement. With an expressive roll of his faded blue eyes, Patrick excused himself.

After Miranda deposited the tray within Wendover's easy reach, she chose a chair on the other side of his tester bed.

"You must be uncomfortable. Nothing could be more natural. You're bound to be in pain still. I learned the secret of survival when I broke my arm at the age of twelve. It is vital to keep one's mind occupied. Shall I read to you?"

"My eyes are not damaged, thank you, though if I have to lie here much longer, my brain may be."

"What a pity if you are sent off to Bedlam just now when your estate seems in need of your attention. Who will inherit when you go?"

"An avaricious cousin who is welcome to it. I would do better to go back to my regiment."

"Do you find your greatest happiness in soldiering?"

"It is all I have known since I left Oxford." From angry brooding, his mood changed. "There is more to war than killing. The comradeship is more satisfying than the shallow friendships a man makes in London."

"Is not war a great gamble?"

"I found it worth the risk. A man learns to value the simplest pleasures when he knows he may die tomorrow."

He closed his eyes and Miranda noticed that he was very pale beneath the permanent tan that living out-of-doors had colored his complexion.

"Shall I leave you alone?"

He gave her a sudden, startlingly blue glance. "If

it is to be a choice between you and Patrick, I choose you. I am not well enough to listen to another of his sermons against vice tonight."

Miranda bent over the tray to hide a smile. "I brought you hot bread and jam. I hope you like a nursery tea. I'll come back later when you're finished."

"Don't go. Pour the tea for me and tell me about yourself. Why has your father left it so late to give you a season?"

"I could not be spared from Templeton. Now that Charles and Edgar are both gone off to school and Papa has finished remapping the Continent, he has remembered his duty to me, I suppose."

"Are they very studious boys?"

"Charles is bookish and brilliant. He goes up to Oxford in the autumn. Edgar rides like a centaur and dances beautifully but hates to study. However, he is handsome and charming, like Papa, so perhaps he will become a diplomat too. If I fail to make a match this season, I shall retire and prepare to serve as hostess for Edgar in Paris or Rome someday."

Her eyes were unusually luminous, Wendover noticed. He couldn't decide whether they were gray or green, but he did observe that they seemed very clear and bright, as if candle flames glowed behind them.

From judging her a pleasant country girl, he began to wonder if she was not something more. Not a beauty, for she had neither the carriage nor the dignity required, but there was a natural, friendly way about her that made one overlook her undistinguished nose and slight figure.

"Your father obviously intends to see you betrothed this season, Miss Trafford. Will you be content to marry the man he chooses?"

"Indeed I will not!" He had to smile at her fiery

response. "If it is a man I can respect—perhaps. Then again, perhaps not."

"What will you do if you do not like his choice?"

"I shall set up household with Mrs. Shelburne and become an acid-tongued aunt to Charles' and Edgar's children."

Her frank manner amused him. "I find it hard to believe in a young female who has never been moved by a handsome face or charmed by a fine bass voice into thoughts of marriage."

"I learned my first lesson in the most painful way. At seventeen I nourished a·fatal attraction toward my brothers' tutor. He was just twenty-two and he wrote sonnets to me."

Miranda's hands lay demurely in her lap, but Wendover observed the pucker that caught at the corners of her lips.

"The sonnets did not scan?" he hazarded.

"They scanned perfectly. It was only after the twentieth time of hearing that my eyes glimmer like forest pools at dawn that I caught myself yawning."

She shot a glance at him from under her short, thick lashes and, catching him smiling, exchanged a wicked grin with him.

"You are incorrigible, Miss Trafford. No proper young lady ever speaks her mind in the company of a gentleman. If I were a different sort, I might misunderstand you."

"But you are not different. I trust you—at least so long as you are confined to your bed."

Wendover leaned back against his pillows and laughed in spite of the pain it caused him. Miranda chuckled with him, pleased that she had helped him forget his troubles, at least temporarily. But he soon sobered.

"I wonder if you realize the difficulty of our present situation. I am now *your* tenant and I cannot return your money until my steward rises from his sickbed and brings me the funds that were due me on the night you arrived. I hope you will be kinder to me than I was to you."

"I have no plans to dun you." Relieved to know that he was not a pinch-penny, Miranda noticed that he was looking drained and that there were hollows beneath his eyes. "Have you taken anything to ease your pain?"

"Brandy. I shall be better after a night of sleep."

"I doubt if you will sleep without help. I have a potion with me that is infallible. After you've had your dinner, I will bring you a dose."

"It will take more than the poppy to keep me sane until this confounded leg mends. I am already deep in the dismals."

"Do you enjoy cards? We might pass an hour or two at the table, if you like."

"Cards are pointless unless there is a wager set."

"I agree. I will make counters. Whichever of us owns the most when we are finally set free will owe the other—what? A hundred pounds? Five hundred?"

"Do you often gamble for high stakes, Miss Trafford?" he asked, amused.

"Rarely on cards, although when one of Patrick's horses is running, I have him place a fair sum for me. However, if you prefer not to chance your luck with me—"

"The cards are in my desk. If you will move your chair closer and clear away the tray, we can begin."

Tom Groom, arriving with Lord Wendover's supper some time later, was surprised to find Miss Trafford and the injured gentleman laughing together, for until now he had considered milord a dour sort.

"That's a hundred and twenty counters for me," Wendover said cheerfully to Miranda. "Oh, dinner already? Too bad; just when the cards were beginning to fall your way, Miss Trafford."

"Don't pretend to be sorry," Miranda retorted as she gathered cards and counters and arranged the table so that the dinner tray was within easy reach. "There: do enjoy your meal. Mudd went to a great deal of trouble to catch it for you."

"Must you leave? Tom could bring a tray for you. It is confounded dull to dine alone."

"It's time I attended to my other patients, but I'll come back with your sleeping potion."

"In time for another game of piquet, I hope."

"I'm afraid that would be too exciting for an invalid late at night. We can resume our game tomorrow."

He watched her go regretfully. The chit was good company, even though she lacked the polish and charm a man expected in a young girl. If, as now appeared likely, they were to be prisoners of the storm for longer than another day or two, he owed it to her to advise her on the ways of society before she arrived in London and was declared an antidote. At the least he could give her the names of the best dressmakers and shops for millinery and other frippery, thanks to having visited those establishments with Lady Trent.

Though Miss Trafford might not be able to afford the best. Her gown, which became her, nevertheless was not in the latest mode.

Her father should have settled her long ago before she acquired her independent ways. Now the very fact that she had perforce to spend some time at Wendover Manor was certain to cause trouble for her when she reached London.

He scoured his list of acquaintances for possible escorts he might introduce to her. Howells might do. True, he was a widower with two young daughters, but Miss Trafford would make an excellent mama for them.

The more he thought about the possible match, the better he liked it. Not only would he repay Miss Trafford, but provide his old friend with a suitable wife as well.

CHAPTER 4

Snow continued to fall, just as Mag had predicted. Although fevers and tempers sometimes flared, Miranda managed to keep her ill-assorted company as content as possible under the circumstances.

Shelly grew neither better nor worse, hovering in a feverish limbo. The footman, Tom Groom and the postillions made themselves useful feeding fires in the many fireplaces and helping to wait on the bedfast.

Lord Wendover began to look forward to their daily card games at which he had drawn ahead by some four hundred counters, but at the evening chess games, they were even. Dr. Purvis paid regular calls and seldom had any fault to find with Miranda's nursing. On the surface, all was as well as could be expected.

Still, by the fifth day, Miranda was driven to search out Mudd in the kitchen and beg him to venture forth into the drifts after whatever food he could find.

"They's n-naught in t-the village," he mumbled.

"Maybe one of the tenants has a bit of ham he's willing to sell. Even another bag of pheasants will hardly feed thirteen people, and our poor little porker was gone in a day."

Mudd said something to the effect, if she heard

43

right, that milord always had a fondness for mutton and he would see what he could do. If there was a shifty look in his eye, Miranda forbade herself to consider it. She had given him plenty of money to buy whatever he could find.

Next she repaired to Wibberly's room and was relieved to find that his chills had subsided temporarily. She sat down on a low chair beside his cot and folded her hands in her lap.

"Since you have served Lord Wendover throughout his campaigns, Wibberly, you know him better than anyone. Don't you think it would relieve his mind if you got word to the ... the person who was to have met him here?"

"That won't be possible, miss."

"The ... person might have arrived at Wayland if the post road is open."

"The person in question, miss, never left London," Wibberly said repressively.

Miranda ran her fingers through her short curls distractedly. Like a little girl, Wibberly thought, though if there lived a kinder, more sensible lady, he had never met one. It was a wonder she had not fallen ill herself, what with the burdens she took on her shoulders cheerfully. He resolved to relieve her of those cares as soon as he felt able to get about again.

She was looking at him with a perplexed smile.

"Then how are we to keep Lord Wendover quiet until his leg has time to heal, Wibberly? I can't go on letting him win at cards much longer without his getting suspicious."

Wibberly's lids flew up and she caught a glint of understanding in his eyes before he lowered them respectfully. "He reads, miss, and he always enjoys a rousing bit of argumentation."

Miranda's chuckle brought a flicker of answering appreciation to the valet's thin face.

"*That* I can manage quite easily. I seem to arouse his combative instincts." She rose and tucked in his coverlet with deft hands. "It must be hard on him to be weather-bound in the country when he is accustomed to a rakish way of living."

"I don't deny that a soldier lives a rough life, miss. Milord could never put up with losing one of his men. After a battle he dipped deeper than most, and it wasn't my place to blame him. He was one of the bravest, but he never enjoyed the killing like some did."

"I see. Why did he stay in the Army, then?"

"To get away from his home, miss. His father turned against him after he married Lady Jessamin. His men became his family, and most would have died for him if it came down to it."

"Lord Wendover is fortunate, Wibberly. Goodnight. I'll send Ebbets along soon to help you wash and shave."

Miranda stopped next outside Wendover's door. She gave a double rap and was bidden to enter.

Inside she discovered Tom Groom snoring peacefully in the big armchair by the dwindling fire while Wendover leaned at an awkward angle against an untidy heap of pillows in an effort to catch enough light from a single candle to read the book in his hands.

"Tom! Wake up, Tom!" Miranda had to shake her groom's shoulder to rouse him. He was a wonder with horses but hopeless with people. "Lift Lord Wendover up a bit while I give these pillows a good shake. There, that's better. See if you can find more candles while I clear off the table."

When all was tidy and the fire mended, Miranda sent Tom to the kitchen to fetch a hot drink.

"Plato?" She riffled through the book, which had

45

slipped to the floor. "I would expect a soldier to be studying Caesar's campaigns instead."

"What do you know of Plato—or Caesar, for that matter?" he rallied with a smile. "At your age you can only have read fashion papers or wept over romantic novels."

"I've done both, but while I had to oversee my brothers' studies I couldn't help absorbing something of them. There, another candle should give you enough light to read comfortably. I have come to report that Wibberly is doing well and Shelly is no worse. Now that you are settled, I shall leave you to rest."

"I'm not settled. If you want the truth, I'm not the stoic I thought I was. If you have it to spare, I would not object to another sleeping draft tonight."

"Is the pain very bad?" she asked anxiously.

"Bad enough. Even worse is having to lie here and contemplate the mess I seem to have made of my life. When I get back on my feet I may sell out and leave England."

"But the manor is your home! This is where you belong."

"It's been more than ten years since I lived here. It was such an unhappy place after my mother died that I was glad to escape into the Army."

"You're very truthful."

"You're not the sort one wants to lie to."

"Since you cannot lie, tell me why you were reading Greek philosophy."

"I'm not sure. Tied to my bed like this with more time to reflect than I have ever had before, I am trying to understand why I have become what I am and to make plans for the future. In the unlikely event that I ever take up my seat in the House of Lords, I would wish to be prepared to state my views."

"You should have gone up already. A man who

knows war at first hand has valuable experience to offer."

"Who will listen? When I left London they talked of nothing but the latest scandals."

Miranda gave him her teasing smile. "Perhaps you went looking in the wrong drawing rooms."

He leaned up on one elbow painfully with an answering smile.

"Halt! Don't say what trembles on your lips. In future I promise to seek out only wise men and to avoid the fashionable London salons."

"What a shame. That means that I shall miss your maiden speech, and you will miss my come-out." Seeing that she had stirred him out of his lethargy as she intended, she gathered up her skirt with its demitrain and made for the door. "Now I must fetch your medicine."

When she was gone, he found himself wishing for her early return. She was a good sort of girl to have around when one was ill. The man who married her was bound to live a comfortable, contented life. Perhaps she was too clever for good old Howells. If she had a respectable dot, Bettinger might be a better match for her. He was a bit scatterbrained, but on the whole he was a decent fellow and he was nearer to Miss Trafford in age.

He was lying still, staring at the ceiling morosely while he added up his own years to thirty-two and realized that his own youth was gone, when Miranda knocked and darted in, her face glowing with color above the high neck of her unfashionable garnet gown.

"You're breathless. Is something wrong?" he asked, alarmed.

"No more than usual. Since it is impossible to go outside, I flit through the halls for my exercise. I find it quite as healthful as walking in the shrubbery, and at least my feet are dry."

47

He drank off the bitter concoction she handed him, thinking that she looked exceptionally pretty for a rather ordinary girl. Miranda, seeing him glance at her and make some judgment, turned away.

"See, I have brought you pen and paper in case you want to take notes as you read." She made room for these objects on the table at the far side of the bed. "The ink leaves much to be desired, as I found it almost dried-up and had to revive it, but it is better than no ink at all."

"You are very thoughtful. When do you make your bow, Miss Trafford? Has a date been set?"

"In his last letter, which came a week before I left Templeton, Papa spoke of mid-May, but I shan't know for sure until we reach London."

"I wish I could be present. It's not likely that I'll be fit for dancing yet, but I can make myself useful as a spare escort."

"Do you expect that I will lack for partners? Am I likely to be labeled an antidote?"

"Of course not. Any man of sense is bound to appreciate you for your friendly manner and your capabilities."

Her short nose, so unfortunately lacking in Grecian symmetry, wrinkled as she gave a rueful smile. "Since you informed me earlier that the gentlemen you know in London are anything but sensible, I had best not hope for too much. I have no acquaintance in London, though Papa does."

"A father's friends are seldom useful."

"And my brothers' are too young."

"Then you may count on me, Miss Trafford. There is a way I can repay you for your goodness. When I know the date of your first appearance at Almack's, I promise to gather up a brigade of my old comrades in arms and instruct them to fill up any slack in your dance program."

48

"Shall I like them, do you think?"

"Not all of them, perhaps. Several are of ripe years, one limps, and another is deaf from the effects of a cannonade, but at a first assembly, quantity is sometimes as important as quality."

They were laughing together when Patrick entered with Tom Groom to prepare Lord Wendover for the night. It was beneath Patrick's stern gaze that Miranda bade her host a demure goodnight and departed for her own apartment in the frigid west wing.

Miranda wakened another morning to a world of dazzling sunshine. It was even colder than it had been, however, and she hurried to cover Mrs. Shelburne with the fur rug from the coach, for Shelly looked pale and feeble in the pitiless light.

"How long have we been here, Miranda?" Mrs. Shelburne had drunk a little of the broth Miranda coaxed her to take, and now she fell back against her pillows. On hearing that it was the eighth day, she grew disturbed. "You must get word to your papa at once. He will be beside himself with worry."

"I have already written a letter and Jem volunteered to try to get through with it. Lie back now, dear, and I will read to you."

Some little time later, after Mrs. Shelburne had fallen into a doze and Miranda was on her way to the library to hunt for a book Wendover wanted, Ebbets caught up with her, his carefully blank footman's composure disturbed.

"There is a Lady Wendover to see you, Miss Miranda."

"Are you sure it is not Lady Trent?"

Before she could say more, a dashingly dressed woman of late middle years surged down the passage and clasped Miranda in a plump, perfumed embrace.

"I am come to welcome you to the bosom of our family, dear Lady Trent, naughty though it was of you to marry my Anthony by special license! You may count on your new stepmama to hush up any gossip."

Freeing herself with some difficulty from bonnet strings and extravagant drifts of fur, Miranda stood back and regarded her visitor with an effort at friendliness.

"Much as I regret to disappoint you of a daughter, Lady Wendover, I must tell you that I am not Lady Trent, nor have I wed Lord Wendover. In fact, I never saw him before last week."

"Not married!" Anguish distorted Lady Wendover's neat, small features which must have lent her a kittenish beauty when she was a girl but which now showed a distinctly cattish set. "Shame on you then, to take up residence in the abode of an unmarried gentleman!"

"Do please follow me into the library, where there is a fire, and let me explain how my stay here came about. Ebbets will bring us refreshments."

After an indecisive moment of pouting, Lady Wendover agreed with a cool nod. As she shed her costly fur pelisse into Ebbets' hands, it was evident that she possessed an opulent figure under her rich velvet gown. One could almost understand how old Lord Wendover had found her a tempting armful, Miranda reflected charitably as she helped the lady to a seat close to the fire.

But she saw varying expressions of doubt, displeasure, and finally of suspicion flit across Lady Wendover's face as she recounted the story of the storm and her own decision to find a bed for Mrs. Shelburne instead of trying to reach Wayland.

"I'm no pea-goose, Miss Trafford," the lady declared coldly. "It's plain as my nose that you've come here after Anthony. I've known of gentlemen compromising young girls, but this is the first time any decent young lady deliberately put herself into such a situation."

"But I swear to you that I never saw your son before in my life!" Miranda cried.

"Don't try to gammon me, my girl. I know a female on the catch when I see one. I wasn't born yesterday."

Many, many yesterdays ago, Miranda thought angrily, though she managed to restrain her temper.

"Why should I pursue Lord Wendover, madam, when it is known everywhere that he is in Dun Street?" she inquired coolly.

"He has the title and he is a handsome boy, I always said, above even Lord Byron, who is inclined to put on flesh." Catching herself, Lady Wendover composed her tiny features into an icy air of disdain. "Have a room prepared for me at once, Miss . . . Trafford? I cannot go away and leave my dearest son in the grip of a scheming nobody."

"Perhaps you should speak with Lord Wendover before you come to a decision. As I have tried to make clear, he is confined to his bed and in a vile temper."

"I was always able to tease him out of the sullens. I will go to him at once. There is no need for you to come along. The manor is my home, hateful though it is."

Miranda said nothing but followed discreetly as the plump woman rose to her feet and trod unsteadily across the room and along the hall, the elegant flounce of her gown lifted slightly to show a glimpse of morocco slippers with gilded heels. Lady Wendover did not hesitate long enough to knock at her son's door but surged in and rushed over to him, giving little screams of dismay on catching sight of his splinted leg propped on pillows.

51

"My poor, poor boy! It breaks a mama's heart to see you in such a pickle. Oh, how dreadful you look. But do not despair. I am come now to take care of you myself."

By the time Wendover succeeded in escaping from her octopuslike embrace, his face was thunderous and his mouth grim, although he managed to speak civil words of welcome.

"Please do not put yourself to any trouble for my sake, Lady Jess. My housekeeper is quite capable, and Miss Trafford's menservants take excellent care of me."

"The scandal, Anthony! Tongues will wag when it becomes known that you are keeping a strange young female under your roof."

"Lady Jess, you must understand that it is *I* who am a guest in this house. Miss Trafford has entered into a contract to lease the manor from me."

"I don't believe it!" Lady Jessamin sank into a chair beside the bed and poured herself a glass of wine from the decanter at her elbow, which she drank down all at once. Then she eyed Wendover coldly. "So you've not got a feather to fly with, as usual? What's the use of your going off to get shot at if you can't bring home a proper bit of loot, I'd like to know!"

"Surely you would not have me behave dishonorably, Lady Jess," Wendover protested with an ironic flicker of his eyes toward that lady.

"Only if you was sure not to get caught."

Miranda, standing in the shadows near the hearth, happened to catch Wendover's glance and could not avoid exchanging smiles of mutual irony with him at this evidence of his mama's greed. That lady, sharp of eye, swung around to stare Miranda up and down.

"Too bad you are not an heiress, Miss Trafford, or you might have got your way. We could easily

52

have called in the parson and tied the knot before there was time for the scandal to get out." She shrugged. "But a country miss will never do for a Wendover. Anthony, you will have to get that leg fit for dancing and come back to London before the season ends. This time you may leave it to me to pick out the lady."

Lady Wendover had knocked her bonnet wildly askew in her assault upon her prone stepson and in the process revealed a mass of ringlets of a striking orange shade. Poor Lord Wendover, thought Miranda—he will need to find a very accommodating heiress to put up with such a stepmama.

"Kindly forget your matchmaking schemes, Lady Jess," Wendover ordered coldly. "I have no intention of marrying. I can't afford to."

"But you *must* marry, Anthony. Your poor papa would turn in his grave if you got yourself killed in battle and left that Scottish cousin to inherit. He might turn me off without a penny!"

Miranda met her host's eyes again. They were both perilously near to laughter.

"Surely you don't expect me to wed simply for your convenience, Lady Jess. But I'll do this much for you. I have put it in my will that you may inhabit the dower house during your lifetime."

"That horrid, damp place! You know I cannot endure the country, Anthony. I am only happy in London."

"I am sorry to hear that, for I can no longer afford to maintain you there in the style you presently enjoy."

"But you will soon marry," Lady Jess cajoled. "It is early days to despair, dearest boy. If Lady Trent does not come around, we will find you another heiress. You may count on me."

Noting the hot flush of anger that rose to Wendover's hollow cheeks, Miranda hastened to intervene.

"You are still young and handsome yourself, Lady Wendover. It seems most likely that you will marry first."

"Not if I'm buried in that poky dower house," Lady Jess declared hotly. "I'm like to mildew along with the carpets before I ever find a rich gentleman in Babb's Crossing!"

"Of course it would take time to make the house fit to live in," Miranda agreed smoothly. "And the weather at present is most disagreeable. I have no doubt that you will want to return to London at once, lest the snow begin again."

"Oh, no I won't, not while you're in this house, Miss Trafford. You can't flummox me that easily."

Lady Wendover set her sharp, pointed little chin forward aggressively. Wendover looked ready to rise from his bed and order his stepmama from the house. He was still in pain and slightly feverish, and not up to dealing with this odious female, Miranda decided.

She rang for Ebbets. "You are kind to offer your services, Lady Wendover, but I fear I am not able to entertain guests at the present time. You will understand, knowing that I have three people ill in the house. Another time, should I continue to lease the manor, I shall be glad to offer you hospitality."

Lady Jessamin's cheeks flushed furiously beneath her rouge.

"Anthony, are you going to lie there and let that chit insult me?"

"I have tried to make it clear to you that I am only a guest in this house."

"I have never heard of anything so disgraceful. Letting out the manor that's been in the Wendover family since the Flood, almost!"

The erstwhile lady of the house dabbed at her

eyes with a handkerchief trimmed in pink lace and lamented the sorry state of the Wendover fortunes, as well as her own foolishness in having married a man twice her age who had left her practically penniless. As she ranted, her temper rose and her grammar suffered. Wendover turned away on his pillows contemptuously. Miranda felt thankful to see Ebbets when he finally answered her ring.

"Lady Wendover is just leaving, Ebbets. Order her coach at once, please, and have Mag bring a packet of wine and biscuits to sustain her until she reaches Wayland."

"You will suffer for this indignity, miss! The second I reach London you may count on me to set the word about that Miss Trafford is a scheming hussy out to trap my poor, crippled son into marriage!"

She got to her feet unsteadily and marched out of the room without bothering to bid goodbye to Wendover, who watched her departure in grim silence.

Miranda followed her into the great hall, where Mag presently appeared bearing the required packet and a bottle of wine.

Lady Jessamin eyed the wine, then turned on the girl.

"I am surprised that your mama allows you to remain in this house, my girl."

Mag's eyes opened wide. "It ain't what it used to be, Ma says, and we never gets paid, but it's a roof over our heads."

"You and your mother should have nothing to do with this young female. She is out to catch your master. She is no lady, I promise you."

Poor Mag knitted her shaggy brows. "I know she's only a miss, but Ma and me, we think she's as good as any lady even if she ain't got the handle."

Patrick stomped in with word that the coach

waited. Milady had better make haste if she hoped to reach Wayland by nightfall.

Miranda followed the older woman to the door. "If you truly care for your son's welfare, Lady Wendover, I hope you will not spread unpleasant rumors about him. He will not like it, nor will my father, Sir Henry Trafford."

"Sir Henry . . . ?" The lady was daunted, though only momentarily. "He is only a baronet from the country with political pretensions. I have heard of him. Farewell, Miss Trafford. Let us hope we do not meet again, for I could not bring myself to speak to you!"

Patrick watched her go before he turned to Miranda.

"What has that wicked creature done to you, Miss Randa? I never saw your face so white."

Miranda managed a faint smile. "She declares I am a scheming hussy who came here to entrap Lord Wendover into marriage."

Patrick shook his head toward Mag, who hovered in fascination. "Go back to the kitchen, girl. You're not needed here now."

Mag showed signs of objecting until Miranda urged her to obey.

"I'll go if it's you says I should, miss, but don't you let anyone bully you. Ma and me and Mudd'll stand up for you, that we will! And if you was to marry milord, we'd be that glad!"

Miranda sank down on the same decaying tapestry-covered chair she had sat on that first night when she arrived at the manor. It was just as cold now as then, or perhaps a little colder, she reflected wryly, and if she had been in difficulties then, they were multiplied now.

Patrick leaned against the stone mantel and she saw him make an effort to control his temper. It seemed that everyone was angry at her for a variety of reasons, most of them beyond her control.

"The roads opened yesterday, Miss Miranda," Patrick informed her heavily. "There's nothing to keep us here longer."

"Patrick, I *dare* not leave Shelly until her fever peaks. That will happen at any time now, according to Dr. Purvis. If it does not break, she will die."

Patrick shuffled. If there had been candles alight, Miranda knew she would have seen tears in his eyes.

"Aye, you're right. Not but what it's too late anyhow. That so-called lady that's no lady but one of Them, if you know what I mean, is bound to spread her venom before we reach town. You go on up now and have a little rest, my girl. Harris can sit with Mrs. Shelburne, and I'll mind Lord Wendover myself."

"But we haven't had our game of piquet yet, and it's the one thing that keeps him quiet."

"I'll give him as many games as he likes," Patrick replied glumly, "for any wager he prefers."

"Don't you dare! Dr. Purvis says he must be kept quiet until the fever is gone from his leg. I let him win enough to lull his suspicions, but lately I've caught him watching me suspiciously. If only the cards would not keep falling my way, it would be so much easier for me."

"Never you mind, Miss Miranda. Patrick will take care of everything. Now you just go up and stop fretting. By evening we should have word from Jem as to your Papa's whereabouts in London. I told Jem to say to him that we need a nurse sent down to care for Mrs. Shelburne, and I don't doubt he'll see to it, seeing as how I put the case strong. You're wore out, and no wonder. You'll feel better after you've had a good rest."

Miranda struggled to her feet with a yawn. "I

hope so. I *am* more tired than I realized. Patrick, say a prayer for Shelly, that the fever breaks."

The coachman watched her plod up the stairs and shook his head. Something was eating at Miss Miranda, something beyond her troubles with the cold and lack of food and everyone depending on her. If she was falling in love with Wendover, heaven help her. He had better say a prayer for her, too, he decided grimly.

CHAPTER 5

That evening, as she busied herself with setting out the chessboard for what had become their ritual game, Miranda felt Wendover's eyes follow her closely.

"You should set out for town as soon as possible," he said abruptly. "Word of your presence here will spread like the plague as soon as Lady Jess' tongue starts to wag. Your best hope is to be there in person to outface the gossips."

Miranda sat down in the chair opposite him. "I have already discussed our remove with Patrick. I delay only because of Shelly. We must go soon, but we won't leave you in the lurch. I'll take Tom Groom, leaving Ebbets and the postillions to carry on here."

"How is Mrs. Shelburne today?"

"Early this morning her fever shot up and I was frightened, but before I came down tonight, her forehead felt cool and she was coherent, though very weak. Papa has been asked to send a nurse to share her care with Harris until she is able to travel, which won't be soon."

He nodded and stared down at the chessboard, lost in thought.

"So you are preparing to abandon ship?" He

opened with a move she had not encountered before.

"Only because I must, as you just advised. Wibberly will be able to attend on you tomorrow, and if you grow desperate for a hand of cards, Ebbets will oblige."

"You think of everything, Miss Trafford."

"I try to," she retorted, stung by the irony in his voice.

She countered his move. They played in silence. After his third move, she knew herself lost. The game came to a quick end.

"I wonder why you let me win before when I am a rank amateur against your skill."

"For the same reason you've been letting me win at piquet. Your brothers have taught you how to play cards?"

She grinned unrepentantly. "It was Patrick. No, please don't get out the deck. It's late and you look tired and even a bit feverish. Let me help you across to your bed."

"I can manage without your help."

He reached for the crude crutches Patrick and Mudd had put together for him and levered himself upright, but before he could balance himself comfortably, one of the crutches slipped from his grasp. He caught himself only with Miranda's aid. In silence she picked up the wayward crutch and handed it to him.

His blue eyes blazed with fury at himself. "Well? I'm waiting for you to tell me that you knew this would happen. You are always right."

Her merry round face crumpled in dismay. "Oh—am I really such a horrid prig?"

"Not yet, but I advise you to scotch the tendency before it gets out of hand."

"I'll try." She walked along beside him until he came to his bed and sat down on its side with a groan of relief. "Do you think I should work at developing an adorable simper since that's what you gentlemen prefer in a female? Does this please you?"

She drew her wide mouth into a pouting pucker and batted her eyelashes. Wendover's mood, as variable as the weather before a storm, lightened and he laughed, though unwillingly.

"Don't let me encourage you, Miss Trafford. When you go to town you'll have to hold your tongue and smile politely or you will be called odd. Nothing could be more damaging except downright ugliness."

"I'd like to turn around and go back to Templeton," she said, abandoning her efforts to amuse him.

"You would be wise to do just that. If you have an acceptable suitor, marry him and avoid the madhouse that is London in the season."

"There is no one at home I want to marry."

"You need not be in a hurry. Your sort improves with age."

"Since I am nearly twenty-four, I may be said to have improved as far as possible already."

She shook up his pillows and he leaned back, relinquishing the crutches into her care. She saw the sweat on his forehead and worried that he had overdone, but he was not a man who took kindly to advice.

He motioned for her to sit in the chair beside the bed. They sat together in silence, busy with their separate reflections. The firelight etching Wendover's finely drawn features made it clear to her how greatly pain and disappointment had changed him in just this short time. The man of action, soldier and rake, had been transformed into a scholar who lay awake, according to Patrick, into the small hours reading and writing, with consequences nobody, not even Wendover himself, could guess at.

"If you could choose any mode of life, Lord Wendover," she said presently, "what would you do?"

"I used to dream of coming home and living at the manor just as my forbears did, dividing my time between town and country, marrying and rearing a son to succeed me. That was before I discovered that Jessamin Botts has brought my estate to near ruin. Worse yet, I have to acknowledge kinship with her. I might do well to go out to the colonies, where the Wendover name is not known. To carry the burden of the family sins single-handedly is more than I bargained for."

"*I* had never heard of the Wendovers before I arrived at your doorstep, if that's any consolation. And if you want to compare knavish ancestors, I can best you with a baronet who was beheaded for treason."

"That's nothing much. My great uncle was excommunicated for taking three wives."

"You lose to an abbot who absconded with the church funds."

His eyes were brighter as they laughed together, the tension between them banished for the moment. Wendover could be a charming companion when he wasn't in a temper, Miranda reflected. She wondered what sort of a person Lady Trent might be. Intelligent and witty, she hoped, for Wendover's sake.

"I am going to miss you," he admitted, watching her intently.

"But not for long," she answered easily. "Now that the roads are passable, Lady Trent will be arriving any day."

"She will not be welcome." The closed, forbidding expression darkened his fine features again as he turned to look into the banked fire.

"You mustn't blame her for not traveling during the storm. Her coach might well have overturned, or something worse could have happened. She'll come as soon as she can."

"Would *you* have come under the circumstances?"

"If I loved a man enough to want to marry him, I would go to him if I had to walk, but I am a countrywoman and accustomed to doing whatever I want or need to do despite the weather."

"Yes. I thought so." He fell silent.

Miranda, observing him from beneath her lashes, thought she had never seen a face so devoid of hope. Perhaps he had counted on Lady Trent's fortune to help him reclaim his estate. But even if she had changed her mind about wedding Wendover, there surely must be a dozen other women who would give their fortunes to be noticed by him, for there were not many men who could equal him in birth or breeding, and perhaps none in appearance.

Hoping to rouse him from his unhappy reverie, she said, "I see you've been making notes again. I hope you are planning the speech you will make when you take your seat in the Lords."

"I doubt that I ever will. My notes are a waste of time."

"I think you would make a remarkable addition to the Parliament. Only imagine—a peer with ideas! If that doesn't cause a stir, nothing will."

He returned her smile with reluctance. "I have plenty of ideas, but I doubt they would be welcomed."

"You can be persuasive when you choose. You have Wibberly and the Curry family eating out of your hand."

He gave her a challenging look. "Shall I use my talent to persuade you to stay for another day, Miss Trafford?"

"Oh, please don't try, for I might give in. In spite of the snow and the cold and our troubles, I have grown fond of the manor and its inhabitants. I am reluctant to leave."

"You will forget us when you reach London."

"No, I promise I shan't."

"Then stay."

She tried to read his expression, her delicate brows drawn in a frown. It was unlike him to hint that he needed her. Either he was teasing or he meant to use her as a weapon to rouse Lady Trent's jealousy. In any case, he was not joking.

"I really shouldn't. Though perhaps one more day—"

The door opened suddenly and Dr. Purvis entered at a run, as he always did. With a sharp glance at the bemused pair by the fire, he put down his bag and knelt to add a log to the dwindling fire.

"Ebbets tells me that you've been using your crutches freely, Anthony." He dusted his hands before placing them on the bulging pockets of his jacket. "I suppose you forgot my warning to wait another week?"

"I have no time to waste. Lady Jess is selling everything she can put her hands on. I must get up to town in another week."

"You'll be lucky if it's a month," the blunt young doctor advised. "Miss Trafford, you are excused. Do not chivy me, as I can see you preparing to do. I am aware that I have other patients to see. I promise to attend on them as soon as I finish torturing my friend Wendover."

She went away smiling to prepare Mrs. Shelburne for his visit. As soon as the door closed after her, Purvis ordered his friend to open his robe and unbutton his shirt, as he prepared to examine the broken ribs Wendover had insisted should remain a secret between them.

"Healing well enough," he nodded. "The leg too. The old coachman did a prime job when he set it and packed it in snow." He sat down in the chair Miranda had vacated and poured himself a small glass of port. "Now all you have to do is to put that silly Trent female out of your mind, and I will declare you on the way to recovering."

"What do you know of Lady Trent?" Wendover asked coldly.

"Father told me of your plans. The only reason he agreed to marry you by special license was that he feared you might go off to Scotland otherwise. So she backed out? No doubt she feared to catch a sniffle due to the weather."

"If you were not my closest friend, Rob, and if I were not tied to my crutches, I'd call you out. I was a fool to expect a woman of her sort to wed a pauper."

"You're not entirely pauperized yet, or you wouldn't be if you will forget your scruples and exercise due control over Lady Jessamin. True, your papa made you swear to take care of her, but not to set her up in Wendover House and pay her excessive debts. Have you seen the crowd she entertains?"

"Once. I was sickened and came away."

"Then you may not know that your estate is also supporting that old court card, Sir Egbert Dartleigh. He dances attendance upon Lady Jess in the most revolting fashion. He hasn't a penny of his own except what he wins at the gaming tables."

"Lady Jess paid me a visit today, or did you know that too?"

The doctor's square face with its blunt features assumed an air of innocent surprise. "Ah? Where is she, then?"

"Miss Trafford sent her packing. Said *she* was leasing the manor and regretted that she was unable to entertain guests at present."

Dr. Purivs leaned back in his chair and let go a whoop of laughter.

"I like that girl's spirit. I plan to call on her when I go up to town." He peaked an eyebrow toward his old friend. "Unless you have ideas in that direction?"

"Of course I have not. She is an excellent sort, but you know that I am in no position to think of marriage now."

"She may be a provincial, but if she has an adequate dowry, she would be just the woman for you. With her help you could get your estate back in running order. Of course, she can't compare to Lady Trent in beauty or fortune."

"I wouldn't dream of comparing her to Lady Trent."

Dr. Purvis began to repack his bag in a leisurely fashion, while noting that his friend's temper was on the rise.

"I suppose I had best go along and see Mrs. Shelburne next. I held little hope for her when I saw her first, but thanks to excellent nursing, she is going to survive. Goodnight, Anthony. No need to thank me."

"Damn you, Rob! Then I won't!"

"Pleasant dreams, old boy."

He shut the door after himself with exaggerated care, leaving his boyhood chum to scowl into the fire and curse his own helplessness.

Miranda spent a troubled night.

Shortly after a dim dawn crept through the drawn curtains she got out of bed and dressed in her travel gown of deep maroon cashmere. Her face in the mirror looked wan and she brushed her tumbled hair listlessly. How unexpected to feel genuine sorrow at leaving this unfortunate place, and yet she did.

But she had other problems on her mind.

Last night Mudd had come to her with word that he knew where he could obtain a bit of tender beef. Miranda had opened her purse and given lavishly, delighted to know that Shelly and Wendover were soon to get good, heartening soups and roasts to hasten their recovery.

It was only after Mudd went away that Miranda thought to count out the remaining contents of her purse. Where had it all gone? For the first time in her life, she was at *point non plus*. The words to describe her predicament tolled themselves in her mind in a shameful procession: rolled up, without a feather to fly with, possessed of no more of the ready. Scuppered, in fact, as Patrick would say.

For a young woman who had, since she could do her sums, been used to spend as much as she required, it was a plight so far beyond her experience that she fell into a panic. After the way she had flaunted her money when she leased the west wing, now she could not even leave vails for the Currys, or pay Dr. Purvis, and this after all the trouble she had brought down on the manor!

She counted her few remaining coins again. There wasn't enough left for food, lodgings and tolls on the way to London. It was no use to apply to Shelly, who never carried more than a few pounds. Nor to her host, although she could not help thinking of the money she had given him for their lodging and wishing she had struck a better bargain.

Harris came bustling in with a tray of breakfast. The maid's cold had turned into a niggling little cough. She gave a harrowing exhibition of it as she placed the tray on the bedside table before saying that she doubted those who were left behind today would leave the manor alive, though of course she knew her duty and would stay and care for Mrs. Shelburne until the end.

"I've sent to Papa for a nurse, Harris, and I've made up a new syrup for your cough."

"My cough is the least of it, Miss Miranda. With you gone and milord shut up in his rooms, who's to keep matters in hand here, I ask you?"

"Shelly is perfectly rational this morning. You may go to her for advice. In matters below stairs, consult Wibberly. I find him very sensible. Before you finish packing, will you send Patrick up to me?"

As soon as the maid left, Miranda counted her money once more, hoping she had made a mistake. On finding that she had not, she hurried into the state bedroom and borrowed three pounds, all Shelly had with her, on the pretext that it was needed to recompense Mrs. Curry.

Miranda was sipping a cup of tea nervously when Patrick knocked at last. He listened to her tale of woe with a grim countenance.

"So our pockets are to let, eh? Nonetheless, you're not biding here another day," he warned sternly. "My grays are ready and we leave this morning, miss!"

"But we can't pay our tolls, Patrick! What if we are stranded?"

"They'll remember your papa's name in Wayland, I don't doubt. I'll tell the landlord you lost your purse."

"Who will believe a story like that?" Miranda replaced the fold of a gown in a trunk and straightened up with her familiar grin. "Maybe if I were to cast a smile at some gentleman in the taproom at Wayland, he would lend me—"

"You try that, Miss Miranda, and I'll pick you up and lock you inside the coach!"

"I was only joking, Patrick—I think. I've asked Mrs. Curry to pack a basket of food, so if the worst happens, we shan't starve. As soon as I say goodbye to everyone, I'm ready."

The parting between Miranda and her companion was painful to both. Miranda said she could not bear to leave her to Harris' care, but Shelly would not hear of her lingering.

"I only hope your reputation has not suffered already, dear. It was a wise move to take Mag along with you, although she does lack credibility as a lady's maid. Won't you change your mind and take Harris instead? I shall manage without her."

"Absolutely not. It may be days before the nurse can get here, and Harris knows how to care for you meanwhile. And I couldn't disappoint Mag at this late date. She's wild with excitement."

The two women embraced and exchanged promises to write often. It took all of Miranda's guile to offer a cheerful farewell to her beloved companion, and she put away her handkerchief only a moment before she knocked and was admitted to Lord Wendover's room.

He was sitting in his favorite wing chair beside the fire. Her first impression convinced her that he was in a temper about something. Wibberly, looking pale and gaunt but still unobtrusively efficient, drew up a chair for her across the hearth and offered a choice of refreshments.

"One last cup of tea would be nice, Wibberly, if you are sure we have an adequate supply."

"Bring tea if you have to use the last leaf in the house," Wendover ordered sharply. "We owe it to our hostess to give her a rousing sendoff."

Miranda stared into the fire earnestly. After Wibberly was gone, silence fell between them.

"You're blue-deviled, Miss Trafford," Wendover challenged. "I must admit to being surprised. I thought you would be happy to see the last of this benighted place."

"I shall be all right once we're on our way, I suppose," she replied, repressing a sniffle with great difficulty.

"I fear you will have an uncomfortable journey in the rain."

Miranda lifted damp eyes to the windows. "Oh, is it raining? I hadn't noticed."

He leaned forward, frowning at her. "You are deep in trouble, Miss Trafford. Are you afraid your father will be angry when he arrives to find an empty house?"

"It will do him no harm. Papa is badly spoiled, but he knows how to take care of himself when he has to. If I am not there to make him comfortable, he will simply put up at the Pulteney until I arrive."

"Are you feeling unwell? It would not be surprising under the circumstances."

"Oh, I am well enough. It is only . . . I don't know how to tell you, but suddenly I find myself without enough money left to pay our way to London!"

His dark eyebrows flew up and then he laughed. "Is *that* all? Not to fret. I have been in Dun Street ever since I received my father's legacy—Lady Jess—so you may count on me for advice. How much do you have in hand?"

Upon Miranda's admitting to the meager sum, he seemed surprised but undaunted.

"Have no fear; a way will be found. But what possessed you to set out for London with so little of the ready in your purse?"

"Papa said he would provide when we reached London."

"I hope he is not a pinch-penny. If you expect to be noticed when the season opens, you will have to patronize the best dressmakers." He tugged at the bellpull so hard that Miranda was glad she had arranged for Mudd to strengthen it. "I gave Wibberly your hundred pounds to provide for such tenants

70

and villagers who might need help during the storm, but there may be something left."

Wibberly entered shortly, as if he had been waiting outside. He appeared unsurprised to learn his master's wishes.

"There is thirty-odd pounds left, milord. If more is needed, I have a small sum you are welcome to take."

Miranda, pink with embarrassment, protested that she could not rob the household of all its ready money.

"Nonesense! Without you we would have been in the soup, and you know it, Miss Trafford. As for money, as soon as my steward recovers from whatever mysterious ailment has kept him from meeting me here with my quarterly rents, we shall be well provided for."

Miranda felt a stab of relief. So that was why Wendover had taken her money instead of offering the hospitality any gentleman would have accorded the least traveler in distress!

Wibberly bowed his way out as Wendover went on to say that he would repay her the money she had lent him as soon as possible.

"I hope you understood that it was only a loan. I have been expecting my steward each day, and each day he disappoints me."

"If you wish it that way," Miranda said, getting to her feet. Absently she straightened the pile of books on the table at Wendover's elbow. "I hardly know how to express my gratitude for your hospitality, Lord Wendover—with the exception of the night we arrived. Was it after all so dreadful to have us in your house?"

"Now you are asking for a compliment, which I am glad to offer. Without you and Patrick, I would have been in the soup." He made a move toward his crutches, but Miranda's exclamation of reproof halted him.

"You are not to use those sticks any more than necessary, or you won't be fit to attend my come-out." She noted with relief the beginning of a reluctant smile on his lips. "Now I really must go, but first I have another confession to make. I cannot pay my gambling debt until I reach town. I pray you will extend my credit for another week."

He caught the wicked glint in her eyes before she cast them down in a maidenly way.

"What irony! If I had your knack for piquet, I would set up shop with Lady Jess and win back the family fortune. To make my humiliation complete, I never was able to work out how you went about losing so convincingly."

Miranda's wide mouth tilted slightly at each corner, an expression he recognized as meaning that she found it difficult to contain a smile.

"It was the luck of the draw. The cards fell your way. Now I must say goodbye, Lord Wendover. Patrick will bring back the books and papers you wanted when he returns in a few days. Is there any other errand I can do for you?"

"Only be sure to send word how your journey goes and where to reach you—in case Mrs. Shelburne should need you."

She extended her hand. He took it between both of his and held it there for a long minute as if he had forgotten it. Miranda smiled down at him.

"I thank you again for letting us invade your privacy, Lord Wendover. You have been all that is kind. We will always be in your debt."

He continued to scrutinize her face as if something he saw in it puzzled him.

"Well, what keeps you?" He looked down and released her hand. "Go, since you must, but remember those you abandon here."

"Oh, I shall. I expect to be overcome with nostalgia every time I taste pheasant. Fond memories will fill my mind—of Mudd and Mag and Mrs. Curry. And of you, of course."

"Miss Trafford!"

But she was across the room and out of the door already. He kicked his crutches with his good leg and sank back into his chair in a fit of gloom.

CHAPTER 6

Under Patrick's expert hands Miranda's old-fashioned travel coach edged its way through crowded London streets with sometimes no more than an inch to spare here or there.

Mag, at Miranda's side, babbled with wonder at sight of so many vehicles and such elegantly dressed people. Miranda had visited the city once before when she was sixteen and so managed to restrain her excitement to a degree, but she could not keep back an exclamation of wonder when they drove into Halsted Square and halted in front of an imposing town house the size and style to make anything less than a palace look poor in comparison.

"Patrick must have mistaken the directions. Papa would never take the trouble to set himself up so neatly without my help," she said.

A row of shining windows perfectly draped confronted them. A competent butler let them in and a footman took Miranda's cloak. While Mag, stunned into silence, was led off to the servants' quarters, Miranda was ushered into a handsome salon, where a blazing fire reflected itself in the marble of the hearth and bowls of flowers lent the large room a springlike fragance.

Sir Henry came forward to embrace his daughter. He looked as sleek and contented as a well-fed cat.

"Miranda, my dearest girl! Until your message arrived, we were fearful for your safety. Come and greet your Aunt Louisa. She is your new mama. We met in Vienna and came to an understanding. You must know that she was widowed when Prince Demerov died at the Battle of Leipzig. I have been lonely these many years since I lost your mother. I hope you will wish us happy."

"Of course I do! Aunt Louisa, how wonderful to have you home with us again after so many years in Russia!"

Miranda knelt beside her new mama's chair and was kissed on both cheeks by the elegant, still beautiful woman who was the twin of her own mother. Physically there existed a great resemblance between the two women, but in their personalities they were very different. The princess exuded charm and poise, while Miranda remembered her mother as being timid and gentle.

"Let me look at you, Miranda. Ah, fresh as a primrose. But where have you found that dreadful costume?"

The princess's husky voice quivered with amusement. An emerald necklace shimmered above the décolletage of her satin gown which was cut so exquisitely it might have grown on her still slim figure. Miranda, after her first pained reaction, found herself returning her aunt's smile.

"My seamstress at Templeton assured me that it is the *dernier cri*."

"Indeed it was, five years ago. But do not worry, little one. You have been neglected far too long. I shall change all that."

"You have accomplished wonders already, Aunt Louisa. This house is lovely. I expected to hire staff and prepare for Papa's homecoming, but I never could have made it so welcoming."

"I always travel with my own servants and familiar objects." The princess gestured toward a Persian carpet that made a square of glowing color before the hearth. "I cannot endure to live without fresh flowers and hot fires after having spent much of my life in arctic Russia. My husband taught me to appreciate comfort. A girl growing up in England knows nothing of these matters. Hold out your hands, child. Just as I thought. As chapped as a scullery maid's, and there, I believe, is a chilblain."

"If you had been snowbound in a primitive country manor house as I was, your hands would look equally dreadful, Aunt Louisa."

The princess leaned back and invited Miranda to tell them everything.

"One hears rumors of a secret marriage between the recently widowed Lady Trent and the handsome rake newly home from Waterloo. What happened? Henry, send for more champagne, please."

Miranda chose to sit on a velvet stool at her aunt's feet.

"Sadly for poor Lord Wendover, it was I and not Lady Trent who appeared on his doorstep. He was quite angry with me until he broke his leg. After that, of course, he was forced to depend on me and we got on well enough."

The princess demanded more details. She laughed over Mag, sighed over poor Mudd, and agreed that Patrick had done just as he should when he set Wendover's broken bone.

Sir Henry did not find the tale amusing. "Do you mean to tell me that Wendover did not recognize my name?"

"He was off in Europe with the army for some ten years, Papa."

"That is no excuse. The impudent fellow, to treat

you as if you were any ordinary young lady! The Wendover title dates back only to Queen Elizabeth, while ours is much older."

"If Wendover's ancestor was as handsome as the present owner of the title, I can understand why the Queen gave it to him!"

"I hope you haven't conceived a fondness for the fellow. He is not to be received in my home."

"I intend to receive him whenever I choose, Papa. He was all kindness after that first night."

The princess intervened in her husky voice that held authority.

"He may call, of course, but there has already been a flurry of gossip. It think it best that you treat him as only a casual acquaintance."

Miranda grinned. "I may need him. He offered to provide me with a corps of beaux when I make my bow."

This news so incensed Sir Henry, who took his consequence seriously, that he spilled a drop of champagne on his burgundy velvet coat.

"My daughter will not lack for suitors! I have already had to refuse three offers because you would have none of them. This season I won't put up with your finicking ways. I intend to announce your engagement before summer comes, Miranda."

Miranda's cheeks blazed. Father and daughter, so alike in some ways and unlike in others, faced each other furiously until the princess intervened.

"Let us not spoil our first evening with worrying about what may happen, Henry. I suggest that we have a little more wine and talk of other matters. After dinner, Miranda, you papa wishes to present you with your mama's jewels. I, of course, have my own."

A week later Mag, freshly arrived back at the manor, thrilled her mother and Mudd with a description of those jewels.

"Rubies and pearls and little crowns made of dimings that sparkled till your eyes fair watered, Ma, and that were nothing compared to them the princess wore. And there was a cook that talked Frenchy and a Messoo that came to do up their hair every day."

"The little miss must have come into money," Mrs. Curry opined, going across to add barley to her simmering soup. "Tell us about the kitchens again, Mag."

She resumed her seat at the long table and listened rapt as a child at Christmas to Mag's description of cookstoves and spits of every size and complexity as well as a bewildering variety of pots to use for each different dish. "Oh, Ma, if you could see the Frenchy cook roll up a tender of beef in pastry crust! And oncet he set a lot of thin little pancakes afire and sprinkled them with sugar after!"

Word of Mag's arrival home seeped through the household. Presently Wibberly came with word that Lord Wendover wished to see her. The excited little maid, on being asked how Miss Trafford had found matters in London, edified her master with a detailed description of the elegance of Sir Henry's establishment and the beauty of Miranda's new mama.

"You are certain she is comfortably situated?"

"Lor', sir, Miss has fell into the cream."

"She deserves her share of gaiety. Does she enjoy the routs and balls a great deal?"

"The princess said as how she weren't fit to go about until she gets proper gownds made for her. Ma and Mudd and me, we think she's sweetly pretty in any gownd, and so did the gentleman that kept calling to see her."

Lord Wendover's dark blue eyes rested on Mag kindly. "I suppose you don't recall his name?"

"It were Sir Frederick. Stocky-built with reddish hair, my lord. He brung pink rosebuds oncet and grapes in a basket another time." Mag blinked hard in an effort to jog her memory. "He'll be younger than you, sir, about the age of Miss. He calls her Randa, so Ma reckons it's as good as settled between them."

"Thank you, Mag. That will be all."

After the maid had gone, Wendover leaned back in his chair and regarded his splinted leg with disgust. It was the more painful because he had no one to blame but himself. In his hurry to get to London and have it out with Annabel, he had permitted his famous temper to overrule his reason.

He should have realized then what he admitted to himself now. Annabel was not the sort of woman to expose her famed complexion to inclement weather, no matter how fond she might be of the gentleman she had almost been persuaded to wed. She must have had second thoughts as soon as he left town to make arrangements for the secret nuptials, must have taken time to consider what a scandal their elopement would cause, and decided that he was so well and truly caught that she need not risk it. He would be available later when she was ready.

He hadn't intended to keep her here at the manor, for Annabel had been accustomed to the utmost in luxury after her marriage to the elderly Lord Trent. It had been his intention to carry her off to a comfortable inn after Mr. Purvis performed an early-morning ceremony and from there to proceed to the Continent for their honeymoon. Later on he expected to deal with Lady Jessamin.

However, all those plans belonged to the past. As soon as possible he determined to be off to town. Certain formidable tasks had to be undertaken in London, and the sooner the better.

The tall clock in a corner chimed. He threw it an irritable glance. Not yet six, and another long, lonely evening lay ahead.

Odd, that he had never minded solitude in the past. Now he felt cheated without someone to talk to, or to play cards or chess with. He had never thought of a woman as a companion before; to him they were delightful creatures made to be flirted with, or if they were of a certain class, to be pursued and hopefully won, then forgotten, all of them, when a man went off to battle.

Only, Miss Trafford was different. Like bread, he mused, substantial and nourishing and not a confection that palled after a few servings. He smiled, remembering one evening when she had paused during their heated argument over what constituted happiness and directed his gaze toward Ebbets.

"We have bored the poor man to sleep," she murmured.

The footman, plump and stolid, sat in a chair near the door nodding, lulled as usual by the incomprehensible words his lordship and Miss Trafford used when they argufied together. Listening to them affected him the same way Reverend Watts at Templeton did when he got to preaching hard of a Sunday, Ebbets thought as his eyes closed and his head tilted to one side.

"Perhaps that is happiness," she remarked in her soft voice that always seemed the prelude to a smile, "to be satisfied with whatever fate serves up to you."

"Would you be so easily satisfied?" he challenged.

"No, but not everyone is free to choose. I have been lucky."

"What if you make the wrong choices?"

"I would expect to make the best of it. So long as

one has health and the means to live comfortably, there are compensations. There are books to read and horses to ride and sunny days to enjoy under even the worst circumstances." She looked across at him with her teasing smile. "If all else fails, one can enjoy observing the follies and idiosyncrasies of humanity."

Ebbets muttered a mild oath in his sleep. Wendover would have wakened the man, but she stopped him. "Let him sleep. He is dreaming of his Saturday pint at the pub, and he deserves to finish it."

Now the clock struck the half hour. Wendover rang impatiently. When Ebbets appeared, he demanded, "Do you know how to play cards?"

"I do, milord. Everyone at Templeton does, milord. Patrick teaches us when we starts to work there. Of an evening we gets into a game in the kitchen and the losers has to scrub the pots after supper. The young masters likes to play with us better than with Miss Miranda because she always wins."

"I can believe that. Before you sit down, go and fetch another bottle of brandy."

On the following day, which began with a warm rain that melted some of the piled snow at the manor, Mrs. Shelburne was surprised by a visit from the vicar.

She was still confined to her bed. The nurse Miranda had sent down was in attendance, for Harris, complaining of wind in her stomach again, had laid down on her bed.

The pastor began to offer prayers for her recovery. How very different he appeared from his bustling, impatient son, Shelly reflected as she peeped from under her lowered lids at the pastor's kindly, lean face and obediently said "Amen," all the while feeling a mild embarrassment under the protruding eyes of the nurse, who stared at them as unblinking as a lizard.

"Now, Mrs. Shelburne, may I offer you any kind of nonspiritual comfort?" Mr. Purvis asked after he had drawn up a chair and settled himself beside the bed. "My housekeeper makes excellent calves' foot jelly."

"We have been fortunate in procuring plenty of fresh lamb and even some beef. It seems that Mudd is well acquainted in the neighborhood."

"Indeed!"

Mr. Purvis, schooled in maintaining a benevolent expression, took care not to reveal his thoughts, although he was glad to solve the mystery of Farmer Griggs' missing calf. He must have a talk with Mudd soon: the poor lad was not very bright and could hardly be expected to know right from wrong. To change the subject, he commented on the pile of periodicals lying on the table nearby.

"You are welcome to them, for we are finished with them. Miranda sent both reviews, so whatever your political leaning, one is bound to please you."

"I shall read both. I try to keep an open mind in order not to inflict my political views on my congregation. It is enough if I can win them to my side spiritually."

Struck with admiration for his sensible point of view, Shelly told him that her father, also a clergyman, had been of the same opinion. He was much beloved and was deeply mourned when the smallpox took him and her mother in the same week.

"What a terrible sorrow for you, Mrs. Shelburne. I trust you had brothers and sisters to sustain you."

"I was their only child. However, I married shortly afterward, so I was not entirely alone. My husband died in the Peninsular War. It was shortly after his death that I went to live with Miranda. In truth, I think of her as my own daughter."

"She must be a most excellent young lady. My son was impressed with the way she coped with your troubles at the manor."

Thus encouraged, Mrs. Shelburne became loquacious, describing in detail how clever and kind and cheerful Miranda was, while agreeing that young Dr. Purvis was a perfectly admirable young man also. Half an hour passed in this pleasant exchange until the nurse, who had nodded off, startled them with a snort.

The vicar rose hastily. "I hope I have not tired you," he apologized, his gentle face wrung with remorse. "I had not meant to linger so long, but it was a particularly pleasant visit. I shall return often and I hope you will make use of me to fetch and carry for you meanwhile."

Her cheeks flushed, Shelly thanked him and said she would look forward to his visits. After he left she asked the nurse for her hairbrush.

"For my hair is in a sad tangle after the fever. Perhaps Harris will help me wash it tomorrow."

"I wouldn't if I was you," the nurse warned ominously. "I knew a lady once that washed her hair too soon after the lung fever. She died two days later."

At least the poor soul went to meet her Maker with clean hair, thought Mrs. Shelburne, who had begun to recover her spirits, but such was her habit of pacifying those around her that she only said, "Very well, then. I'll wait another day or two if you think it best."

CHAPTER 7

"Our first task," the princess declared on the morning after Miranda's arrival, "must be to quiet the rumors about your unconventional stay at Wendover Manor."

"Am I disgraced before I have even made a run for it?"

The two women were sharing a pot of tea in the princess's large, cluttered sitting room. Miranda had been engaged in petting her new mama's handsome blue-eyed cat, but now she sat back with a look of half-laughing alarm.

"Not disgraced yet, I trust, but matters are bad enough that something must be done. I have decided to give a small, exclusive breakfast in your honor next Friday, even though I am not ready to present you to society in general until I've made changes in your appearance. I have invited London's most celebrated gossips to meet you. Lady Jersey and Countess Lieven have already accepted."

"Heavens: I shall be speechless in their presence!"

"I hope so, dear girl. You are to wear the dreadful plum-colored gown you had on yesterday, and when spoken to, you must say only yes, or no, or thank you."

"They will go away believing I am an idiot."

"Precisely the effect I am aiming for. After seeing you in that frumpy gown and discovering that you have nothing to say for yourself, they will go forth and tell all of London that Lord Wendover would have to be blind or in his dotage to have made advances toward you."

Miranda could not repress a wry grimace at the picture of herself her aunt was painting.

"After I have convinced Lady Jersey that I am too plain and stupid to be compromised, what must I do next?"

The princess did not answer at once. She appeared to be making a great fuss over the pouring of fresh tea into her glass.

"Did I mention that Lady Annabel Trent will be among my guests?"

"You did not. I have no wish to meet her."

"Ah, but I have heard that she is curious about *you*. Nothing will do more to clear your name than to have her treat you as a friend, for that will prove that she doesn't consider you a rival for Wendover's affections."

"How do you suggest that I win her friendship, supposing that I want it, which I do not?"

"Admire her beauty. She absorbs flattery like blotting paper. Ask her advice about where to shop and what colors she thinks will suit you. Then later on, when we have stripped you of the bucolic air that clings about you, she will believe it was her doing."

The princess bent her fascinating, heavy-lidded gaze upon Miranda, who suddenly found it impossible to refuse her.

"Oh, very well. I'll make a fool of myself if you ask me to, but tell me—does nobody in town behave naturally?"

The princess gave her husky laugh. "Who would

dare? London would be like a costume ball with everyone portraying Hate or Envy or Malice." She leaned toward her niece with a confiding air. "Why do you treat Sir Frederick so unkindly, Miranda? Your papa wishes for the match. You have known each other from the cradle and he seems devoted to you."

"He is such a creature of habit that he believes he loves me simply because we were of an age and were thrown together as children. When I am with him for more than five minutes I begin to fidget. Be honest, Aunt Louisa—have you ever met a greater bore?"

"Quite often when we were at court, though never such a talkative one. He has told me that story about your hitting him with a fishing rod at least ten times already. Did it really happen?"

"Of course it did. He tried to prevent me from swimming in our own lake with my two brothers— said it wasn't decent! I sent him home with a welt on his arm and jumped in as soon as he was gone. In a decent bathing dress, and I was only twelve."

"He seems very protective toward you. That can be a comfortable trait in a husband."

"Not the way he does it. I could live with a man who showed his anger if I did something foolish or dangerous so long as he treated me as an equal, but I refuse to be condescended to as if I were weak-witted simply because I am a female!"

"Goodness, Miranda, you need not shout at me. I quite agree with you about Sir Frederick, but your papa asked me to sound you out, and now I have done my duty. Since you won't have him, I shall aim much higher. With your fortune, and once you are decently outfitted, not even a duke is beyond our reach, although those few I have met are too old and corpulent to be of interest."

Miranda grinned. "Can you imagine me sharing enormous meals with a fat duke?"

"Frankly, no. Still, one ever knows. After this first little breakfast, while the gossips are telling everyone how hopeless you are, you're to go into seclusion until the season actually begins. Then, after your complexion turns decently pale and your new wardrobe is completed, we are sure to find you an eligible match."

Miranda stretched out her toes toward the hot fire her aunt required and rumpled her brown curls thoughtfully.

"Was your marriage arranged, Aunt Louisa? Were you happy with Prince Igor?"

"Igor and I chose each other. We met when he visited London. He was twenty-one and I was seventeen." The princess tilted her head back with a reminiscent smile. "Were we happy? Sometimes madly, sometimes not. We fell in and out of love a thousand times during the years of our marriage. When he was killed I suffered agonies."

"You were fortunate to have Anna and Boris to console you."

"I love them dearly, and my four grandchildren, but I fear they are a little ashamed of my Englishness. They are very Russian. It was a relief to turn over the estate to Boris when I married your father. Now, that is enough about me. Miranda, you have carried the burdens of the Trafford family far too long. It is time for you to enjoy the pleasures of a young and carefree girl."

"I have forgotten how. I feel lost without my usual duties to occupy me."

"Then please let me advise you a little. To begin, I must say that although it is admirable of you to be careful with your money, a certain amount of extravagance is expected of a great heiress."

Miranda hung her head. "I only came into my

inheritance when I was twenty-one. By that time I was used to being careful, for Papa is rather a spendthrift and I was determined to keep his estate in good order for my brothers."

"Your man of business informs me that you have spent very little on yourself."

"I pay all my own expenses and I have agreed to foot the bills for Charles' and Edgar's schools. That in only fair since my godmother left all her money to me and nothing to them."

"Fair—what nonsense! It means nothing in a world where some are born clever or beautiful or wise while others arrive sadly damaged in one way or another. Of course you will always do more than your share to help those who need you, but dear Miranda, the feast of life is spread before you. Enjoy it while you may. A woman has only a short time to be free."

"Is marriage very difficult, then?"

"Difficult, though not impossible if you are willing to compromise. With Igor it was either ecstasy or grief. With your papa it is quieter and more comfortable. I am helpful to him in his work and he can give me the cosmopolitan life I have always enjoyed. A marriage of convenience can be a happy one."

Miranda shook her head. "It would not suit me."

The princess threw her a shrewd glance. "I wonder if you have not developed a tenderness for the handsome Lord Wendover."

"He was a delightful companion when he was not in a temper, but he is deep in love with Lady Trent."

"Some say it is her fortune he loves."

"Not to judge by the way he kissed me when he thought I was the beauteous Annabel."

The princess shrugged expressively. "Ah, well, men lose their wits over a pretty face, and Lady

88

Trent is so sweetly forlorn now that she is supposed to be mourning old Trent that she calls out all their chivalry. You might well take a lesson from her, Miranda. Men like to have a woman lean upon them. You need not remind me that you are quite as capable as many gentlemen. That is a trait you must keep hidden until you are safely married."

Miranda got up and poked at a log that sat too far forward. Her face was flushed when she turned back to her aunt. "That is the equivalent of lying. I can't pretend to be a goose when I am not. I could not respect a man I had to win with those tactics."

"I don't ask you to giggle like a schoolgirl, but we might work toward acquiring a more melting demeanor. Yes, Wilson? Ah, Monsieur is here. We will let him have you first, Miranda, for it is going to take time to tame those wild curls into something like a coiffure."

Since Princess Demerov was the most exotic hostess of the season which was yet to begin, her invitations were accepted eagerly. Adding to the attraction were the scandalous rumors going round about her niece, who was said to have pursued Lord Wendover to his country house and there somehow caused him to break his leg.

Few of the guests troubled to hide their surprise when they were introduced to the small, quiet, ordinary young woman who was the notorious Miss Trafford. Whispers of doubt and smothered smiles were exchanged while the ladies fed upon fabulous dainties from Russia. The princess entertained them with a tale of wolves that pursued her sledge one winter night when she was alone, and made casual references to the interesting peculiarities of the Russian royal family, which stories the countess confirmed.

It was considered to be one of the most successful parties of the late winter, though a few of her guests offered the princess their sympathy when they made their farwells.

"Perhaps your little Miss Trafford is only shy in company as yet, Louisa," Sally Jersey murmured, giving the princess's hand a consoling squeeze.

Countess Lieven was more forthright. "Get the girl something presentable to wear, Princess. Since she seems to have no conversation at all, let us hope she has other talents. If she sings acceptably, or plays the harp—"

"Miranda has no voice and she plays only a little. She tells me that she rides extremely well."

"Much good that will do her at a ball. I wish you luck with your new daughter, but do not set your heart on too great a match for her."

It was Lady Annabel Trent who behaved with kindness and sweet condescension to the shy little girl from the country after Miranda paid her a quiet compliment and asked for her advice about the gowns she hoped to have made. During the crush of farewells, Lady Trent drew Miranda aside and asked to know everything about Lord Wendover's accident.

Miranda recounted the bare facts in a colorless voice, her hands clasped on the skirt of her dowdy, plum-colored gown. Lady Trent smiled down on her from her stately height.

"How fortunate that it was someone as sensible as you who happened to be there when he was hurt. I am so sensitive to pain that I would have gone faint. When dear Trent lay dying, I had to keep to my bed, for I could not bear to see him suffer."

"I sympathize with you in your loss, Lady Trent," Miranda replied through stiff lips.

Mourning became Lady Annabel. The severely simple black gown she wore, accented with only a touch of white lace at her breast, enhanced the pallor of her perfect complexion and set off the gilt of her thick, fair hair.

"I try not to burden others with my grief." Lady Trent's soft pink mouth drooped at the corners appealingly. "I hope we can be friends, Miss Trafford. Tell me, do you enjoy London?"

"I have seen little of it yet, Lady Trent."

"Then let me take you up in my chaise tomorrow. I promise to show you all the best shops. Afterward we might drive in the park and I will point out to you everyone of importance."

"You are very kind, but my aunt doesn't wish me to go abroad until I have rested."

The princess had been standing close and listening intently. Now she broke in on their conversation.

"An outing in the fresh air is just what you need, Miranda, and I am too busy to take you myself. Of course she will be delighted, Lady Trent."

That same evening, while Miranda and the princess sat together in the withdrawing room waiting for Sir Henry to finish his port, the princess put down her tea, which she insisted on drinking out of a glass as they did in Russia, and said, "I had some anxious moments when you were cozing with Lady Trent, Miranda."

"So you should have! What kind of female is she to be so preoccupied with her own comfort that she does not take the trouble to visit the man she is to marry? I can understand why he is charmed by her beauty—she is lovely—but what will they talk about?"

"A man in love is not interested in conversation."

"He can't expect to sit and look at her for a lifetime."

"I doubt if he thinks beyond the honeymoon. I wonder what is delaying your papa. We are due at the theater in half an hour. Are you sure you don't mind being left alone?"

"On the contrary: I would do anything to avoid exposing myself in my Templeton wardrobe again. Must I really drive out with Lady Trent tomorrow?"

"Of course you must, and be sure to wear the maroon gown you had on when you arrived. That should put the final seal on your dowdiness."

Miranda gave her a pleading glance. "You are cruel, Aunt Louisa."

"For your own good, dear child."

"Exactly what Dr. Williams always said when he gave me a bitter medicine. Very well. I'll go tomorrow, but when I come home I shall give all my dresses to the new little maid you hired for me. Or else I shall burn them."

The princess's large, dark eyes rested on her niece thoughtfully.

"You are very different from your mother. Where have you come by your reckless ways?"

"Grandpapa, perhaps. Mama never quite admitted it, but I have an idea that our esteemed ancestor was not above doing a bit of smuggling in his time."

The princess laughed. "Which explains why we have an exceptionally fine cellar of French wines and brandies. Poor Papa: he had hoped to rear a clutch of seafaring boys. In the end he had to make do with your mama and me, and your Uncle Bracebridge, who turns queasy at the sight of water. Ah, here is your papa at last. Be sure you stay up and read your new books until the small hours. You must look your worst when you go driving with Lady Trent tomorrow."

Miranda was overcome with laughter. Tears stood on her cheeks as she said, "I have heard of cruel stepmamas, but you take the prize, Aunt Louisa!"

"Miranda!" thundered Sir Henry. "Apologize at once!"

The princess glided across and tucked her arm through his.

"Never mind, Henry dear. Miranda and I understand each other. How handsome you look tonight, sir. I expect to be the envy of every woman present at the theater."

After they left, Miranda sank back into her chair listlessly.

Tonight's moral is that a female should learn to calm the beasts with flattery, she reflected. It seems false and shameful to me. Why can't men and women be as open with each other as Wendover and I were? I suppose it was because we were strangers, and not in love.

Certainly he thought of her only as a younger sister or as a friend. She was less sure of how she felt about him. She did miss their evenings over the card table and especially their tempestuous discussions afterward during which he gave no quarter because she was a female and she fought him on equal terms, now and then even agreeing with him, to her own surprise, but that was hardly what people called love. It was only that she had got used to him.

Presently she went up to her own room and settled down with her new book from Hookham's only to find that it did not hold her interest. Nightfall was a lonely time.

On her desk lay the letter she had received that morning from Mrs. Shelburne. She read it over again with a sense of longing for all that she had left behind down in the country.

"Lord Wendover has been all that is kind. Often we share supper, and he invites Dr. Purvis' papa to dine with us whenever Mrs. Curry has prepared something special.

"Lord W. is nothing like the man I was prepared to dislike. He and the vicar are the best of friends and share a love of learning I admire. Mr. Purvis is very kind to me. I know I shall miss him when I leave the manor. Though he is sometimes absent-minded, particularly when he is preparing a sermon, Mrs. Curry says he is beloved by his parishioners, and this I can believe.

"Young Dr. Purvis tells me that I must gain strength before I dare attempt the journey to London. This distresses me, for I feel I have failed you. However, for the present I am helpless.

"I miss you more than I can say. I hope your new mama takes you about to all the parties and balls you deserve to enjoy after your long years of service to your family. Write me of your successes, for I am sure that everyone who meets you must love you."

Miranda grimaced. Not in my maroon gown, without a word to say for myself! She folded the letter away and dismissed Benson, whose anxious hovering distracted her.

And they certainly won't fall in love with me when they compare me with the exquisite Lady Trent tomorrow when we drive out together, she thought as she got into bed. Nor if they've heard the ugly rumors about me. As Patrick always says, I'm a slow starter. I wonder if I am not entered in the wrong race.

CHAPTER 8

After her humiliating experience in Lady Trent's chaise as they drove in the park together, Miranda was glad to go into seclusion at the princess's bidding. She had passed unnoticed as she sat beside the lovely Annabel save for an occasional amused glance from one of that lady's admirers, and once a frosty stare from a dowager who must have heard the rumors about her.

Day after day she underwent stringent applications of various esoteric lotions and creams the princess concocted herself.

"Like an alchemist, Aunt Louisa," Miranda commented toward the end of ten days. "You've turned my complexion several degrees lighter, it's true, but I think I miss my freckles. Who ever saw a lily-white countrywoman?"

"You're a Londoner now, dear child. And there are still a few freckles we shall have to hide if we can't eliminate them. The chamomile and lemon have done wonders for your hair, too."

"I'd forgotten that my hair was almost blonde when I was growing up. I like it this way. Shall I have to use the rinses forever?"

"Until you go gray. Then I'll have another receipt for you. Now please go and dress quickly. Madame Francesca has a new shipment of silks and we'll want first choice."

Miranda, accustomed as she was to having her gowns made up twice a year by a seamstress from nearby Horton, was stunned at the variety—and the cost—of the clothes the princess insisted that she order.

"Six walking costumes? And a dozen pairs of kid gloves?"

"Not enough, to be sure, but sufficient for a start." The princess frowned over a handful of ostrich plumes. "Try this one against the green silk. No, it won't do. We shall have to look further."

Recovered from her first shock, Miranda entered into the spirit of the game of fashion cheerfully. The princess noted with approval that the girl had a discriminating eye and a flair for the newest colors that suited her wild rose complexion, avoiding pastels in favor of interesting deep shades that set off her hair and enhanced the brilliance of her unusual eyes.

At the end of three weeks of seclusion, Miranda announced that she was frantic with being pent up indoors and begged to be allowed to take a walk in the fresh air.

"I suppose it will do no harm," the princess agreed with some reluctance. "Your marine-blue walking costume has come. You may as well wear it and get used to being decently dressed. Take Benson with you, and remember that one does not speak to strangers in London as you might in the country. If a gentleman accosts you in the park, stare him down. Not that I expect it to happen."

"Neither do I. I am beginning to feel like the idiot child the family has to hide in the attic," Miranda protested. "Will I have to stay indoors and incognito the whole time until my come-out ball in May?"

"Certainly not. I have made up my mind to bring you to notice quietly, at the ball of my old friend Lady Alston is giving for Mary. Will you mind playing second fiddle to Mary for a night?"

Miranda brightened. "Nothing will suit me better! I'm very fond of her."

The two girls had become fast friends, for Mary was no trembling bud fresh out of the schoolroom, but a girl of twenty whose original debut had been delayed owing to her having contracted typhoid, which illness caused her to lose most of her hair when she was eighteen.

"It was all for the best," Mary confided to Miranda soon after they met. "My hair was carrot-colored and now it has grown back much darker. At least it's not noticeably red, do you think?"

Miranda had assured her that it might almost pass for auburn. No one would label Mary a beauty, but she possessed a lively intelligence and a quick wit. The two girls had made it a habit to walk together very early in the morning before society went abroad.

Miranda wished she had her friend at her side now as, with her timid maid Benson hanging back, they entered Hyde Park at the most fashionable hour of the day. Throngs of dandies rode along the bridle path, or drove to the nines in dashing vehicles. Exquisitely dressed ladies displayed themselves in open carriages, and one could easily pick out the beauties from a distance by the number of gentlemen clustered around them.

No one paid any attention to Miranda as she walked along at her usual brisk pace. It was heaven to be out on this springlike late March day, she thought, and interesting to watch the parade of fashion around her.

"Oh, miss, my side is killing me," Benson complained after the first five minutes.

With a smothered sigh, Miranda slowed and looked around for a place to rest. She had just settled on a suitable vantage point when she heard her name called.

"Miss Trafford! I hoped to find you here!"

She looked up to see Wendover seated high above her in a high-perch phaeton drawn by a handsome pair of grays, with a small groom grinning in the seat behind.

Her eyes sparkled. "So you've escaped too! How are you? How is everyone at the manor?"

"Come up beside me and I'll tell you all."

"My maid . . . ?"

"She can wait there for you. Help the lady aboard, Freddy."

Miranda climbed up eagerly and watched from the high seat as Wendover guided the matched pair between a pair of lesser curricles with an expertise that impressed her.

"I am surprised to see you," she said as soon as she settled herself beside him. "Should you be out and about so soon?"

"Not according to Rob Purvis, but I have urgent business in town. I arrived only late last night or I would have called on you today." His blue gaze swept over her and took in her new walking costume and the bright curls that showed beneath her smart bonnet. "You've changed, Miss Trafford. What has become of my small country mouse?"

"She is disguised beneath a wardrobe of new clothes, but she's there. I never saw such a handsome equipage, Lord Wendover! And you are a veritable whipster!"

"I borrowed it from Bettinger, an aide of mine with whom I am staying temporarily. Don't try to change the subject. What happened to your freckles?"

She turned a little away from his intent gaze. "Bleached out with my new mama's creams."

"I'm not sure I approve of the new Miss Trafford, but no doubt she is a very popular young woman. How many proposals have you received to date?"

Miranda grinned. "None, since I told my old beau from home that he was tiresome. In fact, I have not even met any gentlemen, for my new mama has kept me secluded as if I lived in a Turkish harem."

"Wise woman. I am anxious to meet her. I wish I might call on you tomorrow, but the business that brings me to town can't wait and I shall be occupied all day. You may count on me to present myself as soon as possible. Now, tell me all that you have seen and done."

Miranda poured out a budget of news that caused Wendover to smile, and frown, and look down at her with a warmth in his eyes that was new and very pleasant.

"Now it's your turn," she said. "I want to know everything about Shelly, not just that she's better. And did Mudd get the beef he promised? Was it good? Have Ebbets and the other boys behaved and made themselves useful?"

"One question at a time! Mrs. Shelburne is able to walk out a little now that the weather is better, quite often in the company with the vicar, who calls almost every day. The beef was excellent, and your servants are proof that you know how to manage your staff. I have taken an aversion to pheasant for the moment, which you will understand. For myself, since you are so kind as to ask, I have discovered that my bailiff has long been in league with Lady Jess. He never did appear with my rents, but as soon as I have seen my solicitor, you may count on being repaid."

"I think our debts cancel each other out. If you will forgive my gaming debt, I will do the same."

"You haven't changed at all," he said, smiling down at her. "Are you happy with your new mama?"

She made him laugh with her story of the breakfast of gossips though she took care not to mention the fact that Lady Trent had been present. They were so occupied with their exchange of news that they did not notice they had become the cynosure of all eyes. Wendover nodded to an acquaintance occasionally but did not stop. Miranda replied to Lady Jersey's small nod with a beaming smile. An hour had passed and the park was beginning to empty before Miranda realized how late it was.

"Oh, poor Benson! I forgot all about her. Can you deliver me back to where I left her quickly?"

He touched the ribbons lightly. Ten minutes later they swept to a halt in front of the awed little maid, whose large, dark eyes looked swollen as if she had been weeping.

"Forgive me for not getting down," Wendover said, taking Miranda's hand while the groom waited to help her down. "Next time I shall have to bring my canes along." He kissed the hand he held before he released it. "Until the day after tomorrow, then. I have many tender messages from the manor to deliver to you when we are alone."

The intent blue look he bent upon her confused Miranda. He meant Mudd and Mag, of course, although one might be excused for thinking he intended to deliver a tender message of his own if one did not know that he was going to marry Lady Trent.

She found herself thinking about his words oftener than she liked that evening, which she spent alone, as Sir Henry and the princess had gone out.

The next day was occupied in running errands for the princess, so that it was late in the afternoon before Miranda returned to Halsted Square to find

Sir Henry and the princess gone again, this time to attend a diplomatic reception.

Miranda slept uneasily that night and rose early in the morning. After a light breakfast she bathed and dressed in her favorite new rose-colored muslin and settled herself in the library, where she watched the clock while she made an effort to read. Wendover hadn't said at what hour he would call, but she meant to be at home to receive him whenever he came. Because I'm anxious to hear about everything that has happened at the manor, she told herself, then had to admit that it was mostly because she wanted to talk to Wendover again.

She had never had a friend like him. With most of the men she knew, she felt perfectly confident and capable of getting along with them on easy terms. Wendover was different. She was never sure of him. There were times when she thought of him as dangerous as the lion he reminded her of, and other times when he was as natural and open with her as one of her brothers. Most of the men she knew welcomed her help and advice concerning household matters or even estate affairs. Not Wendover. He seemed to resent her efforts to domesticate him.

By three o'clock that afternoon Miranda had changed her dress twice and snapped at poor Benson, who looked ready to cry until Miranda apologized.

At five, Lady Alston and Mary stopped in to visit the princess. Miranda was in such a ferment in case Wendover should call while they were there that she failed to notice her friend's agitated grimaces across the tea table and was surprised when Mary drew her aside after the two older women had gone toward the hall.

"Miranda, I have something to tell you that's terribly important," Mary whispered. "Be ready at nine in the morning. I've told Mama we're going to Hookham's to change our books."

"I'm not sure I'll be free. I'm expecting a caller—"

"You must get away! Something has happened that concerns you, and I have to talk to you in private."

"Very well, if we'll be gone only a short while. Wendover is to call later today or tomorrow with news of Mrs. Shelburne."

Mary's face showed shock. "Oh, no! I hope not. Not after what's happened."

"What *has* happened, Mary? Don't be so mysterious."

At that moment Lady Alston bade her daughter to stop whispering like a silly kitchen maid and show that she had been taught proper manners. Mary obediently curtsied to the princess, threw an agonized look at Miranda, and let herself be borne away by the large, domineering woman who was her mama.

The next morning sparkled with sun. A soft breeze hinted that spring was almost here. Recent rains had washed the pavements clean and colored each shrub and tree a tender green. Even the sky had a scrubbed look, for not a cloud was in sight.

"I'm positively swollen with curiosity," Miranda complained when she settled herself beside Mary in the Alston barouche. "What is it you have to tell me?"

"Before I begin I have to ask your forgiveness, Miranda. I'm presuming on our friendship to warn you that you are the object of everyone's gossip. How could you have driven round the park for hours with Wendover, of all people! And in a high-perch phaeton! The story of your stay at the manor has been resurrected and embellished beyond belief. Some people even believe that you are Wendover's . . . that he has given you a slip on the shoulder."

102

Miranda laughed in relief. "Oh, if it's only that same old story about the snowstorm, I needn't worry. Anyone with a grain of common sense must understand that I had no choice. It was either find a refuge, or let Shelly die. What a tempest in a thimble."

"It's much more than that, I'm afraid. The old tabbies pretend they're scandalized. One woman warned my mama that she will not attend my ball if you are to be present."

"I'm sorrier than I can say, Mary, but it need not be a problem for you. I shall simply come down with the influenza and beg off."

"Indeed you will not! If nobody comes to my ball except you and those who are loyal to me and my friends, it will suit me perfectly. That is the least of my worries. Miranda, there are dreadful rumors circulating that you will not receive a voucher for Almack's, and you know what they will mean."

Miranda nodded soberly. Lady Jersey was one of the patronesses, and she remembered her cool nod in the park day before yesterday. To be barred from Almack's meant social ostracism. Sir Henry would never forgive her. After a long moment of thought, she pushed back her smart new poke bonnet impatiently and said, "In that case I shall pack up and go home to Templeton, where people know me too well to listen to malicious talk."

"You can't do that. It would be an admission of guilt. And what's worse, you would be showing yourself a coward."

"Then what am I to do? Ah, I have it! I'll simply insert a notice in the *Times* saying: 'Lord Wendover kissed Miss Miranda Trafford once only, and that was by mistake.' "

Mary's brown eyes gleamed excitedly. "You never told me that. What was it like to be kissed by the handsomest gentleman in all England?"

"It might have been pleasant if he had known who he was kissing. As matters fell out, at the time I would have preferred a decent fire on his hearth."

"I despair of you, Miranda. You'll never marry if you go on making light of your emotions."

"Since I am already deep in disgrace, it would sink me even lower if I were to fall in love."

"Well, it's too early to despair. Listen: I have an idea. If you were to become engaged, the gossip would end. Isn't there a faithful beau you can turn to?"

"There is Frederick, but I would rather be called a member of the muslin company than marry him."

"You needn't go so far as to marry him. Only accept him and let him squire you around until the rumors die down. When the season ends and you go back home, you can tell him you have changed your mind."

"That would be a shabby thing to do. I think I had best go back to Templeton after all. I'm not in need of a husband. I wonder why I ever agreed to undergo a season at my age. It was Papa's plan, of course. He's determined to get me off his hands before he leaves for his new post in the States."

"But Miranda—think again. If you do not marry, you'll never have a home of your own. When your brother inherits Templeton he'll take a wife, and she won't want you there interfering. You will be bored to distraction without an estate to manage." Mary's kind, plain face clouded. "For myself, I shan't have any choice. I'll have to accept the first eligible gentleman who offers—if one ever does."

"No, you need not. You can come and live with Shelly and me and take your time about finding a suitable husband."

They were now arrived at Hookham's. Since there were not many customers about on such a beautiful day, the girls felt free to browse. Mary discovered a forbidden volume of Lord Byron's poems, while Miranda hunted for another novel by Jane Austen, whose dry wit delighted her.

She happened to be standing near the front when she heard a familiar voice. She turned and recognized with pleasure the broad shoulders and tawny hair of her erstwhile host.

"Lord Wendover!" She went toward him with a smile. "This is the first time I've seen you walking without your crutches!"

"It is better described as hobbling," he replied with a glance down at his pair of canes. There was no answering smile on his face. Instead he said in a flat, bored voice, "I trust you are comfortably settled with your father. Good. Now, if you will forgive me, I am already late for an appointment."

He looked entirely different today, so haggard and ill that Miranda had to restrain herself from begging him to sit down and rest.

"Please don't go yet. You promised me more messages from Babb's Crossing last time we met."

"Be assured that Mrs. Shelburne is mending as well as can be expected. I left a packet of letters for you at Halsted Square the day before yesterday. Now I must beg you to excuse me, Miss Trafford."

Miranda watched him limp away, too stunned to think reasonably. What had happened to change him? He had been warm and friendly during their drive in the park. He must have heard the ugly rumors too, and felt embarrassed by them in light of his attachment to Lady Trent. At least it was better to believe that than to think he regarded her as no more than a tiresome former acquaintance he had to put in her place lest she encroach.

"Miranda, are you ill?" Mary whispered, coming up behind her with *Childe Harold* in her hands. "You had better sit down while I call for the carriage."

"I'm perfectly well. Just . . . surprised."

Mary followed the direction of her friend's eyes and saw Lord Wendover mount into his borrowed rig with some difficulty.

"What happened, Miranda? Did he insult you?"

"He barely recognized me. I wonder if I have done something to offend him."

Mary had never seen Miranda's composure in such disarray.

"Let us go," she urged. "People are beginning to stare. We can come back for our books tomorrow."

So it was that Miranda arrived back at Halsted Square in low spirits, uncertain whether or not to inform the princess of the unpleasant news Mary had imparted to her. Thompson came forward to remove her light shawl.

"I understand that a packet of letters was handed in for me the day before yesterday, Thompson. Has it been mislaid?"

"If such a packet was delivered, it will be in Sir Henry's hands, Miss Trafford," the butler replied austerely.

Thompson had grown fond of the little miss, who was free with her smiles and her purse. She never failed to inquire about his son, who was in training at Ponsonby Place. Thompson thought her sweetly pretty and had risen up to defend her at the Crown last night when a butler from a lesser household had cast slurs on her name. Thompson disdained to involve himself in public squabbles as a rule, being above vulgar exchanges with his inferiors, but he felt a certain satisfaction as he recalled how he had faced down the upstart. Nobody was going to insinuate that little Miss Trafford had carried on with Lord Wendover, not in the presence of Herbert Thompson!

Still, it was with trepidation that he watched Miranda trail up the stairs and enter the rooms of the princess. Lady Trafford could be formidable when she chose, and she had appeared very angry after Lady Jersey's short visit earlier.

Miranda found her aunt reclining on her satin-upholstered French chaise. Despite her relaxed appearance, she was plainly disturbed.

"So, Miranda! You have heard the rumors too? *Why* did you behave so foolishly? Certain ladies may drive in the park with gentlemen, but not a girl who has yet to make her come-out, and above all, not *you* with Wendover!"

"He had news of Shelly that I was anxious to hear. Is that a crime?"

"In London it is. I wonder how a girl as sensible as you are can stir up so much trouble."

"I wonder too," Miranda admitted ruefully. "Mary advises me to become engaged to Frederick, just temporarily, of course. I suppose it might work, though I couldn't do it unless I told him first that I have no intention of marrying him ever."

She dropped into a low slipper chair and removed her bonnet. The princess turned her hands palms up in a gesture of despair.

"My dear girl, it is too late for that. When you refused him for the fourth time, he turned to the Stanley girl for comfort. You must have noticed that he has called only twice in the last two weeks."

"If I did notice, it was with relief. Hester will suit him perfectly. She will admire him and tell him that he is always right, which is what he wanted me to do, but I never could. Aunt Louisa, must I go to Mary's ball? I do not like to embarrass the Alstons. Neither do I want to expose myself as an object of scorn before people I neither know nor care about."

"Of course you will go. I have ordered your Uncle Bracebridge to escort you. No matter how painful it may be for you, you must keep up an appearance of innocent enjoyment to let people know that the gossip has not disturbed you."

Miranda got to her feet in a hurry. "I only regret that if I must bear the shame, I never had the fun of the game! Wendover conducted himself in every way as a gentleman should. I give you my word that nothing unsuitable happened at Babb's Crossing."

The princess raised her heavy eyelids to peer at Miranda keenly.

"I can't say I blame you for defending Wendover. I saw him at the theater last night. Debt-ridden and plagued by scandal he may be, but the women fawned over him as if he were Byron himself. Lady Trent pouted and finally dragged him away before the last act."

So he was still a slave to her whims, Miranda thought as she took her leave of the princess and went toward her own rooms. Not that it mattered to her what he did, except that the gossip should cease as soon as their wedding plans were announced.

Benson was waiting to help her undress. She sent the little maid to ask Sir Henry for a few moments with him. Benson returned shortly with a packet of letters in her hands.

"Your papa is engaged to dine at the Austrian embassy tonight, and cannot see you. He said he has looked at these letters and you may have them as there is nothing objectionable in them."

Miranda had been standing by a window swinging her bonnet by its ribbons. Now she flung it across the room. It landed on her dressing table and knocked over a china figurine.

"Oh, miss, are you ill?" Benson quavered.

"I am only cross. Go away, please, and leave me to wrestle with my temper in solitude."

CHAPTER 9

What a night to have to escort his niece to a ball! Uncle Bracebridge gave his silk-lined cloak to Thompson and groomed himself fussily as a plump cat. Outside the rain fell steadily and looked to continue throughout the night.

In the salon he found Sir Henry standing before the hearth, the epitome of elegance in a coat of dark blue superfine, his still slim figure defined by the excellent cut of his waistcoat, his dark hair arranged to emphasize its abundance.

Bracebridge accepted a glass of brandy after the two men exchanged cool civilities and raised it to his lips.

"Hmm. Excellent in its way, but not to compare with what Papa laid down before I was born. So you are finally going to introduce your poor, neglected daughter to society, eh? A bit late at her age, though with her fortune she may still make an acceptable match."

"I daresay she will do better than that. The Traffords have always been fortunate in love."

"Indeed? At the time my sister chose you, she could have had an earl."

"If you mean Sparling, that would have been a mistake. He took to the bottle and had to be pushed about in a wheeled chair when he became too obese to walk."

"A few pounds of flesh never hurt any man over thirty." Bracebridge endeavored to suck in his paunch. "Insurance in case of illness, m'doctor says. I hope your Miranda don't expect me to squire her on a regular basis, Trafford. I'm a busy man."

Sir Henry, who ignored his diplomatic training when he was with his brother-in-law, laughed. "I trust you can spare a few hours from the whist table for your poor niece. From what I hear, you will be saving yourself a considerable sum."

It was fortunate that the ladies made their entrance at this moment. Princess Demerov glided in first. She wore a gown of stiff white brocade embroidered thickly with gold thread. Around her throat lay a circlet composed of six strands of perfectly matched pearls centered at the breastbone with a huge emerald.

Miranda lingered in the background until her new mama had received lavish compliments from the two men before presenting herself.

"You look very pretty, Miranda," Sir Henry observed after a critical appraisal. "Louisa has worked wonders."

"It is only too bad that she could not manage to change the shape of my nose," Miranda replied with a smile.

"You and I," her uncle reproved, "have our noses from your grandmother Bracebridge. Small and tilted they may be, but often admired. The regent himself said to me once, I am glad to have one friend who does not boast of a Roman nose; after all, we are Englishmen!" He studied Miranda's gown of palest pink satin with an overskirt of soft green net and shook his head. "Gals making their come-out always wear white, niece."

110

Miranda went across and slipped her arm through his.

"I don't wish to present myself as a girl fresh from the schoolroom, Uncle."

"No one need know how many years you've been kept down in the country if you don't tell them."

"But *I* know. I can't pretend to be a simple young thing when I have been used to ordering the estate and mothering two big boys."

"Gad, Miranda, don't speak so blunt! It makes me ill to think of a young female being acquainted with such sordid matters. What gentleman will want to think about pasturage when he is dancing with a pretty girl?"

"I can't imagine, Uncle, but if ever I meet one, I promise to engage myself to him the moment I am asked."

The Trafford party arrived a little late owing to a congestion of vehicles outside the Alston town house.

"Never mind," Mary said in answer to Miranda's apology as they passed down the reception line. "You look as appealing as an apple tree in bloom. Go away before you make my poor blue pale into oblivion."

"I'm half-afraid to enter the ballroom," Miranda murmured. "What if your guests rise up in a body on catching sight of me?"

"If they do, they'll never be invited here again. But do take care, Miranda. The Wyndhams are here. Wendover paid some attentions to their daughter before he met Lady Trent, and they long to hurt him in any way they can—through you if need be."

"Where are they?"

Mary drew Miranda to the door of the ballroom. "There: she's the woman wearing the purple turban with the curled feather. Or is it a viper's tongue?"

Miranda peered in cautiously and drew back with a grimace.

"An adder's tongue, I think. Aunt Louisa is beckoning. Wish me luck, Mary."

"I do. I've arranged about supper already. You're to go in with my Cousin Keniston."

Miranda gave her a grateful smile as she followed her papa and mama into the ballroom. So at least she was sure of three partners: Uncle Bracebridge, her father, and Cousin Keniston, whoever he might be.

Her hand on her uncle's arm, Miranda crossed the polished floor slowly. A sudden hush fell over the crowded room, followed by a murmur as heads turned for a better look, and then by a spate of whispers that rustled like a breeze running through dry leaves.

Miranda's heart was thudding uncomfortably by the time she took her seat in the gilded chair her uncle held for her. Suppose no one asked her to dance? At home she had always been sought after, so she had no idea how to behave in the event that she was shunned. Hide upstairs in Mary's room? Pretend to be overcome by the heat and ask to be taken home? But those were cowardly strategies. She had to see it through, no matter how painful it proved.

Uncle Bracebridge and Sir Henry, standing behind Miranda and the princess, were innocently gratified at the attention Miranda was attracting.

"You've made a fine impression, Miranda," her uncle said. "Of course everyone must know you are my niece, and I am close to the regent."

"It is enough that she is a Trafford," Sir Henry declared.

The music began. Uncle Bracebridge bowed be-

112

fore Miranda, wheezing but gallant. Curious eyes followed them as they joined the set. Though Uncle Bracebridge puffed and creaked, he proved light of foot and they managed comfortably together.

Sir Henry claimed the second dance, which was a reel. So elegant and graceful was he that he drew the eyes of the gossips away from Miranda temporarily. More than one widow lamented that the princess had captured him before she had had a chance.

When Sir Henry returned Miranda to the princess, who sat serene in her gilt chair, he excused himself with a murmur that he and Bracebridge were off to the card room now that all was well in hand.

"Not yet, my dear," the princess warned. "Not until Miranda has a partner for the next dance."

At that moment Mary hurried up to them with a tall gentleman in tow. "May I present my Cousin Keniston?" she panted. "Oh, bother: mama is beckoning again. I must fly."

Cousin Keniston bowed formally, his face serious. Miranda noticed that his evening costume, though made of fine cloth, was old-fashioned in its cut. He wore his dark hair somewhat shorter than the current style, and his plain white waistcoat sported only a single fob. He was no dandy, she noted with approval. More than likely, he was a country cousin who could not be bothered to follow the whims of fashion.

He bowed to Miranda and held out his arm with the stern air of a man determined to do his duty no matter how painful it might be.

Miranda tilted her face up toward him with a smile.

"Do you dislike dancing very much, sir? If you do, we can as well sit this one out. I shall pretend that I am tired."

He had to bend down from his height to hear her over the hum of talk. His eyes, a cool gray, rested on her suspiciously, as if he thought she meant to make fun of him.

"We will dance, of course. Mary is my cousin and I am here to take part in her come-out."

"Very well then. The country dance is my favorite."

Nothing more was said until the music began, when they were parted. After they came together later, Cousin Keniston said abruptly, "I apologize if I seemed brusque. I like dancing well enough. It is only that this is an awkward time for me to be in London. We are in the midst of spring planting at Malburn."

Instantly sympathetic, Miranda replied, "How well I know. It is a bad time for me too, for at Templeton we are trying out several new strains of corn and wheat."

The music carried them apart again. As she danced away, Miranda caught a glimpse of Cousin Keniston looking back at her over his shoulder with a doubtful frown.

She hoped she had not upset him. He was a pleasant-looking sort, she reflected, though not to compare with Wendover. She rather liked his lack of polish and was amused by his suspicious attitude, for she well knew how testy a country squire could be if he thought he was being looked down upon by a member of the *ton*. She was glad he was to be her partner for supper. They had a great deal in common.

As they left the floor together when the dance ended, she smiled up at him and said encouragingly: "There, that wasn't so dreadful after all, was it?"

"Quite the contrary. Tell me, what do you call this new strain of corn you spoke of?"

Miranda offered the name and estimates of yield.

He listened, then gave her a direct challenge. "You are young to be so knowledgeable, Miss Trafford. I think you and Mary have got up a tease together. Or are you being pert?"

"At almost four and twenty, I am too old for pertness, sir."

Her frank admission struck him into silence. He bowed and departed hastily for the other end of the ballroom.

"What have you done to him?" the princess begged to know.

"Only told him how old I am."

"I despair of you, Miranda! Thank fortune I have found a partner for this next dance. Ah, here he comes. Miranda, may I present Mr. Wilmot?"

Her new partner had a dashingly poetic look. He wore his dark hair in painstaking disarray in imitation of Lord Byron, and as they took their places, he quoted with a meaningful look into her eyes, " 'She walks in beauty, like the night . . .' "

He began to pay her extravagant compliments. No doubt he had learned that she was an heiress, she thought distastefully. By the time their dance ended, Mr. Wilmot had managed to compose a four-line verse of his own, likening Miranda to a wild rose. It was not very original, but at least it rhymed. Miranda thanked him sweetly.

He bowed and left with a lingering smile. Miranda took her seat beside the princess, who sat waiting for her with an air even more regal than was usual.

"Smile, Miranda. All the gentlemen I talked to are engaged for the next dance, I fear. I shall go to the card room and have a word with your papa. Meanwhile it won't do for you to sit here alone. Pretend you have torn a flounce and retire."

"But I am not wearing flounces."

"No matter! Follow me. Keep smiling and chatting as we leave the room. It must not seem to be a retreat."

Aunt and niece parted in the hall outside the ballroom. Miranda found her way to the room set aside for the ladies. There she retied the ribbon she wore woven through her curls and stared at herself in the mirror as if she were a stranger. No beauty there, she admitted critically, yet nothing to mark her an antidote, either. When she had lingered as long as she thought proper, she draped her net shawl through her elbows at the correct angle and dawdled her way back to the ballroom for all the world like her brothers used to do when she had taken them to their dancing class. She must tell Wendover that: he would laugh with her.

The princess's chair was empty. Miranda sat down to watch the posturing couples on the floor with an air of interest, only partially assumed, for in her mind she was busy describing them to Shelly in her next letter.

The French windows near her chair were open, she noticed, and she inhaled the damp, fresh night air gratefully. At home the early vegetables would be drinking in the rain. She worried about Molesby, her head gardener, who suffered from rheumatism in the spring, and hoped he had found a sturdy young boy from the village to help with the planting.

In the midst of her musings she saw the Wyndhams come across the floor and take seats just on the other side of the French windows. They looked over at her and Miranda endeavored to smile with a cordiality she did not feel. Sir George and his lady turned their heads in the other direction like a pair of angry geese, Lady Wyndham's feather bobbing indignantly.

It was the cut direct. Miranda's face went hot, less with hurt than with anger. She stared straight at the ugly couple with a faint smile of contempt on her generous lips.

The dance seemed to go on forever. By the time the princess returned, escorted by a gentleman of middle years got up in the very crack of style, Miranda's face felt as if it had turned to stone.

"May I present Lord Depew?" the princess said. "He is anxious to dance with you, my dear."

She looked up into a raddled face and noticed that the gentleman had heightened his color with cosmetics, which did little to hide the lines and veins of his years of dissipation. He gave her an intimate wink as they took the floor.

"I admire a young woman who has the courage to defy convention," he drawled. "You are as pretty as you are daring. I am getting up a little party to picnic at my estate just outside the city next week, and I do hope you will be my guest."

"You are kind, my lord, but I cannot accept until I have asked my aunt's permission."

"Humbug. You slipped off to stay with Wendover. Give Lady Trafford the same sort of Banbury tale that got you off before, and I promise you won't regret it."

He squeezed her arm meaningfully. Raising her eyes to his, Miranda said with a melting smile, "How delightful. But are you sure you have room to accommodate the train I brought with me to Wendover Manor? I never travel without my companion, my maid, a coachman and a footman, and of course a pair of postillions."

Lord Depew's gaunt face was a study in frustration.

"Don't try to gammon me, girl."

"I would not dream of it, my lord, for I can see that you are a man of wide experience, and I am only a country girl."

"A demmed shrewd one!" he replied crossly.

"And not such a girl, if what I hear is true. How comes it that you are not married at your age? No takers, eh?"

"I did not fancy any of the gentlemen who offered for me."

"Well, you had better settle for what you can get. Not many men would be willing to take Wendover's castoff."

Miranda, caught with her arm in his as they trod the final measures of the dance, said nothing. It took all her self-control to keep from slapping him across his evil face with the fan that hung from her wrist.

She waited, instead, until the music came to an end and they approached the princess, who sat chatting with the Countess Lieven. Then she removed her hand from his arm, brushed her long glove with great care, and said, "Kindly leave me, Lord Depew. I do not care to be seen in your company any longer."

Fury soon replaced his stare of incomprehension. "Nor I with you, Miss Trafford! You had best return to the country, where your crude manners may be acceptable!"

Miranda went to stand in the open French window, where she fanned herself vigorously until she regained her composure. Upon her return to take her seat beside the princess, she saw Lord Depew talking with a pair of cronies. They looked across at her and sniggered together. It was not difficult to imagine what Lord Depew had told them.

"What is the matter with you, Miranda?" the princess inquired after she had bade the Countess Lieven goodbye. "Are you ill? I've never seen you so pale."

"I have just sunk myself beyond hope."

"*Now* what dreadful thing have you done!" The princess, who was not given to nerves as a rule, longed to throw a spasm. Her niece seemed fated to fall into one disaster after another, and if there was anything she loathed, it was unpleasantness of any sort.

"I told Lord Depew that I did not care to be seen in his company."

The story came out in such hot accents that the princess begged Miranda to lower her voice and to keep smiling unless she wished everyone present to know what had happened.

"It was indeed wrong of Depew to insult you as he did, but could you not have turned him off with more tact? I agree that he is unspeakably vile, but he is an intimate of the regent and is received everywhere. Let us hope he does not inflict his bile on your poor papa, for he has important connections. It appears that we are in the soup, indeed." The princess raised her chin another half inch and put a white hand to her throat. "However, we must continue to smile. If matters do not improve, I shall send for the carriage and say I am feeling ill."

"But everyone will guess—"

"Of course they will, but one must pull a decent veil over uncomfortable situations." Seeing Miranda's rebellious expression, she sighed. "I have arranged to have young Thomas Alston partner you in the next dance. Then it will be time for supper. Your papa and Bracebridge will join us, and no one will notice that you do not have a partner."

Young Tom came up then and bowed to Miranda formally, after which he gave her a familiar grin and led her off to the floor. It was the pleasantest dance yet, Miranda thought as she and Tom teased each other and laughed together over Tom's occasional missteps.

"I wish I could take you in to supper," Tom confided as they walked across the floor toward the princess, "but Mama has ordered me to partner that giggling Parton girl. I told her I prefer older women, but she wouldn't listen to me."

He took his leave, and a few minutes later Miranda saw him going toward the plump little Parton child with the air of a man heading up the steps of the guillotine.

"I'm glad I'm not that young," she remarked to the princess.

"I wish you were. This season would be easier for all of us," the princess retorted. "If your father and Bracebridge do not come soon to take us in to supper, I shall have to send a servant after them."

"Mary's cousin from the country was to have had the supper interval with me, but I suppose he will beg off."

"Miranda, I see a tall gentleman coming this way. Is it—I do believe it is her Cousin Keniston after all!"

Miranda looked up toward the lean figure threading through the crowd toward them. There was no mistaking the solemn look on Cousin Keniston's face. He intended to do his duty by her, however odd he considered her to be.

The princess greeted him with rare effusiveness. "Please do not think of waiting for your papa, Miranda," she urged. "No doubt they are in the midst of a rubber and they will come when they have finished. Do go along and find your own table. We will follow later."

Cousin Keniston offered Miranda his arm. He might be lacking in town polish, but he was good at getting what he wanted. It took only a word to a footman and they were seated at a choice table located beside a window that overlooked a narrow balcony. A gesture ordered the other two chairs removed so that they were alone.

Miranda gave him an inquiring look. "I wished to have some time to talk with you away from the mob," he said bluntly, "for you are the only person present who has anything interesting to say. After I've brought you whatever you like from the buffet, I hope to hear more about the changes you have made at Templeton."

While they ate their salmon and new peas, he bombarded her with questions which Miranda answered with complete candor. Instead of being shocked at her unorthodox background, Cousin Keniston was all admiration.

"Your father was wrong to put such a burden on you, but you have handled it well. I believe most young women should learn something about estate management, for very often, in cases of war or sudden death, they are left to handle these affairs alone, as my mama was when Papa died. I was only six at the time. Under her care my property grew and flourished. You remind me of her."

"That is a pretty compliment, for she must be a remarkable woman.

Cousin Keniston described his sainted mother in full detail. Invalid though she was, she never failed to join him for breakfast. Every day she visited such tenants as were in trouble or ill, and she had established a home for Unfortunate Females in conjunction with an orphanage, which she supported out of her own pocket. As he talked, Miranda hoped she herself didn't fall into the category of an Unfortunate, and wondered whether Cousin Keniston had heard the gossip and was trying to warn her in a roundabout way.

"Do you plan to stay in London long?" she asked him when he finally subsided.

"I am not certain as yet. Tell me, Miss Trafford, how do you like London now that you have begun to sample city life for the first time?"

"If I'm to be honest, I would rather be at Templeton. I left too much work for poor Molesby. He will be bent double with his back in this rainy weather. And I wanted to separate the dahlia tubers myself before planting begins, because they are a special variety I received from a friend of Papa's in Spain."

"We haven't tried dahlias yet at Malburn. Do you recommend them?"

They were so engrossed in their conversation, for it developed that Cousin Keniston grew certain rare tropical plants in his greenhouses, that they found themselves the last ones left in the supper room. With some reluctance Cousin Keniston escorted Miranda back to the ballroom and requested another dance before releasing her into the care of the smiling princess.

Miranda, too, was sparkling, for she had enjoyed their talk, and Cousin Keniston had promised to give her a pair of orchids to try for herself at Templeton.

"How did you do it, my dear?" the princess murmured.

Miranda stared. "Do what, Aunt Louisa?"

"Capture Lord Keniston. He is the greatest catch in London and known to be as wary as a deer about women."

"You can't mean Mary's Cousin Keniston? Why, he is only a country squire, but I found him excellent company. We had a good talk about composting after supper."

The princess rolled her large eyes heavenward.

"Lord Keniston owns one of the richest estates in the country. Malburn is his main seat, but he has a number of other properties. He is noted not only for his wealth but for his sterling character. There's never been a whisper about him, or so I am told. You clever child, to annex the most eligible bachelor present."

Miranda rolled her own blue-green eyes, which were twinkling more merrily than usual.

122

"To think that I was only trying to be kind to Mary's awkward country cousin! Virtue is always rewarded."

"Do you like him?"

"Very much. If you're asking whether I am smitten, the answer is no."

"It is too soon to make up your mind. You are bound to like him better as time goes on. Aha, just as I hoped. Now that Keniston has taken notice of you, you are about to be deluged with offers to dance. Don't put on that obstinate face. Forgive them for having little faith. Try to think of them as brothers and you will get on nicely."

So it happened that by the time Sir Henry and Uncle Bracebridge left their final card game and appeared in the ballroom, they found Miranda the center of a group of gentlemen all vying for a dance or asking permission to call upon her soon.

"There is Keniston speaking to her," Uncle Bracebridge exclaimed with surprise. "Keniston, of all people, to admire our little Miranda."

"She is a Trafford," Sir Henry needled him, "and though not a beauty, she does have a charming smile and a friendly manner any sensible man is bound to appreciate."

On the way home in the carriage together at something after three in the morning, Sir Henry remarked complacently to his only daughter, "You could not have found a more suitable match than Keniston. He is everything I could ask for in a son-in-law."

"Papa, I met him only tonight. Don't plague me with talk of making a match already!"

"What is the matter with her, Louisa? What did I say to upset her?"

"Miranda is overtired, my dear. It has been a long evening. Ah, here we are at Halsted Square at last.

123

I confess that I am past the age when I find it enjoyable to stay up all night."

Thompson himself waited to take their wraps. Their glum faces disturbed him.

The little miss must have got off to a poor start for all she's in looks tonight, he ruminated. If it's loose talk that harmed her, I'll give that Mattern a facer next time I see him.

Miranda followed the princess up the stairs wearily. Sir Henry, flushed with pride at having a handsome wife and a daughter who was turning out to be satisfactory despite his earlier doubts, repaired to the library to drink a final glass of brandy.

Keniston, he gloated, a man known to be aloof and uninterested in females! Though he had not admitted his fears to the princess, Sir Henry had been convinced that Miranda lacked the soft, sweet airs and graces to attract the right kind of husband. Otherwise he would not have tried to hurry her into an alliance with her beau from Templeton, for Sir Frederick was nothing in comparison with Keniston.

He drank another small glass of brandy. Some time later, after he retired to his room and was helped out of his evening dress by his sleepy valet, he went to knock at the door of his wife's bedroom.

"Go away please, dear Henry," the princess called feebly. "I am prostrated with a headache."

Sir Henry retreated to his own domain. What was wrong with his household tonight? All had gone better than even he, with his usual optimism, could have hoped for, yet his women hadn't the gumption to celebrate with him.

He stumbled into bed and fell asleep still puzzling over the strange moodiness of the female sex.

CHAPTER 10

"Everyone is marveling at the way you have be-witched Cousin Keniston, Miranda," Mary con-fided. "He is known to loathe London, but he has stayed in town for almost a month now. He posi-tively glows when his eyes light on you. Will you marry him?"

"He hasn't asked me yet."

"He will, unless some busybody tells him about the time you stayed at Wendover Manor."

"I've told him the story already, the second time he came calling. He was surprised that people in town should make a fuss over our taking refuge from a winter storm, as any sensible countryman would do."

The two girls were bowling along in the Alston carriage on their way to visit the dazzling shops in Bond Street.

"Then if he knows and doesn't mind, it's all but settled," Mary decided with a satisfied air.

"Don't be too sure." Miranda assumed the lan-guid pout of a reigning belle. "I am simply besieged by suitors, my dear. There is Mr. Langton, for one. He delights me with a newer, more fanciful waist-coat almost every day. Think what an interesting husband he would make."

"Miranda, you can't be serious. He is the most odious fop. Who else has offered?"

"Mr. Wilmot: he offers as regularly as the sun rises. And Sir Arthur Phelps. I lean toward him at the moment because he dances so gracefully. As long as my money lasts to provide him with the best of everything, we may dance down the years together in perfect accord."

"You say the most unusual things, Miranda. No wonder you are declared this season's Original."

"Last month I was accused of being fast. The simple truth is that I haven't changed, I have only gained consequence because your cousin Keniston has noticed me. Nobody is willing to offend the possible future mistress of Malburn."

"No more snubs from horrid Wyndhams?"

"Only a few bitter glances before they bow frigidly. I have more invitations than I can accept in a year. I won't deny that it has been pleasant to be feted, and yet I am anxious to go home to Templeton soon, before all my spring blooms are gone."

"Oh well, when you marry Cousin Keniston you'll be mistress of the finest conservatories in England. I can't wait to visit you at Malburn. I shall expect you to give all sorts of balls and picnics for me, and it will be your duty to produce the perfect husband, if I am not engaged as yet. Miranda, do you like Sir Peter Oakes?"

"Indeed I do, and so do you, I gather."

Mary blushed up into the roots of her red hair. "I hope I haven't been too obvious about my preference, but I'm wild with love for that man. I dream about him. If he married someone else, I should wither away and die, but he has done nothing to give me hope as yet."

"He hasn't a very large estate, but in other ways I think he would suit you well."

"I never expected to fall in love this way. Oh, Miranda, will you do what you can to help me?"

Miranda promised, wondering meanwhile why she did not experience the same sort of transports over Keniston.

"It may be that I am too old to be carried away," she brooded as she followed Mary through the shops. "Or possibly I am too particular. I could never adore Sir Peter. He is *too* agreeable, like a milk pudding."

She helped Mary choose a length of muslin in the shade of green she favored, and herself bought pale lilac-colored gloves and a dashing blue bonnet she would probably wear only this once.

The two girls went on to Hookham's, where they lingered so long that it was midafternoon before Miranda arrived back at Halsted Square. She had hardly taken off her new bonnet before Thompson sent a footman up with word that Mr. Wilmot had called to see her.

"Tell him I can spare him only a few minutes."

Mr. Wilmot had become a perfect pest, but she did not like to hurt him. She brushed her hair hurriedly and descended to the small family sitting room prepared to explain that she had another engagement in half an hour, although she intended going alone for a ride in the park.

Mr. Wilmot had brought a new poem. It was filled with melancholy ruminations upon a love unrequited. After he finished reading it to her, he got to his knees suddenly and announced in a stifled voice that he would put a pistol to his forehead unless she consented to marry him.

Miranda explained kindly that although she liked him very much as a friend, she did not feel the affection that would allow her to accept his offer.

"At least give me reason to hope," Mr. Wilmot pleaded. His flowing cravat was in disarray and his

127

brown eyes resembled so closely those of her faithful spaniel at Templeton that Miranda had to look away.

"I am sorry, but I cannot." Seeing that he meant to plead his cause further, she decided it would not be wrong to tell a small falsehood. "I am already bound, in a way."

"To Keniston, of course!" Mr. Wilmot got up and dusted off his tight pantaloons angrily. "I might have known I did not stand a chance against a man who owns a third of England! You have broken my heart, Miss Trafford. I hoped you were not so mercenary. I begin to fear for my reason."

Sir Henry, arriving home at that moment and learning from Thompson that his daughter was in the small salon with a gentleman, smiled contentedly as he proceeded upstairs to that apartment.

It would be Lord Keniston, who was certain to offer for Miranda any day now. His girl had proved to be a thoroughbred after all, though he'd had his doubts. Leave it to a Trafford to make the match of the season. It was a family trait.

Just as the footman was preparing to open the door to the small salon, it flew open from inside and a gentleman with disordered locks, wearing an air of tragedy, rushed past Sir Henry without a word of greeting or apology.

"Who was that?" he asked his daughter with raised eyebrows as he sat down across from her and studied her downcast face.

"Mr. Wilmot, Papa. You have met him here before."

"What is the matter with him? Is he ill?"

"He says he is driven mad with love for me, Papa," Miranda replied demurely.

"Bless my soul! It's lucky Keniston didn't come calling while that fellow was here. It might have put him off. Miranda, I've brought you a gift." He presented her with a small box he had been carrying in his pocket. "I knew you would like these earrings. Sapphires suit you. They are my engagement gift, and I have already bespoken the necklace to match, which you shall have when you marry."

She closed the little box in a hurry. "You are beforehand, Papa. If you expect me to marry Keniston, you will have to wait until he asks me."

"He will; the fellow dotes on you. Your Aunt Louisa tells me that he plans to bring his mother to town to meet you. The sooner the better, I say."

"You may be in a hurry, but *I'm* not. Who will care for Charles and Edgar if I marry? Who will see to our tenants?"

"The boys will be at their schools. They can spend vacations with you and your new husband. As for Templeton, I have been busy making arrangements. I have found an excellent man and wife. He will serve as assistant bailiff to Holmes, who is getting old, and she can replace our housekeeper if you want to take Kelton with you when you leave."

"You have thought of everything." Miranda's face, usually open and lively, had turned expressionless. "So I am no longer needed at home."

"Your husband will need you now."

"It is quite possible that I shan't marry Keniston even if he offers."

"What fault can you find with him, may I ask?"

"Nothing to put a finger on. He seems reasonably intelligent, his appearance is satisfactory, and he behaves just as he should. But still I am not sure! I have never heard him laugh."

"A man in love is in no mood for humor. When you visit Malburn you are bound to be impressed. Well, well, women take strange notions and there is no great hurry. A summer wedding at Templeton might be best after all."

Miranda rose. "Excuse me, Papa. I must go up and change."

A short while later Miranda, clad in a handsome new dark blue riding habit, knocked and was admitted to her aunt's dressing room, where Monsieur Giles had just finished piling up the princess's thick hair into a dark gold heap garnished with dainty ringlets. The hairdresser showed pain at sight of Miranda's tousled curls and volunteered to stay on to attend her, but Miranda said there was no point since she was just on her way out for her afternoon ride.

"What has upset you, Miranda?" the princess inquired nervously as soon as Giles had gone. "You're a veritable storm cloud."

"It is Papa again, pushing me to marry Keniston, and he has not even offered yet."

"How do you feel toward him, dear?"

Miranda swung her neat, small hat by its ribbons and shrugged.

"I like him very well. When he forgets how important he is, no one could be kinder. He turns almost boyish when we are alone. I feel as comfortable with him as I do with Charles and Edgar."

"My dear Miranda, you can't go through life collecting brothers! Have you never fallen deep in love, even as a schoolgirl?"

"Lord Wendover asked me the same question. Of course I have. There were several gentlemen I sighed over—for a little while, until I knew them better."

"Was there no man you would be willing to die for if it became necessary?"

"Never, I'm afraid. If that is what it means to be truly in love, then I have never felt that emotion."

"I pray that you will one day and that the man is Keniston, for you deserve a special husband, and he is a rare catch. I have not heard the least whisper about his morals, which is wonderful in a man of his age and consequence."

"Who knows?"

Miranda put on her hat in the casual way her aunt despaired of—the girl didn't even bother to look in the mirror!—and said she was off for her ride.

"Oh, I mustn't forget to thank you for soothing Papa, Aunt Louisa. I thought he would have an apoplexy when he discovered that I had sent Patrick down to Templeton to fetch my horses to town."

"I reminded him that a country girl needs a daily draft of fresh air to maintain her looks. Miranda, before you go, tell me why you call your mare by such an odd name."

"Xantippe? I did it to make it up to the poor woman. She was wife to Socrates, the famed Greek philosopher, and the poor thing is known to history only as a shrew. I suspect she had good reason to be shrewish. Her husband spent all his time drinking and conversing with his friends and must have neglected her terribly. To top it off, he got himself condemned to death for treason."

The princess raised her heavy eyelids. "That must have been more painful for him than for her. Go along now before it rains. I had forgotten how it rains in England."

Scattered purple clouds hung low in the sky, but no rain had fallen by the time Miranda arrived at the park. Few people were about on this threatening day, so after a decorous canter, she decided it was safe to give Xantippe her head for a brief gallop.

The vigorous exercise drove away the uncomfortable thoughts that plagued her. She let out the reins a little more. How lovely it was to be free of the constraints of society for even these few minutes!

Horse and rider raced along the bridle path in perfect harmony until they both became aware that another horse was gaining on them from behind. Miranda knew that Xantippe hated to be passed. Patrick had been training the mare to race before she had stumbled and fractured a small bone in her leg, thus ending her career before it began.

Scenting a challenge, Xantippe took the bit between her teeth and lengthened her stride. Miranda gave her her head, as ready to race as her mare, and well aware that nothing less than a bolt of lightning could stop her when she was in this mood.

All might have gone well had not a large dog escaped from the footman who had it in charge and dashed across the path, barking furiously.

Xantippe lost her temper and reared. To her chagrin, Miranda was thrown, while the mare, having shaken off her burden, streaked off ahead of her challenger.

From her painfully prone position, Miranda watched the other rider catch up to the mare and seize her flying bridle. She wished him to perdition for having caused her humiliation even while she had to admit that he was a capital horseman.

She pushed herself upright and looked around for her groom, who appeared trotting along slowly. Aware by various painful reminders that she had fallen hard, Miranda shook her head to clear the haze away. The second rider had turned and now cantered back toward her, leading the reluctant Xantippe, who nipped at his tall bay whenever she managed to get close enough.

"Lord Wendover! What a surprise. I would be happy to see you if I had not just made a perfect idiot of myself."

"You rode like Diana. Between that fool dog and your bad-tempered mare, you're lucky to be alive."

"Poor Xantippe. This is her first day in London. She's not used to the city nor to being outrun by another horse."

"Xantippe?" He slid to the ground, a sudden smile lighting up his face, which Miranda thought looked thin and ill. "What a suitable name. Here comes your hopeless groom. He took a tumble just after you entered the park. I was trying to warn you when your mare took offense. Come, lad: walk these animals until they cool. And take care not to let your mistress out of your sight again, do you understand?"

"Yessir, milord." Poor Ned, who now had three beasts to handle, straggled off down the path beyond reach of further scolding.

Wendover gave Miranda his arm and helped her across to a bench despite her protestations that she was not really hurt.

"Then why are you nursing your left arm? Sit here and let me have a look at it." He stripped off her glove and turned back her sleeve. Miranda became aware of an odd sensation as his hand encircled her wrist, and told herself that she must still be a little dizzy from her fall. "Just as I expected—sprained, but luckily, not broken. Any other bruises?"

Miranda grinned. "None that I care to discuss with a strange gentleman."

He laughed, releasing her wrist only when she grew conscious and made to withdraw her arm. "Hardly a stranger, Miss Trafford, after we shared a snowstorm. In fact, I once believed that we were friends."

"So did I until we met at Hookham's that day. It was my first snub, though not the worst. The Wyndhams are past masters of the art."

His face darkened. "I regret deeply the pain I have caused you through my unfortunate stepmother. My only idea when we met at Hookham's was to avoid making matters worse. Believe me, Miss Trafford, I have never mentioned your stay at the manor to anyone. I said as much to your father when I called on him and offered to do all in my power to quell any gossip that might arise."

"You talked to Papa when you left the letters at Halsted Square? I didn't know that."

"Your father made it plain that I was not welcome. He is right, of course. I went there to offer for you, but he let me know that my offer would not be acceptable."

He was watching her reaction intently. Miranda pretended to massage her swollen wrist, not sure what he expected from her.

"That was brave of you," she said lightly. "Imagine your dismay if Papa had accepted."

"I assure you that I would have been more than happy to be accepted as your suitor," he said formally. "I would not have made my offer otherwise."

Miranda could not help admiring the way he carried it off. Of course he was only doing his duty as a gentleman since he was suspected of having compromised her. If she hadn't known of his attachment to Lady Trent, she might almost have believed him.

"I hope Papa was not unbearably rude."

He shifted a little apart from her and laid his arm along the back of the bench on which they sat. On his face was the same half-rueful smile she remembered seeing across the card table when he had made a reckless play and lost. She noticed that his eyes lacked luster, as if he found little joy in life.

"I had not much hope of being welcomed, not after I learned that you are a great heiress. Why did you lead me to believe that you were a country mouse?"

"Because that is what I am in spite of having inherited a storehouse full of cheese from my godmother."

"Not so poor as all that," he jeered, "with Keniston at the head of your army of admirers. Rob Purvis told me that every time he called on you, he found Keniston there. Am I to wish you happy?"

"Certainly not. I haven't even met his mother yet. Why do you look that way? Is there something I should know about Lord Keniston?"

"Only that he has a doting mother. She ordered Wellington to send her son home from Brussels when he developed a mild jaundice. Keniston is her sole consolation in her widowhood."

"Poor Lord Keniston. He has my sympathy."

"Do you find him an entertaining companion?"

"We share an interest in the land. There is a great deal I can learn from him."

"Rumor says your father hopes to set the wedding for this summer."

"Papa has no authority over me. I am in control of my own fortune and have been since I was twenty-one."

"It was confoundedly dull after you left the manor. Ebbets was a poor substitute. I didn't discover until you were gone that it was you who provided the excellent meals we enjoyed. Accept my gratitude."

"What else could I do in all decency after you shared your pheasants with me? I still sigh over the poor little pig, though."

"I began to understand why you left with a light purse. The beef must have cost a pretty penny."

"Oh, that? It was to strengthen Shelly and poor thin Wibberly, though of course I told Mrs. Curry that she might serve you a bowl of nourishing broth if there was plenty."

His listless air disappeared. He threw back his head and began to laugh, and they were once more on their familiar footing.

"You are the most impertinent young woman it has ever been my fortune to meet. Between you and Mrs. Shelburne, you persuade me that females can be good company after all. Your Shelly grew tiresome only when she sang your praises endlessly."

"Then we are even. Wibberly swore you won the battle of Waterloo single-handed. I see a pair of riders approaching. Perhaps you had better leave me flat the way you did at Hookham's lest we set off another round of gossip. Lady Trent would not approve."

"Neither will Keniston. All the Kenistons are famed for their goodness."

"Was there a drop of acid in your tone just then?"

"It was more like reverence. You will find his mama, and his cousin Mrs. Pelham, who lives with them, overwhelmingly sweet when you meet them."

"Can there be too much of goodness?"

"Wait and see. When you meet Lady Keniston, I suggest that you wear the same wardrobe, buttoned to the chin, that you wore at the manor. And if you are invited to play cards, shuffle with care, for her eyes are still keen."

Miranda stood up. Wendover got to his feet and put his hand under her elbow to help her. He was so close that she could see the healed scar on his temple which she used to dress under Dr. Purvis' supervision: it hardly showed now.

"What a dismal picture you paint, Lord Wendover. Are you trying to discourage me from making an eligible match?"

His intensely blue eyes were serious as they met hers. "I am concerned for your happiness. I can't imagine you living in that household, where duty is everything and gaiety is frowned on."

"What—no Venetian Breakfasts? No routs or masked balls? Ah, well, a quiet life will suit me very well. I am already tired of this frantic pursuit of pleasure. Dancing once a week will satisfy me when I am married."

"There are suitable entertainments at Malburn but no pleasure, I believe. Lady Keniston is convinced that suffering and misfortune are dealt out by a stern Creator in punishment for our sins. When one is being chastised from above, it is wrong to laugh or even to smile."

"Then I should be safe, for I haven't committed many sins. At least nothing unforgivable, except for allowing myself to be thrown."

He took her swelling wrist in both his hands and massaged it gently. "Not yet, perhaps. Only wait until you have spent an evening watching Lady Keniston sew aprons for the poor souls in her home for Unfortunate Females while her son expounds on the blights that struck in fourteen, or was it fifteen?"

"I remember the blights very well, so we will have grounds for conversation. But I am not a good needlewoman. Even an Unfortunate would be ashamed to wear my handiwork. Tell me, have you recently come up from the manor? You look as if you've been spending time out-of-doors."

"Yes. Wibberly and I have been trying to set affairs in order now that we are rid of the scoundrelly bailiff. I left Wibberly in charge and came to town to interview a new steward. If all goes well, I'll send the new man down next week."

"Is your land productive? I couldn't get an idea of what it is like, for I saw it buried under all that snow."

"Wendover was once famed for its wool. However, since Lady Jess sold off most of our breeding stock, the quality has declined."

This was the moment the lowering clouds chose to let down their burden. Large drops of rain spattered loudly on the leaves of the oak under which they sheltered. Ned Groom, who had been walking the horses with many an anxious look back over his shoulder, now hastened toward them wearing an anguished expression.

"I suppose I must go," Miranda said reluctantly, as she freed her hand and attempted to draw on her glove. "I wish we had more time to talk. We have quite a respectable flock at Templeton and something might be arranged—"

Wendover seized the glove she was struggling with and ripped it up the side seam.

"Wear it this way until you reach home, then bathe your wrist in cold water to bring down the swelling. Why didn't you tell me you were in pain?"

"It is not so bad, truly, and I have enjoyed our talk."

The rain began to fall more heavily. Miranda's hair curled around her glowing face and she laughed aside his concern as he tossed her up into the saddle.

"Shall I see you at the ball Papa is giving for me?" she asked, pulling Xantippe's head around, for the restive mare was trying to bite Wendover's hand.

"If you want me there."

"You shall have an invitation this very day. Where shall I direct it?"

"I am staying at Wendover House at present."

A shadow darkened his face as he spoke. Miranda hid her surprise and rode off with a wave of her good hand.

Wendover staying with Lady Jessamin? Either he was in worse financial straits than she guessed, or he was not as disgusted with the riffraff that thronged Lady Jess' gaming rooms as he pretended.

Miranda arrived at the house in Halsted Square just as the princess, clad in precious sable-trimmed taffeta, emerged under the shelter of Thompson's large umbrella. She stared at Miranda's dripping habit and shook her head.

"What will you do next, child? Fortunately, you can look pretty even when you're half-drowned. You missed a call from Keniston's cousin. Mrs. Pelham invited us to dine *en famille* at their town house on Monday if Lady Keniston is well enough to make the trip to town."

"How kind," Miranda muttered, dismounting with an effort she took pains to conceal, for Patrick was watching from his box as he waited to drive the princess to her musicale. "Don't let me keep you standing in the rain. Do go along and enjoy yourself."

She managed to get into the entrance hall and trailed across the marble floor, but by the time Thompson reentered with his dripping umbrella, she was sunk down on the lowest step of the divided staircase with her hand to her forehead.

"You're ill, Miss Trafford! Let me call your maid."

"No, no: don't make a fuss. I took a tumble in the park, but I'm just shaken up. I'll rest here a minute before I go up to my room."

Thompson slipped away to the dining room and returned shortly with a small glass of brandy. "Medicine, miss. Swallow it all at once and you'll feel better."

Miranda did as she was told. Shortly the fiery liquid rose to her head and she stood up and prepared to mount the stairs.

"Thank you, Thompson. I'm fine now. Were there any messages?"

"Lord Keniston's man stopped to say that Lord Keniston will call on you at six o'clock this evening. Shall I send word that it is not convenient?"

It could hardly be more inconvenient, but Miranda had no excuse short of admitting that she had let herself be thrown and had spent a half hour chatting with Lord Wendover in the park.

"Of course I will see him. And Thompson, remember—not a word to anyone about my tumble."

"You may count on me, miss."

CHAPTER 11

Miranda's young maid gave a squeak of alarm when she caught sight of her mistress's swollen wrist.

"Never mind. I'll be all right as soon as I have my bath. Nobody is to know that I took a tumble, Benson."

The warm bath water brought out a bouquet of purple and blue bruises all over Miranda's body. To hide them she chose a gown of pale pink muslin with long sleeves, and after a glance in her mirror, she brushed her light brown curls into a fringe across her forehead to cover a bruise on her temple she hadn't noticed before.

She felt curiously light-headed as she wondered whether Keniston had come to make her the long-expected offer. She might as well accept him and be done with it. It was what everyone expected. Keniston was a good man in his own way. If he lacked a certain spark she would have chosen in her husband, still he made up for the lack by being gentle and kindly.

"Milord is waiting, miss," Benson said, hovering anxiously.

Miranda stared at the girl. Benson would be thrilled if her mistress made an exalted match. They all would, including Thompson and even Patrick, although he had some reservations. "Only if he suits you, Miss Miranda. Don't be in any hurry."

Benson almost herded her out of her room. She went down the stairs slowly. When she entered the small sitting room at last, Keniston jumped to his feet as eagerly as a young and inexperienced suitor. He had brought her a large bouquet of pink and white roses from his greenhouses.

"They reminded me of you," he said in his abrupt fashion. It was not his habit to pay compliments. Coming from him, the words hinted at a powerful suppressed emotion.

Tonight Keniston had obviously dressed with more than his usual care. Tall and thin, with his dark hair a little longer on his neck and a fashionable cravat at his throat, he cut a fine figure. Almost as impressive as Wendover, Miranda thought hazily as he led her to a sofa and sat down across from her.

"I have come with good news, Miss Trafford," he began. "My mother is anxious to meet you, and as she had already arranged to see Dr. Grayson on Tuesday, I am planning a dinner for the Monday evening beforehand. Cousin Cora Pelham will be with her, of course, and with your mama and papa, we shall be only a family party."

"Monday?" she inquired. Keniston had not asked her whether she had other plans. To be bidden to a Keniston family dinner must supersede any other engagement. "I am not quite sure if Monday is free."

She had meant it half-jokingly, but Keniston took alarm.

"It would not do to disappoint Mama after she has taken the trouble to travel to London, for as you must know, she is very nearly an invalid."

"I hope the journey will not prove too tiring for her." It was half a day's trip, no more.

142

"It might be, save that I had a coach made especially for her to lessen the jolting. She suffers from pains in her head and neck which Dr. Grayson has never been able to cure, and her heart is not strong, but you will find her a courageous woman. Even when she is confined to her bed with palpitations, she manages to keep up with her needlework."

"That is admirable." Miranda's smile felt unnatural. "And your cousin, Mrs. Pelham? Your mother must be grateful for her company since they are both widows."

"Poor Cora. She lost her husband when they had been married less than two years. George's estate was entailed, so Mama suggested that she come to live with us. My mother is the soul of kindness."

"Was he not young to die?" she asked idly, simply to keep the conversation alive.

"It is a strange story. He and Cora were staying at Malburn for the hunting. Not that Mama and I liked the fellow, but we asked him for Cora's sake. I won't try to hide the fact that he was a man of irregular habits. There was a female at an inn near Malburn—but I shall say nothing more on that subject. George disappeared one day when we were hunting and didn't fetch up until the next morning, in a farm cart and with a fever. In spite of Mama's nursing, he died that night. Mama collapsed and Cora stayed on to nurse her, so it seemed natural to ask her to make her home with us."

"Perhaps your mother hoped you would marry her."

He did not hide his surprise. "Cora is like a sister to me. And I am much older than she is. I am thirty-five. Do I seem ancient to you, Miss Trafford?"

"Indeed not. You are in your prime, as Patrick would say. You do not even suffer from the gout as most gentlemen do."

"I am fortunate in that respect, but as I have

often told you, I have to be careful of my diet, for I have an extremely sensitive digestive system. I cannot tolerate rich foods or wine." He warmed to the subject, which was his favorite. "For breakfast I must have an egg boiled no more than three and a half minutes and a piece of dry toast. If I take a single rasher of bacon, I know I will be ill all day. At midday Mama sees to it that we are served something light such as a bit of poached fish or chicken followed by a jelly of some sort and a custard with stewed fruit. For dinner . . ."

Miranda listened, smiling or shaking her head at decent intervals. The poor man couldn't be blamed for being something of a hypochondriac, considering that his mother had probably hovered over him since birth and fallen into hysteria if he so much as had a stomach cramp. When he had finished telling her that he liked a cup of hot milk before he went to bed, sometimes sprinkled lightly with nutmeg, she agreed that nothing was more conducive to a good night's rest.

She had pulled out her kerchief and was occupied in hiding a wrenching yawn behind it when she was startled to see Keniston dart across and occupy the seat beside her on the sofa.

"Miss Trafford, I must speak! I had intended to wait until you meet Mama, but I find I cannot. I have never felt this way before. To be near you is to—"

At this perilous moment Thompson entered with the tray of refreshments Miranda had rung for earlier. Miranda welcomed him so warmly that he raised his eyebrows. Not ready yet, he opined, bowing to Miranda's request that he send someone to Patrick for the parcel she had asked him to bring from Templeton when he was sent for her mounts.

Temporarily put off, Keniston accepted a glass of

sherry, though not before he assured himself of the vintage.

"Please do try one of these cakes," Miranda urged. "They are made of the best butter and flour and should be most easy to digest."

Keniston accepted glumly, and they talked about the weather like strangers for the next few minutes. But the wine had fortified her suitor. He put a second cake aside after one taste and moved closer to Miranda.

"When Mama comes to London I shall take the opportunity to get her permission before speaking to your father, Miss Trafford. Monday is only a little while off, and in the meantime I would like to—"

"When do you leave for Malburn, sir? Tomorrow morning? Then I am glad that I decided to give you my little gift now. I meant it for a surprise, but it is better that you take it with you when you go."

Thompson, having hemmed outside and knocked discreetly, made his entrance carrying a basket with a pained look as if it contained something unspeakable.

"The parcel from Templeton, miss," he announced, handing it to Miranda with a bow.

Later in the kitchen, Thompson declared that whatever was in the basket smelled of the fields. It looked to him like a heap of lumpy potatoes that had gone off.

"With dirt still stuck on them and knobby shoots coming out, but Milord handled them as if he was seeing the crown jewels. He made for Miss Miranda again and I was sure he was about to embrace her, but then he remembered me and drew back. I blame myself. He might have come up to scratch today if I hadn't been prompt."

"He'll wait until his mama looks her over," said Mrs. Green, the chef's helper. "Rich marries rich, I always say. Here's our little miss with enough for two and his lordship the same, and do they share it around? No, they lumps it together and gets richer."

"If I was to judge by the look on her face, she's not ready to marry. It's Sir Henry pushing her into it."

"That's life, Mr. Thompson. Like it or not, we all do what we have to. Here, taste a bit of my pork pie. Mister Jean Paul says my pies are only good enough for the staff, but Miss Miranda ain't above asking me to save her a piece."

"If she marries Lord Keniston and asks me to go with her to Malburn, I fear I shall have to say no. I'm London born and bred. Country air don't suit me."

Mrs. Green shrugged. "I go where my princess goes. She sent for me to go out to Russia when I was only a girl. It was there I learned to use heathen spices and eat fish eggs. Ah, but it was cold! I hope it's warmer in America."

"You'll have to watch out for red Indians. I've heard they have a way of scalping their victims."

"In Russia it was wolves," the cook said philosophically. "I don't worry. Her and Sir Henry will have everything comfortable. Another bit of pie? I wouldn't say no to a sip of that wine to go with it. What was it you said was in the basket Miss Miranda gave Lord Keniston?"

"Doll-ears, by the sound of it. Some foreign flower roots that came from Spain. He looked at them as if they were bars of gold."

"Doll-ears or no, they'll never make a right pair," Mrs. Green predicted, tossing down her wine, "milord being a plodder and Miss Miranda a sprinter. You mark my words."

Miranda lay abed late the following morning coddling her multitude of aches, rising only when she was summoned to see Dr. Purvis, who waited in the small sitting room. He had called around without first sending word.

"I've come to look at your wrist," the stocky young doctor greeted her by way of apology. "Knowing you, I'm certain you've done nothing about it."

"How did you know . . . ?"

"Wendover. He was right: it's only a bad sprain. I'll bind it temporarily and leave you an ointment to rub on that may help a little." He paused in wrapping the swollen wrist and scrutinized her wan face frankly. "You're more shaken-up than you admit, Miss Trafford. Are you concealing other injuries?"

"Only a rainbow of bruises, all minor ones. Nothing I want to show you. It's embarrassing enough to have taken a tumble." She gave him her small, tucked-in smile. "I'm fine as long as I remain standing."

"Why isn't Keniston here to commiserate with you?"

"He went down to Malburn to fetch his mama to London. She is anxious to meet me, it seems."

Dr. Purvis finished binding the wrist and led Miranda across to a chair equipped with a deep, soft cushion. "Can you really be contemplating marriage with Keniston?"

"Why not? Has he some dreadful illness or a vile past I should be warned of?"

"Not at all. He is too good to be true. His mama's own boy, in fact. It is his mama I warn you of. She wears all the airs of a saint, but from what I hear, she would not hesitate to push you over a cliff if she could save her beloved son from you that way."

"You are funning, of course."

"Unfortunately not. I am suggesting that you

147

watch your step in the presence of Lady Keniston and her familiar, Cora Pelham."

"I can't believe you are serious. Do you have proof?"

Dr. Purvis shrugged his wide shoulders. "None. Keniston's papa died shortly after the boy was born. Mrs. Pelham's husband also died young. Both men suffered unknown ailments that struck them down before a doctor could reach them."

"But Lady Keniston is an invalid, I understand."

Dr. Purvis gave a bark of amusement. "I treated her once when Dr. Grayson was ill. The woman is as strong as a plow horse. If she suffers from an illness, it's in her devious mind. People who displease her are often struck down unexpectedly. It is the Lord's will, according to her. More like the broths and medicines she concocts with her own hands!"

"She can't be that evil! It must be coincidence. You don't think she would poison me the first time we meet, before she even knows me."

Dr. Purvis laughed. "If she waits, she may like you, which would make it harder. Miss Trafford, I wish more females were like you. If they were, I might think about matrimony with a glimmer of hope. Which reminds me, did you know that my father and Mrs. Shelburne are becoming the best of friends?"

"She hinted as much in her last letter. I'm happy for her, though I will miss her terribly. We had planned to set up our own household if I chose not to marry."

"I see." It was plain that he understood what she did not say. "And Sir Henry leaves for the States this autumn. That explains a great deal. Well, I am due at the hospital. Let me see, this is Friday. I'll call around again on Tuesday, after you have dined with Lady Keniston, to administer an antidote and to see how your wrist is mending. Don't get up. I can find my own way out."

Miranda smiled after him as he departed at the brisk trot that characterized him. It was odd how fond she had become of the people at the manor during her stay there, almost as if they were a part of her family.

She hoped Malburn would prove as welcoming if she went there to live.

Lord Wendover had found Lady Jessamin partaking of a hearty early supper in the family dining room when he returned from his encounter with Miranda in the park.

Lady Jessamin noted his weary air as he took his chair at the head of the table. "Roach informs me that you were very late arriving home last night, you naughty boy!"

"So I was." He motioned to a footman to bring him the decanter of brandy.

"Is that all you have to say for yourself?"

"Where I spend my evenings is no concern of yours, madam."

"Nonsense! I have always been extremely fond of you, Wendover. If there is anything I can do to forward your match with Lady Trent, only let me know."

"There will be no match."

"Did she refuse you again? How does she dare, and her only the daughter of a country squire before she landed poor old Trent!"

"I did not offer for her a second time. Now, may I be permitted to eat without interruptions?"

He got up and filled his plate sparingly from the sideboard.

"Oh, you are impossible." Lady Jess pushed aside a scrap of ham with a peevish gesture. This evening her hair looked more gray than orange under an elaborate ruffled cap, and there was no hiding the veins in her long-fingered, grasping hands. "I have tried to give you a mother's love and to do everything just as your own mama would have done, but you show no gratitude."

"My own mother would hardly have sold me up. I doubt if she would have turned Wendover House into a gaming hell for the convenience of a slug like Dartleigh."

Lady Jess was past blushing, but her cap trembled and her slanted green eyes spat fire.

"So this is the thanks I get for my years of devotion! Very well. Expect nothing more from me, ever!"

"I won't. All I ask is that you pack up and be prepared to remove to the dower house within the month. You may have managed to dispose of the jewels and the plate and certain parcels of land, madam, but this house and the manor still belong to me."

Lady Jess' tiny mouth curved in a feline smile.

"I do not deny that this house is yours. I only wonder how you will manage to pay the interest on the loan I was forced to take out against it in order to repair and refurnish it as your papa would have wished."

Wendover put down his fork and turned on her so fiercely that Lady Jess hastened to ring for the footman.

"If you were a man, Jessamin Botts, I would call you out and kill you," Wendover said softly as soon as the man was gone to fetch the fresh tea Lady Jessamin desired. "How much is the loan?"

She hesitated. When she named a figure, he repeated it twice, staggered by the sum.

"If you've gone to the moneylenders, the interest must be astronomical! Little wonder that you've had to sell off my livestock and let my tenants go without seed. Tell me, how have you managed to

150

meet the interest yourself? I am curious to know in case I have to follow your example."

Lady Jess pushed her plate away nervously. Anthony had always been gentlemanly with her in the past. Suddenly she felt almost afraid of him. He wore a certain taut, frustrated look that reminded her of his father when she had driven the old man too far.

"Lady Jess, I asked you a question. Kindly give me an answer. Do not bother to lie."

The cold blue gleam of his eyes frightened her even as it softened her toward him. He was so handsome. If only he had been a little older or she younger—but that was not in the cards, as Dartleigh had reminded her often enough.

"If you must know the truth, dearest boy, I have been forced to countenance gambling here in this house, as you have guessed, though I have always done my best to keep our more unpleasant guests away when you are visiting."

Wendover's smile was grim. "Gamblers seldom make a living at their business unless they practice certain illegal tricks. Shall I ask Dartleigh how to fiddle the cards so that I can make myself useful until the mortgage is paid off?"

Lady Jess dabbed at her lips with a tiny kerchief.

"Sir Egbert has been kind to me, Anthony. Without his help I could not have afforded to live in this house at all. Why, he would no more dream of trifling with the decks than you would. He simply happens to be skilled at such games. After all, Dartleigh is a gentleman."

"By birth, perhaps. Tell me, my devoted mama, if Dartleigh is so fond of you, why do you not marry?"

"Your father's memory—"

Wendover's laugh was ironic. "My father's property is more like. If you remarry, you lose your

151

rights. I have no doubt that the shady solicitor Dartleigh found for you has already exploited them to the limit."

Lady Jess squeezed out a genuine tear. "What was I to do, left a widow and with my dear son gone off to war all those years? When Dartleigh found a way to bring me in an income, of course I was grateful. True, I do not always like the crowds who come here, but I cannot afford to offend them."

Wendover pushed aside his scarcely touched plate of food.

"Suppose I promise you—and Dartleigh as well, if you can get him to the altar—a reasonable income if you will set your sights lower and consent to live within my limited means."

"I've no intention of living in damp poverty in the dower house, and that you may count upon! I'm still young. I deserve to have the pretty clothes and the parties I expected when I gave in to your papa's pleas and agreed to marry him."

Wendover sent her a look down the table that made her draw her shawl close around her shoulders. As if he saw me in my petticoat, she thought indignantly.

"You and the dower house are both a bit mildewed around the edges, Lady Jess, as you might notice if you ever really looked into your mirror. It is somehow sad to see a woman of your age still playing at the games of youth. Do you never long for the children you might have had?"

"Never! I've seen too many figures ruined by childbearing." When he said nothing, but continued to look at her as if he knew everything about her, Jessamin Botts cried out, "I don't blame Lady Trent for refusing you, Wendover. You would have buried her in the country and set her to produce a child every year, I suppose, and all for what?"

The faintest smile touched his finely engraved

lips. She wished again that he were less handsome so that she could hate him as she ought.

"You are invariably right, my clever mama," he said. "Since you have left me almost nothing of my inheritance, our children would have come into a sad estate. I am only now realizing that you and Lady Trent are very wise women."

"Anthony, listen to me. You're a handsome boy; you can win her back if you try. They say she had forty thousand from Trent. With that much we can pay off the mortgage and have enough over to establish a suitable separate residence for Dartleigh and me."

"I do not expect to have any further dealings with Lady Trent. Now, if you will excuse me, I must go about the business of discovering what you have left me of the family holdings."

At the door he turned, an erect and soldierly figure despite the stick he still used, and sent a final searing glance over the woman who had caught his father during his first grief after his wife died and married him before he knew what was happening, the woman whose tempers and demands and cruelty had driven him into an early senility, and finally death.

"You remind me of the moth that hatches in the cupboard and destroys all it finds there in the dark. Lady Jess, I am sending for Wibberly to assume control of this household. He should finish his work at the manor soon, and can leave when the new man I have hired arrives."

"But you can't do that! Dartleigh will never permit—our guests will not—oh, you do not understand!"

"I understand only too well. As soon as Wibberly arrives, we will have a thorough housecleaning."

Lady Jess stared at his departing back. He would not dare—or would he?

She heaved herself to her feet and went away to her desk to dash off a note to Dartleigh. Within half an hour a note came back promising that he would be with her by evening, if his gout improved, or if not, tomorrow.

"I shall simply have to make my own plans," she decided, casting his note into the fire angrily. "I should have known better than to depend on any man."

CHAPTER 12

The princess found herself suffering from uncharacteristic nervous flutters during the three days that must elapse before they were to dine with Keniston's mother. As she reclined on her French chaise waiting for her maid to dress her for dinner and the theater on the Saturday evening before the event was to take place, she was prey to conflicting emotions.

If whispers were to be believed, Keniston's parent would do everything in her power to prevent her precious son from marrying. All would depend upon the impression Miranda made. It was possible, of course, that the dragon-mama might take to her, for the girl was nothing like the kind of society beauty Lady Keniston undoubtedly expected to meet.

The princess turned on her side restlessly. On the other hand, if Lady Keniston was clever enough to have kept her son to herself all these years, she was certain to sense the strength in Miranda and to realize that it would pose a more potent threat to her dominance than mere beauty.

There was one bit of luck in their favor. Lady Keniston seldom mingled with the *ton* in London. If the rumors about Miranda, which had all but died away, ever reached her, all was lost. Lady Keniston was famed for her stand on morality.

It troubled the princess to turn poor Miranda over to an impossible mama-in-law, but she saw no other choice as matters stood. Once the girl was safely engaged to the most upright nobleman in the kingdom, no one would dare whisper about her unfortunate stay at Wendover's country place.

Wilson entered and the princess sat up, reflecting that it was just as well that Miranda had chosen not to accompany them tonight. The less the girl was seen, the less occasion for gossip. She had managed to keep Sir Henry ignorant of the extent of the rumors, for he was unpredictable in matters pertaining to his daughter and might well fly into a rage and ruin everything.

Really, it was enough to spoil one's pleasure in the evening ahead. But after Wilson finished arraying her in a new rose-colored gown and clasped her pink pearls around her throat, the princess felt more cheerful. It was not in her nature to worry unnecessarily. After all, Keniston and his mama were out of reach of vicious tongues until Monday night when, with luck, the engagement would be settled.

If Miranda behaved as charmingly as she could, and if Lady Keniston took to her, all might be well. *Of course* all would be well, the princess promised herself, smiling at her handsome image in the mirror.

However, the evening got off to an unhappy start. The Keniston town house proved to be a square, forbidding structure that gave the appearance of being uninhabited when Patrick brought their carriage to a halt in the brick-paved turnaround.

A butler with the air of a pallbearer took their wraps. At the door of the drawing room they were met by a pretty, dark-haired woman with a full figure who introduced herself nervously as Mrs. Pelham.

"Please do come in. Lady Keniston was prostrated by the journey to London. I begged her to stay abed, but she is so brave, she will never give in to her pain. I helped her to dress. Oh, do sit down. No, not there by the fire—that is Lady Keniston's particular place. My cousin Keniston has gone to escort his mama down. I am sure they will not be long delayed. Will you take some refreshment while you wait?"

Sir Henry made introductions with practiced aplomb despite Mrs. Pelham's constant distracted glances toward the door. When it was Miranda's turn to be presented, she was startled at what she saw in the dark eyes that flicked over her and away quickly.

She hates me! she thought. And she is not so fluttery as she pretends to be. She must want Keniston for herself.

They had all subsided into an uneasy silence before Keniston came in slowly with his mother on his arm.

Expecting to see a tottering invalid, Miranda learned in one revealing glance that while Lady Keniston might suffer from some nervous ailment, it had not affected her tall, lean body nor aged her sharp features beyond what was normal for her years. There was only the slightest touch of gray in her abundant dark hair. She was a commanding presence as she crossed the room leaning on her son's arm, though she gave them all a martyr's smile.

Keniston led her to the low sofa close to the fire. Her guests were invited up one by one to meet the lady, though not until her son and Cora Pelham assured themselves that she was neither too hot nor too cold, that her special pillow was in its proper place at her back, and that she lacked nothing they could fetch for her.

When it was her turn, Miranda made a proper curtsy and was startled anew at meeting a cold, searching stare from Lady Keniston's deep-set gray eyes, although the lady's lips maintained a long-suffering smile and her words of welcome were all that was suitable.

"Come and sit on this little stool beside me, Miss Trafford. You are so tiny you will be comfortable there. I must own that I expected someone more impressive after my son told me that you are a paragon of wit and charm, but I'm sure you have many other talents to make up for being so slight. Do tell me about yourself, Miss Trafford."

Thus challenged, Miranda could not think what to say.

"I fear I am only an ordinary young woman, Lady Keniston."

"My son says you have managed your papa's estate almost as well as a gentleman might, but of course we must allow for his partiality toward you."

Miranda, recovered a little, matched false smile with false smile. "I think we must," she agreed complacently. Let her swallow that bit and digest it!

"Miss Trafford, I could hardly believe my ears when my son told me that you are only now making your come-out. What was the reason for the long delay, may I ask?"

The princess had given up pretending not to listen. She sat forward and intervened before Miranda could reply.

"In her papa's absence, Miranda felt it was her duty to care for her younger brothers just as her mother would have done."

Lady Keniston's martyred smile faded. "Am I to

believe that a young girl lived alone in a house with two growing boys!"

Sir Henry's face reddened. Miranda spoke up quickly.

"My companion, Mrs. Shelburne, has been with me since I was a young girl. It was she who mothered all of us." Miranda leaned toward her hostess and looked straight into her eyes. "I am sure *you* will understand, for Lord Keniston has told me that it was you who kept his estates flourishing until he came of age."

"But *I* had been married. There is a difference."

She fell back as if overcome. Cora Pelham hurried to her side and offered her a glass of hartshorn she must keep ready. Lady Keniston sipped and was seen to pull herself together with an obvious effort.

"Forgive me, but I am a little tired from the journey. Cora, ask Henderson why dinner is late. Our guests have been kept waiting too long. Miss Trafford, will you hand me my basket of needlework? I cannot bear to be idle."

Miranda obeyed silently. Lady Keniston drove her needle in and out of a length of coarse cloth she said was meant as an apron for one of the females in her shelter for Unfortunates with a remorseless regularity that formed a counterpoint to the personal questions she put to Miranda.

How old was she? Almost twenty-four? At that age she herself had already been married six years. Did she play the harp or the pianoforte, or paint watercolors? No? What a shame that she had not acquired any of the gentler feminine arts.

"Have you ever been engaged to marry, Miss Trafford?"

"No, I have not."

"How very odd, for you are not really plain, in spite of being past your first youth."

Sir Henry, goaded beyond endurance, finally spoke up.

"I have refused more offers for my daughter than I care to number!"

Lady Keniston threw him a sweetly understanding smile.

"With an heiress, that is to be expected. I sympathize, for my son has had so many females dangling after him that I cannot begin to remember their names. Ah, Henderson! Dinner is fifteen minutes late. Tomorrow I hope you will explain why. Now, let us go in."

Lord Keniston hurried to help his mother to her feet while Mrs. Pelham folded away her needlework reverently. Miranda noticed that Lady Keniston sat erect easily as her son bent to lift her to her feet. If she really suffered from back pain, she would have found it hard to straighten her spine, Miranda reasoned, wincing herself as she rose from her low stool, for the effects of her fall still lingered.

Once seated in a thronelike chair and attended by a special footman, Lady Keniston ate the choicest of the food that was offered and drank the wine her son urged on her as being good for an invalid, meanwhile complaining that she suffered from a lack of appetite and deploring the lack of morals in England that had led her to found a home for Unfortunates.

"The females we take in are not all from the servant class, I assure you. Many are the daughters of small landowners. We make sure they are thoroughly chastened before we send them out into the world again to take some humble position as seamstress or laundress in a house where there are no young gentlemen to corrupt."

Miranda felt herself flushing. She put down her fork.

"I trust the gentlemen are chastened as well? After all, your Unfortunates didn't fall into trouble by themselves!"

Lady Keniston's smile turned sweeter. "It is a woman's duty to protect her virtue, Miss Trafford. One can hardly blame a young gentleman for taking advantage of one whose morals are feeble. Do you not agree?"

Miranda was about to make a hot reply when Keniston interrupted with a warm look in her direction. "Miss Trafford is too kind and generous to condemn anyone, Mama."

The princess rushed to steer the conversation into safer waters with a comment about the excesses of some members of the court in Russia. Unable to do more than toy with her dinner after that, Miranda was limp with relief when Lady Keniston finally gave the signal for the ladies to retire. Keniston dutifully escorted his mother back to her chair by the fire before returning to the dining room to share the port with Sir Henry. Before he left her, Lady Keniston clasped one hand around his wrist and cast a heavy warning glance up into his face.

So I have failed her tests, Miranda thought. She could not repress a wry smile. Not that she wanted to please the dreadful woman, but it was unpleasant to be found lacking.

Lady Keniston did not miss her expression. "Something amuses you, Miss Trafford? Thank you, Cora, I am perfectly comfortable now. You may hand me my work. Now, do tell us all the secret that makes you smile, Miss Trafford."

"I . . . was admiring your remarkable ceiling frescoes," Miranda improvised.

Lady Keniston tightened her lips. "They are a source of sorrow to me. I cannot approve of art that depicts foreign gods and goddesses in undress, but since they are the work of a master painter Keniston's grandfather brought over from Italy, I am forbidden to have them removed."

The princess described similar frescoes that adorned a palace in St. Petersburg. The conversation grew general, though it never escaped from Lady Keniston's hands. During a lull she directed Cora Pelham to go to the pianoforte. That lady obeyed, making up for a lack of talent by playing a great many lingering chords with a soulful expression on her face.

"What a shame that you are not musical, Miss Trafford," her hostess pointed out remorselessly. "Perhaps you sing. No? What *does* interest you, may I ask?"

Miranda had not resumed her seat on the low stool. From a wing chair where she sat upright and cool, she replied, "My interests are very much like yours, I believe. I care about my family, my land, and my tenants, and of course about my king and country."

She did not know that the gentlemen had come in from the dining room until Lord Keniston spoke out from behind her.

"Well said, Miss Trafford! They are my sentiments too."

Behind Keniston stood Sir Henry with a smug look upon his handsome countenance.

Keniston has asked his permission to address Miranda, the princess thought with a rush of relief. Thank God!

Lady Keniston meanwhile had sunk back against her pillows with a harsh gasp. Her eyes showed white beneath her half-lowered lids and she began to breathe loudly and rapidly as if she had been running.

Mrs. Pelham left off in the middle of a chord and hurried away to fetch spirits of ammonia. Lord Keniston knelt beside his mother and fanned her, murmuring encouraging words, while Miranda and the princess exchanged meaning glances.

Presently Lady Keniston's labored breathing subsided. She opened her eyes and looked around the room at her uncomfortable guests.

"It is my heart," she explained, "but I shall be all right in a few minutes. Cora, will you please go and fetch my brown drops? And ask Henderson to bring in more hot water, for Sir Henry and my son have not had their tea yet."

"Poor Mama," Keniston said. He patted her hand before he went across the room to take the chair next to Miranda. "She has had a heavy burden to carry all these years. It is time for her to hand over some of her duties into younger hands."

Miranda stared at him and wondered how he could be so blind. He went on to discuss the planting of the dahlia tubers she had given him while the princess carried on a complicated medical conversation with Lady Keniston.

"May I hope that you will be at home on Thursday afternoon?" Keniston inquired in a low tone under cover of their talk. "I am not free before then because I am needed to escort Mama to Dr. Grayson and to her man of business, and we are engaged for dinner with relatives both nights. Nothing less urgent would prevent me from calling sooner."

"If you wish to see me, I shall make it a point to be at home on Thursday," Miranda said, not bothering to lower her voice. If it was to be open warfare between her and Lady Keniston, she would return volley for volley.

Henderson and a footman appeared with fresh tea things and little cakes and comfits. Cora came back bearing a small brown bottle which Lady Keniston put down on the tray while she busied herself with the cups behind the large silver teapot.

Miranda accepted a cake and a second cup of tea

at her hostess's urging, praying that the evening would come to an end soon. When Keniston was occupied in talk with Sir Henry, she cast an agonized look toward the princess, who gave her an imperceptible nod in return.

"How late it grows!" the princess cried soon after. "We must not overtax you after your journey, Lady Keniston."

Their carriage was ordered, civilities exchanged, and a final reminder from Keniston to Miranda that he hoped to see her on Thursday, answered by her with a firm promise, before the Traffords were finally in their coach and free to speak.

"That is the most evil, domineering woman I have ever met in my life!" Miranda exclaimed. "I could never accept her for a mama-in-law—never!"

"You won't have to," Sir Henry placated. "Keniston tells me he owns a handsome estate about thirty miles from Malburn, which he has already begun to renovate for his mama and Mrs. Pelham."

"They'll never leave Malburn," Miranda declared, "and I'll not live there with them. That is, if Keniston intends to offer."

"Indeed he does. I knew he would," her father said comfortably. "Promised to set you up in the first style. Swore he never dreamed a female could be as dainty as a wild rose and commonsensical too."

"I don't see how I can accept him."

"Of course you can! Never mind his mama. He says she has agreed to remove whenever he marries."

"He may believe that, but I don't, Papa."

"I trust Keniston to keep his word. He's a solid fellow," Sir Henry answered easily.

How like her father to look on the bright side. Perhaps it was because Fortune had always treated him kindly. Miranda shifted uneasily in her corner of the carriage and touched her lips with her linen handkerchief.

"Papa, please ask Patrick to drive a little faster. I am feeling rather queasy. It must be something I ate."

"The fish, perhaps," said the princess. "I thought it was not quite fresh."

Dr. Purvis put it bluntly when he called on Miranda early the following morning to examine her wrist.

"It was more like something you drank, probably in your tea. Not poison: I would guess it was an emetic, and from what you tell me, you have already got rid of it. Let me give you a soothing draft for your digestion and a word of advice. Don't do it." When she neither laughed nor made any answer, he looked up from the binding of her wrist. "I hope I'm not too late. The odds at the clubs are ten to one that you'll announce your engagement to Keniston this week."

"If you're a betting man, you might put your money on Thursday."

She was half smiling, but he did not respond in kind.

"If you don't care about your own survival, there are others who do, Miss Trafford. No, don't tell me Lady Keniston wouldn't dare. The emetic was only a warning."

"Keniston has her promise that she will remove to an estate some distance from Malburn. Once she's gone, I'll hire my own servants and be mistress of my own kitchens."

Dr. Purvis sat down on one of the pair of low slipper chairs beside the hearth. His brow was creased in a frown, and his square, competent hands knotted together.

"Do you care greatly for Keniston? If you do not,

are you willing to overlook the drawbacks—indeed, the actual dangers—of such a match?"

Miranda rubbed her injured wrist pensively. "We have common interests. That should be enough to satisfy any female who is already on the shelf."

"It is far from enough for a woman like you. You deserve more than a business partner. I would offer for you myself if I thought you'd have me. I've got more heart in my two hands than Keniston will ever have in his entire body!"

Miranda's face, this morning a little wan, lighted in a smile.

"If I believed you cared for me as much as you do for your work, I would accept you."

Dr. Purvis crossed the hearth rug in a bound and knelt before her, taking her wrist in his hand. After a minute of silence, spent by Miranda in thinking how nice he was and admiring his tumbled black hair, he looked up at her ruefully.

"There is but the faintest flutter in your pulse, not enough to afford me any real hope. Tell me, Miss Trafford—does your heart beat faster when you are with Keniston?"

"I can't remember ever noticing one way or another. After all, I'm past the age for that sort of thing."

He kept his hand on her wrist unobtrusively, testing the pulse that throbbed there as he pretended to examine the healing bruise on her forearm.

"Mothers can sometimes be a curse," he remarked in a conversational tone. "Look at Wendover's. I asked him why he chose to stay at Wendover House in company with the impossible Lady Jess, and he informed me that it was the only way he could prevent her from selling the place out from under him."

"Yet Wendover owns the place." Miranda was

staring into the fire quietly, but he felt the telltale surge in her pulse. "Why does he allow her to have her way?"

The doctor replaced her hand in her lap and repacked his bag. Miranda was halfway to being in love with Wendover and either didn't realize it or believed she had no chance against Lady Trent, he concluded.

"Poor Anthony never knew how to deal with women," he confided. "Tears or the threat of a scene confound him worse than Boney's generals ever did. His mother used to fall into a swoon if he so much as cut his finger when he was a lad. Then after she died, Lady Jess moved in and made life intolerable at the manor. It was not until we were sent off to school together that he came into his own. He was at the top in his classes always and a leader on the playing fields."

"What made him choose a career in the Army?"

"Lady Jess. The old man was already half-senile, and Anthony had grown into a very handsome young man. The lady gave him no peace. At his father's request, he signed papers giving over control of the estate to Lady Jess in his absence."

Miranda sat up straight. "But did he never think to examine the books? He must have noticed something wrong."

"He left it to his legal adviser, who was old and easily fooled. He died, and Lady Jess, on Dartleigh's advice, found a sharp man who juggled the accounts well enough to pass muster over the years. It was not until Wendover came home last December that he suspected something of what had been going on."

"It seems to me that these matters belong in a court."

"I agree, but Wendover may be too chivalrous to press the case. He would loathe having to wash the family's dirty linen in public. Well, I must go. I've lingered too long already." He picked up his bag, hesitated, and put it down again. "You won't change your mind and marry me? We would deal very well together, you know."

"Yes, I believe we would. Try my pulse again. If it leaps up, you may speak to my father."

He took her outstretched hand. "Steady as a rock." Their eyes met in mutual regret and understanding. "At least one may hope to remain friends?"

"Of course. I only wish it *had* leaped."

As Dr. Purvis rode off deep in thought, he made up his mind to bend one of the cardinal rules of his profession. He would not go so far as to tell Wendover that Miranda cared for him, but a hint in that direction might change both their futures for the better.

But time was short. Thursday, Miranda had said. She had not sounded like a happy bride-to-be. Once the engagement was made public, it would be too late to save her from a disastrous match.

A physician had a duty to his patients to prevent them from falling ill, as well as to cure them afterward. The problem was how to rescue two stubborn people from their own follies.

CHAPTER 13

"Are you sure you won't come with me to call on Sally Jersey?"

The princess, a shawl of finest China silk draped at a fashionable angle through her elbows, stood beside Miranda's chair. It disturbed her to find the girl sitting listlessly at her window in midafternoon, still clad in her bedgown and robe. "It might amuse you to hear Sally's latest tidbits of gossip."

"I've been the object of them too often to enjoy them. I wish you will make my excuses. The spoiled fish has put me out of temper."

"I can't say I blame you. Meeting that dragon of a mama-in-law can't have been pleasant either. Ah well, when you are married and she has removed from Malburn, you need see her only now and then, when you choose."

"Say rather *if* I am married. It is far from settled yet. Please promise not to drop even the smallest hint to anyone about my possible engagement."

"But Keniston has already won your papa's permission!"

"I know. He has yet to win mine."

"Miranda! You can't mean you will refuse him!"

"Whatever I do, I have an idea that his mama will find a way to prevent a marriage between us.

Don't look so alarmed, dear. We can only wait and see. Go and enjoy yourself."

The princess left with a distressed backward glance. Miranda picked up a novel that lay on the windowsill, then laid it aside and resumed her pensive gazing into the cloudy sky outside. The stomach pains were gone, but she was still in the grip of a dark mood and unsure of the reason for it. She had confidently expected to experience a sense of euphoria once she made up her mind to accept Keniston. Instead she had never felt more depressed.

She made a conscious effort to look ahead in happy anticipation to becoming mistress of one of the finest estates in England. Between her and Keniston, they would make it even finer for their children and those who came after. She tried to envision the greenhouses as Keniston had described them, but her mind shied off like a nervous filly and insisted on going back to revisit the shabby old manor at Babb's Crossing.

I'm being silly, she scolded herself. She could not possibly be in love with Wendover. After all, she neither trembled nor blushed in his presence. Instead, when she was with him she felt strong and confident, as if he alerted a part of her that had never met its match before. She missed his friendly teasing and his sharp wit. Above all, she missed the way he had of expecting her to follow his mind along whatever paths of logic or fantasy he chose to take, as if he believed her his equal and challenged her.

But that is not what people mean when they talk of love, she mused. Love is all sighs and blushes and confusion. No, it's only that in Wendover I've found a friend whose nature suits my own.

Found him and was soon to lose him, she reminded herself as Benson came in. After she went to live at Malburn and Wendover married Lady

Trent, it was unlikely that they would ever meet except on the most formal terms.

"I want a breath of fresh air, Benson," she said suddenly. "You needn't come along. I am only going to walk in the little park in the square. The dark green dress will do, and the straw bonnet and green pelisse. And my purse. I heard a man crying violets, and I mean to bring home an armful for Lady Trafford."

A new footman let Miranda out of the side door a little while later. She crossed the quiet street and passed through the gates of a leafy, small jewel of a park surrounded by a tall iron fence, so intent on her own uneasy thoughts that she did not notice a scrawny man dressed in ill-fitting livery detach himself from the side of the areaway and follow her.

The little man rehearsed his instructions as he sidled through the park gates at a suitable distance behind Miranda, muttering to himself while he dodged past children at play with hoops and balls.

"I don't know nothing, I tells her."

The girl he was following stopped to pick up an errant hoop and return it to a little boy. One of the row of gossiping nannies thanked her kindly as she walked on toward a path that wound underneath an alley of beeches.

No one else was in sight now. Jervey hurried to catch up to the girl.

"Miss Trafford?" She nodded, frowning at him in surprise. "Urgent, to be read at oncet." He pushed a note into her hand.

"Who sent you? Where have you come from?"

"Wendover House, miss."

She raised her delicate eyebrows, but to his enormous relief, she went ahead and broke the seal without further questions and began to read. Just when he judged it safe to slope off, she called him back.

"I'll want a hackney cab at once. Run to the corner and engage the first one you can find. Do you know what has happened?"

"I don't know nothing, miss."

Jervey darted off, hoping to outrun her. If she expected him to escort her, he was for it. As soon as he reached the street, he shot off and away. Something queer was afoot and he wanted no dealings with Bow Street.

"Wretch!" Miranda muttered on emerging from the gates and finding the messenger missing. Though perhaps he had other similar messages to deliver if the situation was as urgent as the note indicated.

No cabs were in sight. She walked rapidly down the street, past the seller of violets and around the corner, where she finally hailed a battered vehicle, ignoring the look of mistrust on the driver's beet-red face at sight of a distraught young lady demanding to be driven to Wendover House in a hurry. No doubt he thought she was in desperate circumstances due to gambling debts.

She opened her purse and offered him a generous fare. With a shrug he helped her inside. She sank back against odorous squabs and read the message a second time.

"Lord. W. is in dyer trouble! Say nothing, only come to Wendover House before the wurst happens. If you have any gratitude after he saved you from frezing, rember it now!" It was scrawled in Lady Jessamin's untutored hand.

Only a disaster could have driven the woman to beg for help after the way they had parted at the manor. Debts? Either Lady Jess' or Wendover's could have brought the bailiffs to their door, although if that were the case, they should have applied to Lady Trent since she was soon to become a member of the family.

It must be something even more frightful than the prospect of debtors' prison.

A duel? If Wendover's hot temper had been aroused, nothing was more likely. In her mind Miranda filled in the circumstances. Perhaps someone had repeated gossip concerning her stay at the manor in Wendover's presence. In that case he would be bound to defend her honor.

But dueling was outlawed. If he survived, he would have to flee England. If he did not survive . . . Forgetting dignity, Miranda poked her head out the window and called to the driver to hurry.

Wendover House looked dark and untenanted, but Miranda did not take time to wonder why. In her haste she only hoped that nothing dreadful had already happened.

The door was opened by Lady Jessamin herself. She was clad in a purple tea gown and her orange hair strayed out in Medusa-like curls from beneath a ribboned cap.

"Come in quick," she urged, looking over Miranda's shoulder as if she expected to see someone standing behind her. "Wendover would strangle me if he found out I sent for you."

"What has happened, Lady Wendover? Is it a duel?"

Lady Jess' green eyes flickered. "Yes. Yes, that's it! On your account. It was an evil day when you stopped at the manor."

"Who is his opponent?"

"I don't remember the name. I only heard him spoken of as a deadly man with a pistol."

"What do you want me to do, Lady Wendover?" Miranda tried to speak quietly in the hope of calming the nervous woman, who alternately wrung her hands and peered around the vestibule where they stood as if she expected disaster to pounce on her at any moment. "How may I help?"

"Only talk to Wendover. Persuade him he must not ruin himself." Lady Jess appeared a little easier now. "There is no time to waste. Come with me."

She seized Miranda's hand and led her past a dimly lit salon furnished with shamelessly overblown elegance, up two flights of steps, and down a long hall that apparently joined the square main house to a separate wing at the back.

Finger to her lips, Lady Jessamin pushed open a thick oaken door a little way and stood back.

"He is in there finishing off a bottle if I know him," she whispered. "Try, if you can't persuade him to apologize, at least to fire into the air. Go in to him while I see to sending up a servant with refreshments."

Miranda advanced hesitantly into semidarkness. After her eyes adjusted to the shadows, she saw that she was in a small, square room containing only an empty bed, a low chest beside it, and a wooden chair. It must be his valet's quarters.

At her left was a window draped with heavy wool curtains which shut out the evening light. On the far side of the room she saw another door. Assuming it led to Wendover's suite, Miranda went across and knocked.

"Lord Wendover?" she called, and turned the latch.

There was no answering voice. Inside she found herself in total darkness. Feeling her way, she finally made out an object that must be a washstand. Ahead of her was the ghostly silver outline of a mirror. This could only be some sort of closet or a room for bathing, and Wendover's rooms were beyond.

She felt around for a bellpull but found none. Pushing open the door to let in such light as there was, Miranda searched for another door that might lead to Wendover's apartment. But the windowless room seemed to have only the one means of entrance.

Perplexed, Miranda returned to the larger room and pulled open the dusty curtains as far as they would go to admit the fast-fading light. Where was Lady Wendover? Beginning to be alarmed, she went toward the hall, determined to search until she found her hostess and discovered the whereabouts of Wendover.

It took her an incredulous few minutes to convince herself that the door leading into the corridor was locked.

Lady Jess must be playing a malicious trick. Miranda pounded angrily against the thick oak panels of the door until she had to stop in order to nurse her bruised hands. Next she tried kicking at the door, but even her sturdy walking shoes were powerless to make so much as a dent in the heavy oak.

She called out again and again, but there was no answering sound from the other side.

In the end she went back to the window. Now she noticed for the first time that it was protected on the outside by a grille of wrought-iron bars. Two stories down there was a slanted view of a bare patch of ground next to an areaway crowded with waste barrels. Lady Jess had lured her into a very effective prison, Miranda realized grimly.

Still, there must be servants about. After a struggle, she pushed the window open a few inches, far enough so that she could kneel and call through the opening for help. Her voice echoed thinly across the empty yard and came back at her from a tall brick wall surrounding it. A gray cat slunk away between the filled waste barrels. If anyone was there and heard her, he or she gave no sign.

Hot with frustration and fury, Miranda dragged off one shoe and used it to pound against the iron bars until they rang.

It was not until a half hour had passed that she admitted to herself that, thanks to her own folly, she was Lady Jess' prisoner. It would not have added ten minutes to have gone home and asked one of the footmen to accompany her to Wendover House, or to have sent to the stables to have her own phaeton brought around.

The floor was bare save for a square of matting. She crouched on the matting and put her shoe back on. It was time to approach her situation coolly and rationally.

First she had to find out why she was imprisoned. The answer was simple when it came.

No decent unmarried female would dream of visiting Wendover House. If it became known that she had been here, she would be ruined socially. Keniston would be shocked. His mama, Miranda thought with an irrepressible grin in spite of her situation, would no doubt consider her a candidate to join her home for Unfortunate Females.

It was entirely possible that Lady Jess planned to exhibit her later that evening when the usual raffish company had assembled. Unless, of course, she had already extorted from Miranda whatever sum of money Lady Jess had decided her reputation was worth.

Five thousand pounds? Ten? Once, such a sum might have satisfied her. Now, with Miranda's engagement to Keniston hanging in the balance, it might be twice that much.

The money was less important to Miranda than her pride. She went back to the window and shouted for help again until her voice grew hoarse. Down below the gray cat ceased fishing in the trash bins and slunk away. Not only was it galling to be caught in such a predicament, it now had begun to seem frightening, especially as the twilight deepened.

Surely someone must miss her at Halsted Square. Benson was bound to wonder when she did not return from the park. Yet all anyone knew was that she had gone walking in the Square. If only she had been less sure of herself—if only she had taken her maid with her as any proper town miss would have done!

Well, it was too late for regrets. Miranda dragged the lone wooden chair across from its place near the bed to the window and sat down to keep watch in the hope that someone—even a scullery maid disposing of potato peelings—might appear down below.

In the lonely silence, she could not help asking herself where Wendover was and what part he had played in this scheme to extort money from her.

She had been so sure he was in the house, preparing to fight a duel, that now it was hard to believe otherwise. Even harder to admit that he could have plotted this clever little trap for her.

She refused to believe it of him. No matter that he was deep in debt and driven to extremity by Lady Jess, he would never stoop to blackmail. Wine and camp followers—Wibberly had admitted as much—but not dishonesty, particularly not at the expense of a girl he had called his friend.

Twilight seeped slowly away, leaving behind cloudy darkness and a creeping chill. Miranda found a partially burnt candle on the chest beside the bed, lighted it with the tinder box, and carried it back to the windowsill. Even if no one could hear her, they might notice the light where one had not been before.

She longed to lie down on the bed and give way to tears, but she put the temptation from her sternly. To be discovered there would put her at a disadvantage when Lady Jess returned with her terms.

No sound came from the hall outside, nor was there any odor of food cooking. In Halsted Square the princess had ordered sole and a bit of baked chicken as being soothing to Miranda's upset digestion. Miranda moistened her lips and put the image of a laden tray out of her mind resolutely.

She had fallen into a semiconscious doze, resting uncomfortably against the slatted back of the wooden chair, when the door opened. Her eyes wide, she watched a monstrously tall, muscular giant of a man with a ruined nose and lumpy ears that grew like fungi from his square head enter and close the door behind him.

"Her sent me to fetch you," he said in uncouth accents.

Miranda jumped up and faced the monster, uncomfortably aware that she must resemble a puppy challenging a bear, for she did not reach to within a foot of his shoulders even on her tiptoes.

"I refuse to go anywhere with you until you tell me where you are taking me and why! Does Lord Wendover know you are here?"

The giant blinked and frowned confusedly. "Her's waiting," he said, and put out his hands toward Miranda, who backed away in alarm.

Without another word, he picked her up and carried her out to the hall and down the stairs to the lower regions, ignoring her fists beating on his back as if he did not feel them.

Expecting either to be abused by the giant or, at best, to be set down in front of a company of gamesters to be mocked and jeered at, Miranda was startled to find herself carried into a sitting room curtained all around with wine-colored velvet and furnished with several sets of chairs and tables for gaming.

A man and a woman were sitting at the table nearest the purling fire. Lady Jessamin, dressed now in elegant ruby satin, with jewels at her neck and wrists, looked almost a lady. The plump man across from her had a face as pasty and characterless as a bread pudding, Miranda thought, until she saw his round little mouth purse in annoyance and heard him say:

"Put her down, Roach. She looks quite plain enough without adding a rumpled coiffure to her dishevelment."

"I never said she was a beauty," Lady Jess reminded him tartly, "and you could hardly expect me to arrange for her to arrive in a ball gown."

The monster placed Miranda on her feet so suddenly that she had trouble keeping her balance. She breathed deeply and stared for a long, cold moment at the couple before her.

"Let me know at once how much you plan to extort from me. The less time I have to spend in your company, the more amenable I may be."

Lady Jessamin gave a falsely polite laugh. "Why, you misunderstand, Miss Trafford. We have brought you here as a favor. Everything is prepared. There is even a bride cake mixing in the kitchen for you and Wendover. Seeing how you doted on my son, I made up my mind to bring you together before it is too late."

"Lord Wendover is to marry Lady Trent, as you well know. My own engagement to Lord Keniston will be announced later this week."

Sir Egbert Dartleigh gave a knowing twist of his lips.

"Not after it becomes known that you spent a night at Wendover House, it won't. You may as well put Keniston out of your mind. You have only to be reasonable, young woman, and you have nothing to fear."

"Where is Lord Wendover? I wish to speak with him."

Lady Jess gave her a sly smile. "Who knows where his fancy has led him tonight? It hardly signifies. When he arrives home at last, the ceremony can be performed at once."

"May I ask what he expects to get out of this farce?"

"Control over your estate, my dear. Less, of course, a fair share for Dartleigh and me to pay us for our trouble in bringing you together."

"You'll never get a penny from me, none of you. That you may count upon!"

"We intend to settle the matter before the wedding," Dartleigh informed her sharply. "You will sign over thirty thousand pounds to Wendover's mama as part of your wedding settlement. His signature will be required as well. You'll remain here until the thing is done."

"You can't force us to marry. I shall tell the clergyman that I am not willing!"

Dartleigh's doughy face turned red with impatience.

"Old Bunce is a bit deaf. He is also well paid. There will be a wedding within twenty-four hours or you will leave here too ashamed to hold up your head in England."

"Wendover will never stand for this. He has no wish to marry me, nor I him. He will find a way to stop this mad proceeding, I promise you."

"He'll do as he's told or lose everything," Dartleigh promised. He consulted the clock, a gaudy French concoction upheld by a pair of cupids standing on tiptoe, in the center of the mantel. "Past eleven already. We will wait here until he returns from whatever rendezvous detains him."

Seeing that his attention was momentarily deflected, Miranda gathered up her skirt and made a dash for the door. Before she had taken three steps, she was picked up from behind like a doll and returned to her place on the hearth rug by the oxlike Roach.

Sir Egbert gave her a cross look. "Come, come: you are too old to behave like a village maiden. Sit down and have a glass of wine and a biscuit. The wedding supper will have to wait until after the nuptials."

"There will be no wedding, and I do not care to sup with you," Miranda stated defiantly.

Instantly she was lifted off her feet and placed in a chair across from Lady Jess, for all the world like a naughty child caught misbehaving. The situation was so improbable and ludicrous that Miranda could not repress a half-hysterical giggle.

"Ah, that's better." Dartleigh turned genial. "Ring for refreshments, Jessie, and let us try to behave as if we are civilized persons."

An aged serving man appeared shortly with a tray on which were a bottle of wine and a dish of biscuits.

"More candles, Beasley," Dartleigh ordered, "and fetch the cards. What shall it be tonight, Jessie? The choice is yours."

Lady Jessamin tossed down a glass of wine quickly before she said that it had as well be piquet.

"Though this is not the way I like to spend the one evening when we have no guests to entertain. Well, it will serve to pass the time. Draw your chair closer, Miss Trafford. You will learn a valuable lesson as you watch Sir Egbert's play. He is an expert."

I have no doubt of that, Miranda thought, and she did as she was told quickly lest the Samson-like Roach attend to it for his master. As she sat looking on, she ate the three biscuits Lady Jess left for her and drank a single glass of wine with the idea of fortifying herself in case a chance came to escape.

The clock chimed midnight. More wine was sent for. This time Miranda only pretended to drink, for she was busy following the movements of Dartleigh's hands and observing his manner of play.

Another half hour passed. Lady Jess yawned. In reaching for her handkerchief she knocked over her freshly refilled glass of wine.

"No more for you, my love," Dartleigh ordered. He was winning consistently as Lady Jess made foolish discards. "The mother of the groom must be at her best when the wedding takes place."

"There will never be a wedding in this house," Miranda said crisply.

Lady Jess cast her a malignant glance. The girl looked positively pretty and uncomfortably sure of herself.

"If there is no wedding, then I advise you to look about for a convenient nunnery! Be sensible, Miss Trafford. If you decide later that you and Wendover don't fancy each other, you can always remove to the dower house. *I* shan't be wanting it."

"Who knows?" Miranda responded enigmatically. "Shall we put a wager on it?"

"Certainly not. What bad taste you show to ridicule the holy state of matrimony." Lady Jess' rebuke was followed by a loud hiccup.

"Then we might try a different wager. Suppose I play your hand, Lady Wendover, against Sir Egbert. If I win, you set me free. If he wins, I accept your terms."

Dartleigh and Lady Jess exchanged glances. The atmosphere in the wine-red room turned from boredom to excitement. Miranda saw amused confidence in Dartleigh's air as he asked her with exaggerated courtesy what game she preferred to play.

182

"We may as well go on with piquet," Miranda replied innocently.

"I'll just go and find out how preparations for the wedding are progressing," Lady Jess said, and departed in a rustle of satin after having spoken a few quiet words to Roach, who sat on a chair near the door like a prison guard.

"Shall we begin?" Sir Egbert inquired in a kindly tone. "If you are in any doubt about the rules, Miss Trafford, you need only ask and I shall be happy to explain them. Would you care to bet a small sum of money on the outcome of each rubber, simply to make it more interesting?"

"I haven't brought much money with me, sir."

"I trust you, dear girl. After all, we are soon to be kin, are we not? Aha, I win the cut. Let us begin."

CHAPTER 14

Intent as they were upon their cards, neither Miranda nor Dartleigh paid heed to a slight commotion outside the closed door of the red room. They were temporarily alone, Roach having been summoned by Lady Jess, and Beasley, after he made up the fire, being ordered to cease his puttering and get out by Sir Egbert, who had just lost another game.

Dartleigh, his face feverish with wine and anger, turned in annoyance when the clock chimed one. Gad, a man had trouble concentrating what with servants scuttling in and out, a clock as noisy as an acre of crickets, and a marriage that had to be celebrated very soon lest he be ruined—not to mention the way a chit of a girl drew cards she should never have drawn, as if Fortune favored her despite his cleverest efforts to thwart that fickle goddess.

Before he could make up his mind what to discard, the door opened and Lady Jess rushed in, her face purple with excitement.

"Wendover's come at last! Dartleigh, put down that glass. I've told Roach what to do. You understand, don't you, Roach?" The monster, who had followed her in like a trained hound, nodded his square head. "Dartleigh, you have the papers?"

Dartleigh threw down his cards gladly. Before he

could rise, however, Miranda picked up his discarded hand and returned it to him.

"Just a moment, Sir Egbert. You must know the rules. If you give up play, I automatically become the winner."

"You cheated!" Sir Egbert accused furiously. He got up and tossed the score sheet into the fire. "You must have cheated, and you a girl from a good family! You should be ashamed of yourself."

The noise outside in the hall now rose to a pitch that could not be ignored. They heard a curse, then a thud, followed by a pregnant silence. The door to the red room opened abruptly. Wendover stalked in, looking as dangerous as a lion at bay.

Miranda saw with overwhelming relief that Wendover was surprised, even taken aback, to find her there. Then he was not a party to the scheme after all! She felt ashamed to have doubted him even briefly.

His expression changed from surprise to anger. He approached the table and looked down coldly at Miranda, who still held her cards in her hand.

"I remember that you are fond of cards, Miss Trafford, but I thought you had better sense than to let your love of gaming lead you into such an indiscretion as this. Put on your wrap and I will take you home at once."

Indignant at being misunderstood, Miranda threw down the offending cards—excellent ones, unfortunately—and stood up to face him with her most quelling expression.

"I came here in answer to a note from your mama warning me that you were in trouble and needed my help. As I counted you my friend, I hastened to Wendover House to do whatever I could. I was then taken to a room with a barred window and locked inside—"

185

"Mad Mortimer's room," Dartleigh murmured suavely.

"—and later carried down to this room bodily, against my will, by that ogre who stands behind you. It seems that your dear mama longs to see us married—though not until we have signed over thirty thousand pounds into her keeping."

"Nonsense! Jessamin Botts, you are a fool and so is Dartleigh. Send Roach for Miss Trafford's wrap and I will take her home and do my utmost to explain matters to Sir Henry." He halted and put out his hand toward Miranda with a frown of concern. "No real harm has come to you, has it?"

"Only to my dignity," Miranda replied with the ghost of a smile.

"Then we can waste no more time. Roach, send around for my curricle."

"Too late, Wendover," Dartleigh advised, seating himself and pouring a glass of wine with a leisurely air. "Everything is laid on: settlements between bride and groom written out in proper legal jargon, clergyman to perform the rites, even a bride cake ready to bake in the kitchen. Might as well accept the good fortune your mama has arranged for you."

Wendover's anger scorched the air between them. "If you think you can force this poor girl to marry me simply in order to line your nest with down, think again."

"As a soldier, you should recognize the truth. You are beaten and you had better retreat gracefully." Sir Egbert raised his glass in a tipsy toast. "To the bride and groom!"

Wendover lunged toward the older man. Catching Dartleigh beneath the arms of his handsome velvet coat, he lifted him out of his chair and shook him so powerfully that his teeth rattled and his wig fell to the floor. Lady Jessamin shrieked. Miranda screamed a second later, but her warning came too late.

Roach stood looking down at the unconscious form of Wendover. In one huge hand he had a small but deadly sapper. Dartleigh struggled to his feet with Lady Jess' help. Wendover moaned and stirred.

"Hit him again," Dartleigh ordered.

It was too much for Miranda. She flew at the monster, kicking and clawing. The last thing she remembered was Roach's scarred face staring down at her. He looked mildly disapproving, like Nanny in the old days when Miranda had disobeyed.

Miranda moved her head from side to side, wondering why her pillow felt so hard and lumpy. She had a headache. Her mouth was dry and she longed for her morning tea. Where was Benson?

She opened one eye painfully and then the other.

"Oh, no!" she exclaimed as she struggled to raise her head off the pillow. She would have sunk back and burst into tears had not a familiar voice from the shadows across the room said quietly:

"Better stay upright if you can. You've got a fine lump on your crown but no serious damage so far as I can tell."

Supporting herself dizzily on one elbow, Miranda did as she was told, first pushing aside the odorous comforter that was all the bedding Mad Mortimer's room offered. Across the room, the lone candle bloomed in the darkness. By its light she could make out Wendover sitting in the straight chair by the window.

She swung her feet off the side of the bed, pausing to straighten her sadly crumpled green gown. When she was sure she would not faint, she sat erect and ran her hand through her tousled hair, only to give a yelp of pain when her fingers encountered the lump Wendover had mentioned.

"Why doesn't someone come to help us? Where is Wibberly?" she demanded crossly.

"I left him at the manor. As for the servants, they've been given time off except for the young footman I had to knock out, and Roach and Beasley. Lady Jess had informed us all that she was off to visit friends in the country. I believed her, fool that I was."

Miranda explored the extent of the lump again, this time more carefully, and winced again.

"Do they mean to beat us into submission? Because if they do, I must say I'd rather marry than be bludgeoned to death."

She saw his lips curve in the familiar wry smile.

"Roach was quite gentle with you, all in all. Marriage to me would be a far worse fate. Do not consider it."

He was making it plain in a gentlemanly fashion that his affections were already engaged elsewhere. Miranda slid down off the bed with an assumption of briskness.

"Your head must be worse than mine. We both need a wash and a cold compress. Are we being allowed water?"

"In there." He inclined his head toward the closet. "After you've washed, we'll need to confer. But first, I beg you to believe that I had no part in this plot. I regret it more than I can say. I promise to get you out of here somehow and to find a way to protect your good name. What are you doing, Miss Trafford?"

With an air of triumph, Miranda, who had been down on her knees scrabbling over the rush matting, held up her purse, which she had found under her pelisse. Both had fallen from the chest.

188

"There is money in here. We can use it to bribe the ogre! Knock and see if you can call him up."

Wendover shrugged. "I doubt if he can count. Roach was knocked down so many times in his last boxing bout that something broke inside his head. Dartleigh and my kind mama gave him a home here. In return for his keep, Roach cracks heads for them whenever one of their gaming friends fails to pay his debts. If he had a soul, the poor simple fellow would sell it for them."

"How long do you think they intend to hold us here?"

"Until we do as they wish."

"That means forever," Miranda reflected gloomily as she shook out her pelisse. "I wouldn't dream of forcing any man to marry me."

"You've got it all wrong, Miss Trafford. If I were going to marry, you would suit me very well, but I would sooner live out my life in this room than take advantage of you." He was staring oddly at the purse that dangled from her wrist. "Is there anything in it besides money? A hair ornament, possibly, with a sharp end?"

"Unfortunately not. If I had known this was going to happen, I would have let my hair grow long and filled it with pins. Don't you carry a pocketknife? My brothers usually do."

"Not when I wear evening dress. My tailor would never forgive me. However, I promise after tonight never to go forth again without cloak and dagger. Tell me, how did Jessie Botts manage to lure you here?"

Miranda explained that she had been led to believe he was to take part in a duel, probably on behalf of her good name.

"It sounded plausible because of my stay at the manor and the gossip it led to. She brought me to this room on the pretext that I might be able to persuade you to apologize, or to delope."

His gaze across the few feet that separated them was keen. Miranda felt grateful for the darkness, which was illumined only faintly by the single candle now burnt down very low.

"What made Jessie imagine that you could persuade me to do anything so cowardly?"

"I supposed it was because I am to blame. If I had not insisted on staying at the manor during the storm, none of this would have happened."

"Surely you can't believe such nonsense. If you hadn't stopped there, Mrs. Shelburne would have died and so might the rest of your entourage. Not to mention your host, who was saved in spite of himself."

"That reminds me—how is your leg mending?"

"So well that I gave up my stick yesterday, unfortunately. If I'd had it with me, I might have put up a fight against Roach."

"He outweighs you by a third at the least, and you were not prepared for his assault."

He laughed. "Thank you for your loyalty, Miss Trafford. Now, please go and wash, and make haste. We've only a few hours left before dawn to make our escape."

"How are we going to manage it? Perhaps, if I have to go without food very much longer, I can squeeze through the bars," she suggested plaintively.

"Leave it to me." He handed her the candle.

Miranda, lightheaded but not without dignity, entered the closet with a swish of green skirt. A basin and ewer containing water stood on the washstand. Using as little water as she could manage with, in case their imprisonment lasted longer than the night, she washed and bent close to examine herself in the dim mirror.

Nothing of what she had been through showed in her face. She looked as rested as if she had just risen from a quiet night of sleep. That was good, in case Wendover did manage to get them free. She would say she had spent the night with Mary, she planned while she smoothed her hair and searched once again through her purse and the pocket of her gown in the forlorn hope of finding something useful—such as a picklock.

Carrying the diminishing candle aloft, she emerged and looked toward the window, where Wendover had been sitting. He was not in the chair. Instead he sprawled face downward on the matting with one arm outflung.

With a little cry, Miranda knelt at his side. He had taken the lone towel from the washroom and attempted to stem the flow of blood from an open wound at the back of his head. He must have fought with Roach after she was hit and won a second, harder blow for himself.

His face and hands felt cold to her touch. She dragged the dirty comforter off the bed and covered him with it, then went back for the pillow to protect his face from the mat. His immobility frightened her. How much blood could a man lose safely?

She was crouched beside him on the floor trying to warm his hands—surprisingly fine hands for a soldier!—between both her own when she heard footsteps outside in the hall. Scrambling to her feet, she ran across and beat on the oak panel.

"Lord Wendover is bleeding to death! We need help, please!"

No answer came from outside. Instead, with a mouselike flutter, a piece of paper appeared under the door. She snatched it up and went to read it by the light of the candle.

It was a legal document written in a precise script unlike Lady Jess' untutored scrawl. Attached to it there was a note, undoubtedly from Dartleigh, she thought as she read.

"Both of you must sign this marital agreement before your wedding rites can take place. Pen and ink will be provided whenever you signify by rapping three times."

Miranda unfolded the document and read it quickly. In legal terms, it stated that she, Miranda Trafford, agreed to settle upon Lady Jessamin Botts the sum of thirty thousand pounds, to be paid in a lump sum within forty-eight hours of her marriage. There was a space for Wendover to sign the agreement as well, "to provide for the future of my dear mother."

Infuriated, Miranda went back and knocked on the panel three times so firmly that her knuckles smarted.

"Yes?"

"Who is it out there?"

"It is your weary papa-to-be, Miss Trafford," replied Sir Egbert in a mock tender voice. "Are you two lovers prepared to sign now? You have kept me up an interminable time, you know."

"Then I would advise you to go to bed, sir. Lord Wendover is unconscious and will be unable to add his signature to mine, even supposing I meant to sign." She paused, then continued in a sweet voice, "Perhaps you should set the figure at twenty-five thousand, since you owe me five already."

"We were only playing in fun, my dear girl. I never dreamed you took our little wagers seriously, or I would have played differently. I am too much a gentleman to take advantage of a country girl."

"Do let us have another game, Sir Egbert— perhaps for the entire thirty thousand? I learned a great deal from you tonight that I would like to put into practice."

"This is not a time for frivolity, Miss Trafford.

You are in no position to play games. It is your duty to get Wendover on his feet and ready for the wedding."

"And if I do not?"

Miranda, leaning against the door, could hear Dartleigh muttering to someone outside and prayed it was not Roach with instructions to beat the bride and groom into submission.

"No one knows where you are. We shall simply keep you here until you agree to our terms. Goodnight, Miss Trafford."

"Wait! Wendover needs medical help, and we have been given nothing to eat."

"Wendover has a hard head, my dear girl. And fasting is good for the soul, as well as excellent for the complexion."

Driven beyond endurance, Miranda snapped back through the door, "Maybe Lady Jessamin ought to try it! Sir Egbert, I beg you to send someone with more water and cloth for a bandage, at the least. You can't want Wendover to die."

From the other side came the sound of retreating footsteps. Two sets, or only one? "Roach?" Miranda called tentatively. A small dry cough was her only reply. It must be Beasley, then, she decided as she went back to kneel beside Wendover. His wound had stopped bleeding, so she removed the bloody towel, and after wetting it with a little water from the ewer, she washed the wound gently.

He stirred. She saw his muscles tighten beneath his ruined coat of dark blue superfine before he rolled over and made to sit up.

"Lie still. You've had two bad blows to your head. Do you want to end up a monster like Roach?"

He reached up and removed the damp towel, which was dripping into his ear. "Did I show signs of being Roach-like when I was unconscious? If I said or did anything to hurt you, I beg you to for-give me."

He spoke quietly. Even though Miranda was re-lieved that he appeared rational, she worried, for she had noticed that his pupils were dilated, a symptom she had learned to fear when it followed a fall or a blow on the head.

"I think you should lie on the bed and keep warm while we plan a way to escape. Your hands are icy. You were worse hurt than you admitted to me."

Wendover levered himself upright with an effort, supporting himself with both hands as he stared glassily at the flickering candle, a grim smile on his lips.

"I spent ten years campaigning on the Continent without suffering any serious injuries. What a set-down, to be defeated by a Botts and a Dartleigh."

"Not defeated, just temporarily set back. Do please get into the bed and let me cover you with this foul comforter."

"Of course I will not. You must take the bed."

"I've had my turn already and am perfectly rested." Seeing the stubborn set of his face, Miran-da was inspired. "You are the only one who can get us out of here, but not until you're feeling more the thing. I depend upon you. Rest for just an hour, I beg you."

Her words appeared to satisfy him. With her help he got to his feet and went across to the bed. She brought the pillow he had lain on and covered him to his chin with the dusty comfort. Once sure that he was settled, she went back and occupied the chair by the window.

Ten minutes of sitting convinced her that the wooden chair had never been intended to accom-modate the human body in any sort of comfort. If she sat back, her feet dangled. If forward, her back suffered from the strain. The carved spindles left their marks if she depended on them for support. Besides, she was cold.

Moving with care so as not to waken Wendover, she lifted her skirt and tucked her feet up beneath her. Next she folded her green pelisse into a pillow to protect her neck from the spindles. In this uncomfortable position she managed to doze briefly, only coming awake when one foot slipped, jolting loose her pelisse-pillow and almost sending her off the chair altogether.

"Miss Trafford, this is ridiculous! Not even Roach could rest in that chair. And it is so cold that you'll never be able to follow me when the time comes to escape from this place unless you come over here and claim your share of this vile coverlet."

"Poor Mad Mortimer," Miranda temporized. "They didn't even give him the comfort of a fireplace."

"I believe he had an unfortunate habit of setting the place afire. Come along. I can't sleep myself while you sit there in such obvious discomfort. This is no time to behave like a schoolgirl."

Miranda got up stiffly. Guarding the precious candle, which was nearly gone, she placed it on the chest beside Wendover. Then she stood for a moment hesitantly before she placed her folded pelisse beside his pillow. Finally she could think of nothing more to delay the moment.

"Naturally I shall sleep in all my clothing except the pelisse," she said, half-shy and half-amused at her predicament, "but what should I do about my shoes?"

"You won't need them to defend yourself against me, I assure you. To keep them on could be uncomfortable—for both of us." She heard repressed amusement in his voice. "I give you my word that I will keep to my own side of the bed. Climb aboard quickly. Your teeth are chattering."

She did as he ordered, lying stiffly on the farthest edge of the pallet. It was heaven to be lying down after her interminable time in the hard chair, and even nicer to feel warmth seep back into her chilled body again.

"If you will move a little closer to the middle, this comforter will cover both of us," Wendover said.

She inched her way carefully to the point where she had enough of the coverlet to pull over her shoulders. Warm and drowsy, she warned herself that she must not fall deeply asleep and roll against Wendover. To keep alert she began to plan ingenious methods of escape. She had only begun to visualize them both crawling up the inside of the chimney stack when she fell into a sound sleep.

She did not know that he reached over to cover her once when she turned and dislodged the comfort. Toward morning she became aware vaguely that her back was cold. Unconsciously she slid a little farther toward him. Warmed, at peace again, she settled back to sleep.

CHAPTER 15

It was past midnight before Sir Henry and the princess returned to Halsted Square from a dinner party. Thompson, who had been told not to wait up, delegated that duty to a footman and went to bed after enjoying a quiet pint at the tavern, so the alarm was not raised until the following morning, when Benson asked to see the princess.

Trembling and nearly incoherent, the little maid reported that Miss Miranda had not come home at all the night before.

"She is certain to have stayed with the Alstons," the princess said, "but it was careless of her not to send us word."

Benson refused to be comforted. "She said she was only going to walk in the square, my lady. That was the last time I saw her, at about five o'clock yesterday."

The princess felt a stab of alarm. "Did she receive any callers during the afternoon or evening? Did a message of some sort come for her?"

"She told Thompson she was not at home to callers. I would have seen it if she got a message, for she never left her chair until she had me lay out her dark green walking gown."

"Was she feeling perfectly well?"

"Except for her wrist and the bruises, she was, my lady."

"Bruises! What do you mean?"

Benson, feeling guilty, told the princess about Miranda's tumble from her mare.

"You say she had a bruise on her forehead?" The princess began to pace nervously. "Why did she not tell us? She might have suffered brain damage and is only now feeling the effects. Have you noticed anything different about her behavior recently?"

Benson hung her head in thought. "Only that she's quieter, my lady. As if she's thinking, like, but she never says why. I know she didn't mean to stay away, because she took her purse with money to buy violets for you."

The princess dismissed the girl. A message was sent to Alston House. Word came back that Miss Trafford had not called there since Thursday. Sir Henry, finally consulted, refused to believe that she was not in her rooms until he had inspected them personally. Then he lost his temper.

"This is what comes of giving a young female her head! She will have run off with that fool poet fellow. He convinced her that he's mad with love for her!"

"Miranda is much too sensible to do anything so scatterbrained, Henry. I fear she has fallen ill. We shall have to search for her, but quietly. If Keniston should hear that she was gone from home overnight, he is certain to back off. I suggest that we consult with Patrick. He is devoted to Miranda."

In due time Patrick, informed of the trouble and barely able to conceal his fury that nothing had yet been done, promised to start a search at once.

In the square he talked to all the nannies and found one who thought she remembered seeing a young lady, rather small, in a green dress.

"She laughed when Ronald bowled a hoop across her path. There was a little footman following after

198

her dressed in a dark red livery that was too big for him. I saw him run out the gate a little later. She went running after him. Did he steal her purse? What are we coming to, when a decent young lady can't walk in her own park without being robbed? Who is the young lady?"

"She lives just across the street."

"Ah, yes, the heiress they say is to marry Lord Keniston. May the good Lord help her to survive longer than some other ladies he admired."

Patrick gave her such a strange stare that she gulped and put her hand over her mouth as he turned and strode away.

"Looked as if he was ready to strangle me," she told one of her cronies afterward, "but I only spoke my mind. My older sister was in service at Malburn until she died last year, and I know all about that family."

"Did Lord Keniston murder the other ladies?" a younger nanny asked in awe.

"Not him. His mama. They don't call it murder if the gentry do it." A thought struck her. "It wouldn't surprise me if his mama hasn't done away with that poor missing girl already."

Some time earlier in the morning of that day, in the silence of predawn, Miranda wakened from a deep sleep and became aware that things were not as they should be. As she pushed aside the heavy comforter, it all came back to her.

She sat bolt upright and discovered that she was alone in the bed.

"Awake?" Wendover's voice cut through the darkness as he emerged from behind the heavy curtains bearing the lighted stub of candle. He looked surprisingly cheerful in spite of a blackening eye and dark clots of blood in his lion-colored hair. "I was about to rouse you."

"With a cup of hot tea, I presume."

He smiled down at her. "A small sip of water unless you insist on using all of our small reserve to wash. But no matter. I've got plans for our escape."

Miranda slid to the floor in a hurry, unaware that she looked her best with her hair in a tumbled halo around her face and the folds of her stiff walking dress molded to the shape of her slight figure. She pushed her feet into her shoes, smoothed hair and gown with an impatient stab at grooming, and went over to stand beside him at the window, where he had parted the curtains to let in the fading starlight.

"I believe I can wriggle through the bars this morning after all," she said. "I've never felt so thin. How far is it to the ground?"

"Too far. Have you a head for heights?"

With his blue gaze on her she nodded, though in truth she had never really enjoyed walking across narrow bridges or standing on tall cliffs. It was only when he surrounded her in the cloak of his own warm confidence that she was sure she could scale an Alp if necessary, and if he asked her to.

"I've managed to work one of the bars free. The roof above us is flat. This room was added onto the main house to contain poor Mortimer, and an attic was considered unnecessary."

"Along with a fire on the hearth," Miranda shivered. "Poor soul. If he hadn't already been mad, the cold and isolation would have driven him into melancholy." She blew on her hands. "A bit of climbing should help to warm us up. When we reach the roof, what next?"

Wendover gave a low, exultant laugh. In spite of his injuries, he was more alive and exhilarated than she had ever seen him, as if he throve on adversity.

"Our first necessity is to reach the roof. Then we

shall see. I had thought to set the curtain afire, but we might have been trapped in here. Our guard has been asleep and snoring for the last half hour." The candle flame flickered and died out. She felt his breath on her hair in the darkness. "As a knight errant, I have been sadly ineffective. Can you forgive me for getting you into this situation?"

"I got myself into it. I have a habit of rushing in where no sensible angel would go."

She felt his hand touch her cheek and heard a smile in his voice. "Thanks to the gods for sending us a few foolish angels. Now, give me your hand. Feel the width of the window ledge on the outside. They built it wider to support the bars. Here in the center is the bar I loosened. I've been through the gap already and stood on the outer sill. From there I pulled myself up to the roof by means of the gutters. If I can do it, so can you with my help."

Miranda obediently examined the gap between the bars. By now the predawn light made the bars more visible and she saw that she could pass through easily.

"It's a long way down," she observed, hiding her dismay. "What's underneath this room?"

"Mortimer's keeper lived there. At the side there's a storage shed. Both rooms are usually empty because of the cold. Will you kneel on the inner sill now? I promise to hold on to you while you slide through the bars backward."

Miranda obeyed, telling herself that she was shivering only because the morning air was so raw.

"Now take hold of the bars on each side and rise to your feet slowly. I'll hold you steady so that even if you should feel dizzy, you'll be perfectly safe. Are you afraid, my small mouse?"

"A little." She was also very much aware of his hands as he helped her up onto the sill. In her hurry to find her footing on the ledge, she put out her left

201

foot too far and gave a small squeal when she touched only air.

"Take it slowly. Move back a little. You're all right. I've got a firm grip on you."

His calm voice eased her panic. Somehow she managed to right herself and fix her hands around the two bars on each side of the bent one. Hoping the rest of the bars were fastened more securely than the one Wendover had loosed, she began to rise from her crouching position, teetering precariously as her center of balance shifted. Without Wendover's firm grip on her waist, she would have fallen, for her hands were at a lower level than her shoulders.

"All right now?" Wendover asked in a low voice.

"I hope so!"

"Then reach for the gutter, one hand at a time," he ordered.

With great care she freed her right hand. The gutter was above eye level. If she raised herself on tiptoe, she could catch a glimpse of the flat roof she must climb to, but whether she dared let go with both hands at once and swing herself up to it was another matter.

Wendover leaned out at a precarious angle to steady her. She let go with her left hand and made a grab for the rough metal of the gutter. Now she was on tiptoe, suspended by her arms, and the rooftop seemed hopelessly unattainable.

"Can you lift me up a little higher?" she whispered desperately.

He braced himself against the remaining bars, and with an effort that made him pant, he strained to raise her some few inches so that she was able to touch the roof slates, but it was not far enough, and her fingers scrabbled helplessly on their dewy surface before she dropped back onto the ledge with a jolt.

"I can't reach it," she whispered breathlessly, crouching on the sill like a large and ruffled pigeon. "Blame it on Harry the Short, an ancestor of mine. If only the wall were built of brick or stone to give me some sort of foothold—but as it is, I just can't do it."

"Rest a little, mouse. Then we'll try again."

"No, it's hopeless. If I had on breeches, I could probably get one knee over the gutter and scramble the rest of the way, but not with this skirt hampering me. You would do better to escape without me. After all, they can hardly force you to marry me if they can't find you."

"Don't talk nonsense."

Before she understood his intention, he gathered her in his arms, lifted her back through the gap, and set her on her feet. His temper was on the rise, she decided as she adjusted her disordered dress.

"It would be my pleasure to marry you, Miss Trafford, but not at the point of a sword—or the nib of a lawyer's pen. Do you think so little of me that you believe I would leave you behind to be bled dry of your fortune by a pair of leeches like Jessamin Botts and old Dartleigh?"

"Of course I don't. Although it would be much more sensible of you to escape alone and bring back help," Miranda murmured, taking care not to remove herself from his sheltering presence.

He loosed his hold a little, shaking from the onset of some powerful emotion. Miranda peered up into his face tentatively, not sure what to expect.

"My dear small mouse, you are that rarest of the female sex, a woman so eminently practical and sane that I can only apologize for the irrational ways of my own sex." He had conquered his inner laughter, but traces still lingered around his eyes and lips. "However, I refuse to leave you here alone."

"I'm safe so long as they're asleep," she argued.

"They'll be up with the dawn. They can scarcely wait to rob you of your fortune. With Roach's help they could persuade you to sign away everything before I came back to prevent them."

"Very well. I'll try the roof again."

"Good girl. This time I'll go first and boost you up. What are you doing now?"

"Fetching my pelisse and my purse."

"We're not going for a walk in the park!"

"No, but I may find a use for them. There. I'm ready. It's do or die this time."

As she stood at the window and watched Wendover work his way through the narrow opening before he rose to his feet, she thought that she had never spoken truer words. She would prefer to die with him than live without him.

For she understood that she had passed the princess's test last night. When she flung herself at Roach to prevent him from hitting Wendover a second time, she had known she might be risking her life and had done it gladly for him. Now she was about to risk it again, this time for the wrong reasons. She would have been more than happy to pay the thirty thousand pounds for the joy of becoming his wife—but not if he did not want her.

While he reconnoitered outside, Miranda had an idea. She wrapped her pelisse around her waist and tied it in such a way that it held up the folds of her skirt halfway between impropriety and decency, to free her legs for the climb. At the last minute she tucked her purse inside the folds of her pelisse at her waist.

"Ready," she whispered in response to Wendover's whisper.

This time all went well. She slid through the bars sidewise, turned and began to rise. Then she made the mistake of looking down. She swayed. Wendover made a human barrier of himself while she shivered against him for a few paralyzed seconds until her heartbeat slowed.

He helped her to stand up straight with one arm and talked away her fears. Her confidence restored, when he told her to transfer her grip to the gutter, she obeyed. Now she was standing on tiptoe again, both arms outstretched above her head.

"In a minute I'm going to toss you up onto the roof," he explained in the half whisper they had adopted for fear of waking their guard. "The sensation will be much the same as being tossed into your saddle. Will you trust me to get you there safely?"

"Of course I will. Tell me when you're ready."

She could feel his muscles tense and she bent her knees slightly to prepare for the lift. Holding on to a bar with one hand, he put his free arm around her waist and, with one powerful gesture, raised her so high that she landed on the roof in a sprawl of skirts.

"All right?" he whispered anxiously.

"Perfectly, but out of my element. Like a beached flounder." She got to her knees and peered back over the edge at him. "What can I do to help you come up?"

"Only move quietly to the wall at your back and give me plenty of room."

A moment later he was on the roof in front of her, lithe and graceful and nearly noiseless in his soft dress shoes.

The early morning light showed them to each other plainly. Wendover looked down at his filthy satin knee breeches with a cheerful shrug.

"If we're accosted by the watch, remember to say that we were set on by thieves and only escaped after a tussle. Are you ready to go on?"

"Of course. Where do we go next?"

Miranda had already scanned the deserted area-way with its laden trash bins and hoped they were not worse off than they had been in Mad Mortimer's room.

For answer he took her by the hand and led her toward the far side of the roof. Perhaps ten feet below, beneath a slight overhang, another roof slanted down to cover a small porch.

Wendover ordered her to sit down on the edge of the overhang with her legs dangling. She watched as he lowered himself over the rim, hung suspended for a long moment, then dropped the remaining distance to the porch roof below. The drop was at least four feet, and Miranda was afraid for him when she saw him stay down on one knee with his head bent after he landed.

"Have you hurt your leg?" she called down softly.

"I'll be all right." He got to his feet slowly. "I want you to turn around and drop down into my arms. Don't fear. I won't let you fall."

"I'm more worried about hurting you when I descend on you. Why can't I just drop down the way you did?"

"Because of your confounded ancestor, Harry the Short. Just do as I ask—please."

She took her time about turning around and made sure she had a firm grip on the roof edge while she waited for him to give the word, although she suffered from a wild impulse to laugh when she imagined how she must look dangling in midair like a circus acrobat awaiting her turn.

He caught her so deftly, she hardly noticed the jolt. It felt so natural, in truth so utterly blissful, to be clasped in his arms that Miranda made no effort to free herself, nor did he put her down at once. Her head was on his shoulder. She lifted her eyes and saw him looking at her with an expression very like tenderness.

He set her down on her feet, then bent his head and kissed her, and afterward smoothed her rumpled hair gently.

"Come along, mouse. We haven't time to linger."

He invited her to kneel at his side as he pointed below to a pair of wooden columns that upheld the porch roof. Both posts were twined with knotted ivy. "They're old vines and strong as ropes. I climbed them often enough when I was a boy. Can you get down alone if I go first?"

"I can try. Go ahead, and hurry! It's almost light, and I'm terrified that someone in the house will wake and hear us. I don't think I could bear to be hauled back to that room again."

The descent proved comparatively easy. Only the tall brick wall around the back of the property now loomed as insurmountable.

"There's a gate," Wendover said, hurrying her along an overgrown path toward the end of the yard. "If it's locked, I'll lift you over the wall."

The gate opened reluctantly under Wendover's hands, the hinges emitting a rusty squeal. A dog barked close by. From somewhere in the house they heard a window open. Miranda scurried through, her heart lurching uncomfortably at the thought that it might be Roach.

The gate squealed again when he closed it. They found themselves in a narrow alley. Wendover took her hand and they ran over the uneven cobbles, panting and laughing like a pair of children escaping from their nurses, until they came to a street which was lined with small shops, mostly dark and shuttered except for a greengrocer's, where a light burned.

"Slip your arm through mine," Wendover muttered. "Lean on me as if you're in distress."

"I *am* in distress. Can we slow down for just a minute until I catch my breath?"

He tempered his long stride to match hers and gazed down at her with a friendly smile. "Will you think me impertinent if I ask how you've managed to grow so plump around the middle on a diet of water?"

"Oh, that! I forgot. I wrapped my pelisse around me for the climb. Set me free until I put myself to rights. There. Do I look more respectable now?"

He struggled hopelessly to keep a sober countenance. At first chagrined, Miranda realized, as she retrieved her purse from the depths of her pelisse, how very lumpy she must have looked, and her own lips curved in a smile.

The street was deserted, but when they reached the second cross street they came upon a seedy, small man who was digging through a heap of rubbish. Behind them a dog began to bark and another one took up the cry. Wendover paused to press a coin into the beggar's hand.

"No one passed here this morning: right?"

"Right, sir. I ain't one to get a lady in trouble, sir."

They hurried on. Two blocks farther they spied a hackney cab standing at the curb, its driver nodding on the box while his swaybacked nag crunched on the contents of its feed bag. Wendover climbed onto the step and shook the driver awake.

"Bestir yourself, man! I've got to get this lady home before her family misses her."

The driver, who looked as decrepit as his horse, shook his head and mumbled through toothless gums that he was waiting for his fare.

"In there he went," he said, pointing toward the dark facade of a narrow brick house, "and tells me to wait. That were a long time ago. But he says wait, so I wait. I has to if I expects to get me money."

"I'll pay you double. We're not going far. You can

get back here easily before your fare knows you're missing."

"How far?" The old man peered down inquisitively. Miranda bent her head, grateful for her bonnet brim to hide her face.

Wendover named the street he wanted. The driver rubbed his chin and shook his head. Wendover stared at him in disgust.

"If you're an example of the people I fought Bonaparte to save, it wasn't worth my while!"

"A sojer, eh? You should've said so at the start. Hop in, Captain, and be quick about it."

The vehicle smelled abominably, but Miranda was grateful for its refuge as a man on horseback passed and a dray appeared down the street. The nag started forward so suddenly that Wendover and Miranda were thrown back against the shabby upholstery together. He apologized and steadied her before withdrawing to the far side of the seat. Miranda was startled to find herself longing to put her head on his shoulder and either weep or laugh, she wasn't sure which. She, who had always considered herself cool and unemotional!

"If you have brought along a handkerchief, Miss Trafford, I will do my best to clean the dirt off your face," he said presently.

"Oh! Am I really dirty?"

"Like a pretty ragpicker. How did you manage to get so filthy?"

"The same way you did," she retorted. "When you finish with me, you had better let me go to work on your face. Although you need a shave even more than a wash." She fell silent in dismay. "Heavens! No lady should mention such a subject, should she?"

"Only if she is a genuine lady and the gentleman in question needs a shave. Your instincts are generally right."

She raised quizzical, bright eyes to his as he scrubbed at her chin with the damp handkerchief.

"I am not accustomed to such flattery from you, sir. Something warns me that you are preparing me for the worst. Where, exactly, are you taking me?"

"To the lodgings of a friend of mine. He can be counted on to keep quiet."

"It's hardly the hour for a female to call on a gentleman at his lodgings. If I can find Patrick at the stables, he'll help me slip into the house at Halsted Square. Or I might stay in the cab while I send in a message to Mary at Alston House. If she'll have me, I can say I spent the night with her."

"Out of the question. A servant would be bound to see you at either place. I have a better plan. You're to go down to the manor in my friend's chaise, after first writing a note to your parents to say you've been called to Babb's Crossing by Mrs. Shelburne, who has taken a turn for the worse."

"They will wonder why they didn't get my note last night."

"I'll send it by a fellow I know who can lie convincingly for money. He will deliver it around noon today with abject apologies for having had a pint too many and forgotten it last night."

"How clever of you to think of it," Miranda agreed. "No wonder you play such an excellent game of chess. I only hope I can play my role of Pawn without being captured."

"Hardly a Pawn. A Queen, I would have said." By this time she was applying the handkerchief to Wendover's face and she noticed that his eyes were surprisingly warm. "Ah, here we are. Bettinger lives on the first floor, fortunately. Take my arm and stop shaking. You've nothing to fear now."

* * *

Half an hour later, Miranda was seated in Mr. Bettinger's salon behind a tea tray while his valet dealt with Wendover in an inner room.

"You've been very kind," Miranda assured the tall, polite young officer as she poured his tea and handed it to him. "I hope we haven't left your larder bare. I've never been so hungry."

"I'm not surprised," he said, blushing. "I mean, after what you went through last night. Gad, to think of a lady climbing out a window onto a rooftop!"

"I couldn't have done it without Lord Wendover. Isn't he ready yet? We really should be on our way as soon as possible."

The young man flushed even more deeply, a guilty expression on his ruddy countenance.

"Er . . . He has gone already, Miss Trafford."

"Gone? But he was to take me down to Babb's Crossing this morning!"

"He has given me that task." He crossed his legs and uncrossed them, kicking the tea table in his embarrassment. "My pleasure, I meant to say, ma'am. I have ordered my chaise brought around. I shall ride, of course. If you are sure you have finished, I think we should make a start. Wendover wants you safe at the manor by midnight."

"Did Lord Wendover not leave any word for me?"

"Oh, yes. I had forgot. Here is his note."

Her face flushed with hurt and anger, Miranda accepted the paper. How craven of Wendover to desert her now!

"You may trust Bettinger with your life. I have arranged for the necessary message to reach Halsted Square as planned. Do not leave the manor until I send word. Keniston will keep!"

She did not trust herself to speak. Cramming the note into her purse, she indicated to Mr. Bettinger that she was ready. As she crossed the courtyard to climb into his chaise, she was too angry to care whether any of his fellow lodgers saw her. "Keniston will keep," he had written. She would never forgive him for that.

But as the day stretched out into an interminable time of jolting and general discomfort, she began to wonder what had become of Wendover. Perhaps he had gone back to confront Dartleigh. From time to time she slept uneasily, waking twice from a nightmare dream in which Wendover was being beaten insensible by Roach.

Bettinger had sent ahead to engage a private parlor at Wayland so that Miranda was able to freshen up and have a hot meal before they embarked on the final stage of their journey. Twilight came and they made good speed. Tall Bettinger rode alongside looking dangerous in a dark cloak, a drawn pistol resting on his saddle in case they encountered highwaymen.

The manor gates stood open. Somebody had repaired their hinges, and the rutted road seemed smoother than Miranda remembered it. In spite of her exhaustion, she felt as if she were arriving home.

When the chaise drew up at the door, Mudd rushed forward to hold the horses, grinning and chattering. Behind him in the lighted hall stood Wibberly.

"Miranda, my dearest girl!" Mrs. Shelburne held out her arms. Miranda ran into her embrace and let her tears flow freely at last.

CHAPTER 16

"When I think of that brazen woman daring to abduct you and have you beaten, I could do murder!" the gentle Mrs. Shelburne declared fiercely.

Mag and Mrs. Curry hovered in the background, twittering with shocked comments on the state of Miranda's clothes mingled with indignant diatribes against the evil Lady Jessamin, while Wibberly expressed his own distress quietly as he led the way to the library. Here a fire burned against the night chill, and two dozen tapers gave the room a welcoming glow.

"How does it come about that you already know what happened, Shelly?" Miranda inquired as she sank into one of the wing chairs by the hearth and flung off her bonnet thankfully.

"Wendover sent a messenger. He arrived some hours ago. You need not worry. We are all prepared to swear that you spent last night here with us at the manor. Heavens, child, your hands are filthy and you're in dire need of a comb. Mag has gone up to prepare a bath for you. Afterward you can put on one of my house robes. Poor love, you look worn out."

"Mr. Bettinger must be even more tired. I hope someone is seeing to his comfort. He's been awfully kind."

Mag, coming in with word that the bath was ready, announced with her best London air, "Mr. Bettinger has went to stay with Mr. Purvis, miss, the way Lord Wendover said as he should do. And Mr. Wibberly says he'll serve you a light supper whenever you're ready." She followed Miranda up the stairs and into her room, all eagerness to be of help.

"Oh, miss, was you truly locked up in an attic and beaten by a giant?" she asked breathlessly as she helped Miranda undress.

"Hit over the head but not beaten, Mag. I'll tell you all about it tomorrow after I've had some sleep. There: I'll be glad to see the last of this dress! It's yours, Mag, and the bonnet too, if you can ever manage to get it clean again. Go and tell Wibberly I'll be ready for my tray in half an hour. Mrs. Shelburne will help me now."

The older woman came in bearing a glass of warm spiced wine she had prepared herself for her charge. Left alone, the two women began to renew their intimacy, exchanging all the information they had not wanted to put into their letters.

Shelly listened to Miranda's story of her imprisonment and escape and, in spite of her indignation, found herself laughing.

"After Wendover caught me," Miranda went on, leaning over so that Shelly could scrub her back, "and he did it very deftly—he kissed me. I suppose he got accustomed to rescuing females during his years in the armed services. Probably he kissed them all and they all enjoyed it just as much as I did."

"I seem to remember warning you against soldiers and their wiles. Miranda, you weren't . . . that is . . . you didn't do anything unsuitable?"

"Not really, unless taking off my shoes before getting into bed was wrong. Wendover thought I

214

would rest more comfortably with them off." She paused, remembering. "It was surely the most innocent night a rake ever spent with a female."

"I have come to view Wendover in a different light lately, Miranda. If he sowed wild oats, he had his reasons. He is much changed, according to Wibberly, since his accident. Did you not notice a difference in him?"

"I thought him more serious, but I laid it to his difficulties with Lady Jessamin. But that's enough of Wendover and me. You are looking even better than I had hoped, Shelly. Do I detect a touch of the sun on your nose?"

Mrs. Shelburne smiled. "Dr. Purvis ordered me to be out-of-doors whenever the weather is fine. It was his father's notion that we begin to restore the lovely old manor gardens. Don't fear: Mudd does all the heavy work. I am allowed to put in a few seeds upon occasion, nothing more. Mr. Purvis comes over every day to direct the work."

Miranda, by now out of her bath and busy toweling her short curls dry, cocked her head toward her companion inquiringly.

"You've found a man you can love at last, Shelly?"

"I know I have," Shelly replied without a flutter, "but he is so accustomed to being a widower that he doesn't realize what has happened yet."

"I shall have to play Cupid while I am here. Shelly, you know how terribly I will miss you, but it's time you had your share of happiness."

"I'm more concerned for you at the moment. My own time will come. From all accounts, you were having a successful season before this unfortunate abduction. Lord Keniston is a match any girl would envy. Do you love him?"

"He is good and kind and has a variety of fine qualities. I like him very much, but I cannot love him. Still, I suppose I'll have to marry him if he still wants me after what has happened. He's my last chance, for if he begs off, everyone will believe I am sunk too low to be marriageable."

"Miranda, tell me the truth. It is Wendover, is it not? Young Dr. Purvis thinks as much. Why in the name of heaven didn't you marry him when Lady Jess made it so easy for you?"

"He wouldn't. In fact, he risked his life to help me escape—just to avoid having to marry me! Not even my fortune is enough to tempt him. I suppose he has gone to Lady Trent. If only I had been born tall and regal, and without a sense of humor!"

Mrs. Shelburne opened her arms and Miranda enjoyed another brief bout of tears before declaring that she was ready for her supper.

"At least I haven't lost my appetite yet, so I can't be entirely lovesick," she commented as they went down to the library, where supper was laid. "Shelly, this hall is as cold as ever. If I lived here, I would keep a small fire burning night and day, and erect a baffle to keep out the wind when the door is opened."

"Wibberly is doing his best to make it more comfortable. I have discovered that the estate is finer than it appeared when we arrived here during the storm, though it has been neglected these many years." She delayed Miranda with an arm around her waist. "Does Wendover guess how you feel about him? With your help, he could make this estate into the handsome property it was once."

"If he guesses, he takes care not to give me encouragement. Why did he not bring me down here himself instead of sending me in the care of a stranger?"

"My dear girl, Wendover's presence here with you would be the last straw! As matters stand, you may survive with your character only slightly dam-

216

aged, though Lord Keniston will have to come up to scratch to save you."

"And if not? May I come and live with you and Mr. Purvis?"

Mrs. Shelburne nodded. "But we won't think that far ahead just yet."

Miranda might have slept on through until afternoon of that Thursday if Mrs. Shelburne had not wakened her with word that Mr. Bettinger and Mr. Purvis had sent to say they would call at eleven.

Attired in one of Shelly's gowns, which she had hiked up with pins after stumbling over its hem, Miranda greeted her visitors in the library and dispensed coffee and Mrs. Curry's heavy but nourishing buns as if she were the lady of the manor instead of an interloper who would be gone forever within the next few days.

Mr. Bettinger, after he ceased trying to arrange his large feet comfortably and found his tongue, explained that he had come to assure himself that Miranda had not suffered from her imprisonment and the fatigue of the journey.

"The colonel—Lord Wendover—wants me back in London tonight unless you need me, Miss Trafford," he explained earnestly.

The vicar tut-tutted. "I wish you ladies will persuade Mr. Bettinger to remain here. I am delighted with his company. You can't know how lonely I am since my son removed to London, where I fear he may stay permanently."

Miranda flicked an amused glance toward Shelly, who gave her back a Mona Lisa smile as she handed Mr. Purvis' cup over to be refilled.

"Your son must miss his home," Shelly said to the vicar, "in spite of the opportunity to study in London. I know that *I* shall miss Babb's Crossing when I leave here next week."

Mr. Purvis spilled his coffee in his distress. "You are not yet well enough to travel! And think of the garden. We've only just begun. You cannot leave us yet!"

"Much as I dislike leaving, of course I must go. Miss Trafford needs me, and as I have told you, my only home is with her."

Miranda watched this byplay lost in admiration at the delicate way Shelly flirted. If only she had taught me a few tricks when she gave me my Latin grammar, Miranda thought.

"I am surprised that you have not married again, Mr. Purvis," she remarked. "You are still a young man, and a wife would be a great help in your parish work."

The vicar's kindly blue eyes turned first toward her and then to her companion.

"I am almost half a hundred years old, long past the time when any lady would wish to marry me."

"Nonsense." Miranda put down her cup. Nothing pleased her more than to make suitable arrangements. "If I were only a little older, perhaps near Shelly's age, I should consider myself fortunate to win such a learned gentleman for a husband. Ah, Mr. Bettinger, must you leave us? Let me go with you to the door. I have a message for you to take to Lord Wendover."

Mudd stood outside holding the young man's mount. The prospect across park and trees was green and lovely, so very different from her first impression of the manor land that Miranda hardly recognized it for the same place. Following her eyes, Mr. Bettinger said, "My father tells me this was once a noble estate, and still might be save for that cursed woman."

"How true," Miranda agreed fervently. "Accept my gratitude for your help, Mr. Bettinger, and assure Lord Wendover that I am safe and well. Tell him that I plan to return to my home at Templeton early next week."

She gave her hand to the young man and he kissed it gallantly. He had started toward his horse when Miranda detained him with a final message.

"Mr. Bettinger! Please do all you can to prevent Lord Wendover from attempting to punish Roach. He might come to worse harm."

"Not if I can help it, ma'am!"

He leaped into his saddle, all grace once he was on horseback, where he felt at home.

The vicar left soon after, striding briskly down the driveway and looking ten years younger. On his long, kindly face Miranda saw an expression of mingled doubt and happiness.

"Did he offer?" she asked Shelly as they walked back to the library together.

"Not yet, but he will." Shelly's face glowed. "I am the most fortunate woman in the world to have found him."

"Won't you mind living in this sleepy little village?"

"Not with Mr. Purvis for a companion. The rectory needs refurbishing to be comfortable, but with my income we shall manage very well. I wish I felt as hopeful about *your* future."

Mag had brought fresh coffee without being asked and the two friends settled down to talk.

"Miranda, are you sure you can be happy with Lord Keniston? From all I have heard of the man and from what little you've told me, I am convinced that you are well suited, but it will never do to marry him if your heart is set on Wendover."

"I daresay I shall get over him once he is married to Lady Trent. Other people survive such losses without going into a decline. After I marry I expect to keep too busy for regrets."

"Of course Keniston is known everywhere for his

upright character," mused Shelly as if to convince herself. "I only wonder if he may not be *too* good for you, dear?"

Miranda choked on her coffee and sank back in her chair coughing and laughing. After a few puzzled seconds, her companion smiled in sympathy.

Both women were in the garden the next morning when Patrick arrived and sought them out.

"Are you certain sure you came to no harm, Miss Miranda?" the coachman demanded fiercely. "If that Lady Wendover that's no lady did you any hurt, I'll throttle her with my own two hands, and that you may count on."

She exhibited the lump on her head, which was healing nicely. When he finally stopped shuffling and settled down, she asked for news from town.

"I went to every place I ever drove you to looking for some hint of where you'd gone, but nobody knew a thing. It wasn't till noon that a stupid fellow, half-foxed, brought your note home. Later that day Lord Wendover came himself and gave your papa the true tale. Mighty relieved we were to know you were safe, though your papa was in a rare temper, it being Wendover's mama that kidnapped you."

"I hope Papa wasn't too rude to him."

"I don't doubt he was. Some of us heard loud argumentation between Wendover and your papa, for Sir Henry suspicioned Wendover was at the root of it, him being known to be on the hunt for an heiress. I was half-afeard of a duel until your mama reminded your papa that Lord Wendover would never have rescued you if he meant to marry you."

"I hope Papa apologized."

"Things quietened down, but I doubt he did." Patrick began to shuffle again. "Leastwise, his lordship came out looking as black as thunder and rode away in a hurry. They say he's gone after

Dartleigh, but nobody's seen hide nor hair of either of them since."

Seeing how upset Miranda was, Shelly drew her down on a rustic garden bench at her side. "Have Sir Henry and his lady managed to keep the affair quiet?" she asked the old coachman.

Patrick's weathered face flushed. "It's the talk of London, what happened, thanks to that old harpy that planned the scheme. The way she told it, it was Wendover stole Miss Miranda away to marry her for her inheritance."

Too stunned to protest, Miranda sat looking dazed, but Shelly burst into indignant speech. "That woman should be imprisoned! How can anyone believe her when it is known that she presides over a gaming house—and perhaps worse!"

"Town's full of pigs, and pigs'll eat any kind of swill that's thrown to them," Patrick replied heavily. "I'd feel better inside if I could hear the truth from you, Miss Miranda."

Recovering a little of her poise, Miranda made Patrick draw up a garden chair and sent Mudd, who was digging nearby with an occasional pause to grin vacantly at the sky, off to the kitchen to fetch wine and cakes.

Patrick looked old and tired, the poor darling, she thought, noticing that his mustache drooped as if he had gone past the point of caring. She began with her walk in the park, and he listened intently. All went well until Miranda described how Roach had struck her. Patrick clenched his fists and leaped to his feet with an oath.

"I'll find that fellow and see he gets his desserts, never you fear, Miss Miranda!"

"Don't you dare approach him, Patrick. I forbid it. Roach would as soon kill you as not."

"I wasn't thinking to meet him fair and square, not at my age and him deserving of no consideration on my part." Patrick was all dignity. "I've got friends that'll help me. Trust old Patrick, Miss Miranda."

"Whatever you do will only cause more scandal, Patrick," Mrs. Shelburne said reasonably. "Stay here with us for now. Then, if nothing happens, if Lord Keniston . . . that is to say, if matters do not improve, we will need you to accompany us back to Templeton."

"It's happy I'll be to go home again," he said heavily.

He had brought a packet of letters for Miranda. When he went off to see his team, Mrs. Shelburne excused herself to take her daily rest. Miranda sat with the letters in her lap, hesitant to open them and let loose new troubles.

The garden was fragrant with the tangy scent of boxwood. The formal hedges were in need of pruning, she thought critically, but the beds Mudd had cleared out showed promise of flowering abundantly.

With a sigh, Miranda opened the letter from the princess. Her pen had sputtered in her anxious haste as she warned Miranda that she must stay in the country until the gossip ebbed or some new scandal arose.

"Sally Jersey had the audacity to laugh when I told her that Shelly had suffered a relapse and you were gone to attend her deathbed. I do my best with that story, but no one believes it.

"Wendover gave us his version of the whole sordid tale in a fair manner and offered for you, as of course he was in honor bound to do, but your father would have none of it, blaming him and his mother for all your misfortunes. If I had my way, I would have accepted the offer, at least until the scandal is forgotten, after which time you could have set him free.

"What a sorry tangle! We can do nothing more until we discover Keniston's intentions. Take care to remain *quiet* and *secluded*, so that no further talk may arise. If anyone should call at the manor, have Shelly keep to her room and preferably to her bed, to lend credence to our story. Of course I do not wish her to fall ill again, but a very slight relapse would not come amiss.

"Your papa and I will remain in town for the time being until it becomes clear whether or not Keniston still intends to make you an offer. Keep me informed as to how matters stand with you. I have had Benson pack a box with such clothing as you may want in the country and Patrick is bringing it to you, but will not send Benson down yet, for though she is loyal, servants will talk, and she would be bound to discover that Shelly is on the mend."

The next letter was a long one from her friend Mary, written with such an outpouring of affection and concern that a thicket of exclamation points stood up all over the pages.

". . . and no one who knows you can possibly believe anything but that you are innocent! But oh, Miranda—why did you not marry Lord Wendover when you had the opportunity? Had he been Sir Peter, I would have done it in a minute, no matter what the price. But in your case there is Cousin Keniston expecting to marry you. You will be good for him, but somehow I can't imagine you at Malburn, for in spite of its perfect beauty, there is a depressing atmosphere about the place.

"I have it from Mama's maid, who is the mother of your Benson, that Lady Jessamin locked you and Wendover in a room together all night! And that you had to climb out of a window to make your escape. If only such an exciting adventure had come my way! If it had been me (I?), I would have expected Sir Peter to offer for me, and the minute he did, I would have said Yes. Sir Peter calls almost every day but has said nothing yet. Nor have I had any other offers. Mama says it is good for the spirit to be humbled, but a little humility goes a long way. It is so *unfair* that gentlemen get to choose their mates, while females have to wait to be chosen!

"Let me know when you are coming back to town. I miss you dreadfully, for with you gone I have no one to laugh with ..."

Miranda smiled as she finished reading Mary's dashing script and folded the letter away. It was just as well that Mary did not depend on her for gaiety now. Her mood hovered between depression and hopelessness, although she made an effort to put a good face on when Shelly was near.

Sir Henry's letter, quite short and curt, advised her to return to Templeton with Mrs. Shelburne as soon as that lady was able to travel.

"The sooner you remove from the manor, thus cutting all connections with the infamous Wendover lot, the better for your family and your reputation. I would myself call out Dartleigh were it not for my responsibilities. I have already suffered as a result of this scandal.

"Your aunt and I have done what we can to scotch the rumors. It may be necessary, however, for you to accompany us to the States eventually if Keniston does not come up to scratch. On the other side of the water no one will have heard of this disgraceful episode and you may find a suitable husband before it is too late."

That was like Papa: appearances meant everything to him. He must be undergoing agonies, for he could not bear the least awkwardness in his social dealings, just as he fretted if a cuff did not sit exactly right and was more disturbed by young Charles' gawkiness than pleased by the boy's brilliance.

Miranda got up and walked up a gravel path toward the house, which sat, at this back elevation, several levels above the grounds and garden. At the railing that separated the highest terrace from the two lower ones, Miranda stopped and looked out over the vista in the direction of a large lake now choked with weeds. From here she could make out the original plan of the garden, which must have been handsome before the trees and shrubs were left to grow wild.

With the practical eye of a woman of property, Miranda began to calculate what work was needed. If the manor were hers, she could work wonders, for the estate was basically sound. Perhaps she could at least help by sending seeds and cuttings from Templeton. She turned and made her way to a small room at the rear of the manor known to Mag and Mrs. Curry as the Orfice, where she found Wibberly seated at a rent desk working on a column of figures.

"I'll be glad to see the new bailiff, Miss Trafford. Between milord and me, we've been trying to straighten out the accounts, but it's hard to tell what's true and what's false, for the old bailiff was a real scoundrel. We caught him just as he was about to sell off the last of the manor's flocks and relieved him of a small portion of the money he had already pocketed for himself and Lady Jessamin."

"I wondered why Lord Wendover accepted my money when we were caught in the storm. He must have been in desperate straits. Is there anything I can do to help you now?"

Wibberly turned a furrowed forehead toward her and nodded. She sat down in the straight chair he offered her and took a long look around the room.

From what she could see, such bookkeeping as had been done by the old bailiff consisted of stacks of papers piled higgledy-piggledy on a set of shelves or enfolded in ancient roll books with their edges protruding, in no sort of order at all.

"If you could tell me whether the prices asked for salt and fodder seem reasonable, I could go ahead and order," Wibberly suggested.

Miranda scrutinized the bills he handed her and shook her head.

"Far too steep. The former bailiff must have had an agreement with the sellers to add on a certain percentage for his own pockets. I suggest that you offer twenty percent less and agree to give fifteen."

Wibberly's dark eyes kindled with new respect.

"A group of tenants asks to meet with me tomorrow morning. If you would be willing to attend, your advice would be helpful."

"Of course I'll come. I owe the manor that much for sheltering me from the storm," Miranda agreed with a smile. "This must have been a prosperous estate once."

"That it was, miss. Each time milord and I came back, we found it in worse repair. He had no idea the accounts were fudged. He was told the estate produced only enough to keep Lady Jessamin. The last time we were here, I remember him saying that half of almost nothing wouldn't keep her in style, so he gave her his share and we went back to our regiment."

"I'm glad that his eyes are open at last. If you'll hand me a stack of those papers, I'll see what I can make of them. And a pen, please, Wibberly. No, I've nothing better to do. I'd prefer being busy to worrying about what is being said in London."

CHAPTER 17

Miranda rose early the next morning. Mag discovered her strolling through the kitchen garden nibbling on a frill of parsley and scolded her as shrilly as a sparrow.

"Wet all over your hem, miss, and look at them slippers, covered with dew and Lord knows what else."

Miranda smiled. "It's a warm day and they'll dry in a hurry, Mag. Can I have my breakfast on the terrace? Chocolate and fresh bread will do."

Mag took the request poorly. "Eat out there with them filthy birds dropping their messes all over, miss!"

"I won't sit under the trees," Miranda promised solemnly.

Mag left muttering that she was sure to catch her death or worse. It was Wibberly who appeared on the terrace ten minutes later carrying a pair of shabby but comfortable basket chairs and a small table, which he placed between them before returning with Miranda's breakfast tray.

"Are you sure my presence won't put a damper on your tenants' meeting, Wibberly?" she asked the valet.

"The men asked to meet you, miss. It has already come to their attention that it was thanks to you that milord survived his accident last winter, miss. They all hope milord will marry and put the manor to rights again."

"I am sure he will marry soon. You will have a new mistress who is very beautiful."

"Yes, Miss Trafford. I'm sure we all hope so," Wibberly said and departed with an enigmatic smile.

Miranda felt shy later when she entered the Orfice and took a chair, but the men asked for her comments and took her advice with goodwill. All went well until toward the end of the meeting, when one of the tenants raised a complaint about missing livestock.

"Might be wolves, not that I've seen any lately," another farmer opined.

"More like a wolf in sheep's clothes," Farmer Griggs muttered. "This wolf likes 'em young and tender. I lost a prime piglet myself."

Miranda flushed up to her curls. Wibberly stepped into the breach quickly. "There were rumors of gypsies in the neighborhood last winter and spring. Let me know what was stolen and milord will see that you are reimbursed."

Mrs. Curry bustled in with a tray of ale and buns. Miranda excused herself, intending to go to her room and write a reply to Mary's letter. She had only reached the great hall when Mag came running with portentous news.

"Mudd says as he spotted a carriage turn in our gates, nor it ain't milord's, being as it's green with gilding on it the like he never seen before, miss!"

"Can it be one of the county families coming to call?"

"It'd be the first time since the real Lady Wendover passed on! Ma says it'll be one of your Lunnon friends, for sure." Mag eyed Miranda doubtfully. "Maybe you should ought to change into a fancier gownd."

"I should at least brush my hair and wash my hands. Mag, warn your mother to expect extra guests for the midday meal."

Since Miranda's bedroom windows opened out over the gardens at the rear of the manor, she missed the arrival of the gilded coach as it swept to a halt before the door, and thus was not present to prevent Mudd from leaping out of the overgrown shrubbery in an attempt to hold the horses. Startled by the sudden emergence of the grinning apparition, the horses reared, the coachman cursed, the groom leaped down with his whip upraised, and a series of feminine screams issued from inside the carriage.

Mudd, even more frightened than the new arrivals, disappeared into the bushes with a wailing lament. Ebbets hastened to attend upon the lady, who was finally persuaded that she would not be accosted by a madman if she dared to step down and enter the manor.

Inside in the great hall, Wibberly appeared and took the lady's wrap. She looked around distastefully. With a shiver, she requested that her shawl be returned to her.

"Where is Lord Wendover?"

"He is not in residence, as I explained, my lady."

"Then I will see Miss Trafford. I know perfectly well that she is here."

"Yes, my lady. She arrived on the Tuesday to attend on her companion."

"When do you expect Lord Wendover?"

"We've had no word. It is not certain that he will come at all."

"Nonsense. He is bound to come here, sooner rather than later. Please see that my servants are cared for, and ask Miss Trafford to attend on me."

"Will you wait in the library, my lady?"

"If it is warmer there, I shall be happy to."

"Yes, my lady."

Wibberly led her to that room and went away reflecting that of the two women his master was involved with, only one was truly a lady.

Miranda had not intended to change her dress. But suppose it was Lady Jersey who was arriving in the green and gilt carriage, come to satisfy herself that the gossip was true? In the end it took longer than she expected to decide on a blue sprigged muslin she thought was suitably demure and to brush her hair into some semblance of order.

Her light slippers pattered a nervous tattoo on the oak staircase and across the great hall. Sally Jersey's watchful eyes always made her feel that a ribbon was undone or that she had said something gauche. Ah, well, she had nothing to be ashamed of. What had happened was not her fault.

"Miss Trafford?"

Miranda came to a startled halt just inside the library door. What was Lady Trent doing here?

"Come in, Miss Trafford. We have a great deal to discuss. I have come to stand by you and Wendover in this crisis."

Seldom at a loss for words, Miranda now found herself temporarily speechless. She had to remind herself that Lady Trent had every right to be here, and yet she felt angry and defensive. She did not want to be saved by Lady Trent, of all people.

Matters might be difficult but not yet at the crisis point before *you* arrived, she thought, but she pulled herself together and said with as much aplomb as she could muster, "How kind of you, Lady Trent, to come such a distance. I fear the manor is not prepared for guests. You will find the accommodations rather primitive."

Lady Annabel turned her soulful brown eyes toward Miranda reproachfully. "I am hardly a guest in this house, which will be my home soon. When does Wendover arrive?"

"He is not expected."

"I find that hard to believe. I was told by a servant at Wendover House that he left for the country yesterday not long before I came away from London."

"I have no idea of his whereabouts. Perhaps he has gone to visit friends. I have not been in communication with him since the morning of our escape."

Lady Annabel's face showed a certain gratification, but she gave a little laugh and said Wendover was very naughty not to have offered for Miss Trafford under the circumstances.

"He did offer, and was refused."

Miranda gave her guest a brilliant smile. Lady Annabel need not know that it was Sir Henry who had done the refusing.

"You must be tired, Lady Trent. Let me show you to my room, which is rather primitive but the best available. You will want to wash after your journey."

As they made their way along the corridor and across the cold great hall to the staircase, Lady Trent remarked distastefully that the manor was in a sad state of repair.

"Yes. It will require a great deal of money to make it comfortable, but Lord Wendover is determined to return it to its former state and make his home here."

Lady Trent did not reply. Instead, having seen a mouse scurry across the worn matting, she squealed and ran for the safety of the stairs.

"There are bats and spiders and other small creatures inhabiting the place too, but one grows accustomed to them," Miranda promised her cheerily.

231

"Here is my room. I'll have your maid bring hot water and fresh linen. Is there anything else you would like?"

"A little wine, perhaps, and a biscuit. I was so anxious to reach here before matters got out of control that I did not take time for breakfast." She peered down at the table beside Miranda's bed, her lovely face contorted with disgust. "What is that?"

"That? Oh, it's an infant mouse I found in a faint when I arrived here the other day. Its mother must have been caught by the cat, poor thing. I feed it tiny drops of milk and it seems to be growing stronger. Isn't it a dear?"

"It is horrid! Miss Trafford, nothing could be more idiotic than to keep one more mouse alive in a house that is already overrun with them."

"You are right, I know, but this mouse is different, I think, because he depends on me. I'll take him away in his box and put him in Mrs. Shelburne's room for the present."

Lady Annabel paused in removing her bonnet and smoothing her beautiful silvery hair.

"Ah, yes: your chaperone who has suffered a relapse. Where is she? I expected you would be at her bedside."

"She is in the garden with the vicar overseeing some new planting. Her illness was only an excuse."

"So they say in London. Now that I am here, it will not signify. After I have rested, perhaps you can point out a comfortable suite of rooms where my maid may unpack, for I expect to make an extended visit."

"Everything here is in need of repair. This is the best room in the house except for the one next door, where my companion sleeps. You won't want to turn her out, but I will be glad to find another place for myself."

Lady Trent showed her irritation. "I know Wendover, and he would never put up with such rough accommodations as this."

"His own room is only passable, no more. There is not enough staff to keep up even the central part of the building, and the two wings have been closed off for years."

Lady Trent shivered. "No wonder Wendover stayed with the Army. I believe I will rest for a little while. Tell my maid to hurry so that I may wash first, and have my footman bring up my boxes."

Miranda went away gladly, wondering whether Lady Trent expected her to say, "Yes, my lady."

In the kitchen she found Mrs. Curry poaching several pheasants with a gloomy air.

"She's come to stay, miss," the housekeeper warned, "as her footman tells us she's brought three boxes. How I'm expected to feed everyone is beyond me, miss, what with nothing up yet but some greens and a bit of sparrowgrass, and my hens not laying proper in this weather."

"I know how hard it is for you, Mrs. Curry, but it will only be for another few days. Mrs. Shelburne and I will be leaving for home on Sunday or Monday."

Mrs. Curry put down her ladle and gave Miranda a scornful look.

"I never would've thought you'd desert my lord, not when he's in trouble, I wouldn't."

"I'm the source of those troubles, Mrs. Curry. Once I'm gone the scandal will die away and he can marry Lady Trent as they planned."

"It's her should go," Mrs. Curry muttered, turning to stir a pot of boiling turnips. "There's some folks belong and some doesn't. Go along now and warn Mrs. Shelburne what's happened. Tell her that if she was to ask Mr. Purvis kindly, his housekeeper might send us some of her baking to fill in, like."

"What a good idea. He may even have lettuce up by this time. Lady Trent asked for refreshments. I'd better prepare the tray, for her maid will be busy unpacking. Too bad Harris is gone back to Templeton. She might have been useful."

"Her! Too good to toast her own bread, that one. Now then, miss, here's Ebbets. You leave it to me and him. It don't look right, you in the kitchen."

Hastening out to the gardens, Miranda came upon Mrs. Shelburne sitting beside Mr. Purvis under the shade of a towering old beech tree. They were looking at each other in such a way that Miranda knew they were opening their hearts. They had not seen her, since her light slippers made no sound on the matted grass. After a moment, she turned around and went back to the terrace.

It seemed that there was no place for her anywhere. Sir Henry had made it plain that she might accompany him to America only as a last resort. From Templeton word had come that the new steward and his wife were settling in comfortably. Edgar and Charles were contented at their schools, and now even Shelly was lost to her forever.

She walked over the weed-grown flagstones toward the door that led to the library. It was her favorite room and yet she hesitated to enter, feeling herself an interloper now that its rightful mistress was in residence.

However, now was not the time to repine. Better to face up to the truth and plan ahead.

She pushed open the door and blinked in the hazy gloom of the interior. Ebbets must have laid a green log on the fire, for it was smoking sulkily. She thought of ringing for him, then changed her mind. Let it smoke. After tomorrow the house and its problems would belong to Lady Trent. Let her worry over the probable dimming of a Wendover ancestor in his gold frame over the mantel as the smoke swirled upward lazily.

Mag, entering a short while later, found Miranda sitting in the leather chair behind the desk, where Lord Wendover usually sat to read or write, and stared at her in surprise, thinking that she was asleep until Miranda lifted her head and gave Mag a blind stare.

"Like as if she never seen me before, me that maided her in Lunnon for near a week," Mag told her mother later in the kitchen.

"The pheasant is near done, miss," Mag announced in a loud voice. "Wibberly laid four places in the dining room, but Mudd says as how a new carriage just turned in at the gates. Should Ma put the soup back, she wants to know."

Miranda shook her head like one waking from a dream.

"Wait until we see who it is. Meanwhile you might warn Lady Trent that you will be serving shortly."

The new arrivals could only be Sir Henry and the princess. Miranda got up with a sigh and, going over to the hearth, gave the green log a hard poke that sent it back where it could smoke up the chimney without harm.

It irked her to be discovered in such a hopeless situation: partner in guilt missing, his kindly fiancée come to save them from utter disgrace, the manor in a shocking state of repair, and the servants, with the exception of Wibberly and Ebbets, so few and untrained as to cause her parents to believe they had arrived at the farthest reaches of civilization.

Misfortune had dogged her ever since she had left Templeton, as if to warn her not to aspire too high.

Not that I meant to, she thought, but neither had she expected to score such a resounding failure. A bleak glimpse into the future gave her a picture of herself going down the years alone, living with a genteel elderly companion in Bath and filling her days with concerts and various harmless diversions, with an evening at whist something to look forward to.

"Miranda?" It was Mrs. Shelburne's voice. She stood uncertainly in the half-opened French door and peered in through the gloom and smoke. Behind her was Mr. Purvis, his arm out protectively to guide her steps.

"Do come in, both of you. We're to dine very soon—or we were, until a strange carriage turned in at our gates. My guess is that we're about to welcome Papa. I need you both with me to help me absorb the scolding I'm about to receive."

"Not while I'm here!" Shelly declared indignantly. "Nothing that happened was your fault. I'll remind your papa that if it had not been for your nursing, I wouldn't be alive today."

Wibberly knocked and put his head in. "Lord Keniston asks if you will receive him, Miss Trafford." Wibberly's pale face was expressionless.

"Yes, of course I will. Show him in. Don't go, Shelly. You and Mr. Purvis must be presented to him."

"But I. . . ."

Shelly looked ready to swoon when Wibberly announced their newest guest. His lordship hesitated on the threshold and finally advanced, only to stumble over the fringe of a worn rug in the gloom while he peered around for Miranda like a player in a game of blindman's buff. Perceiving her slight form near the hearth at last, he hurried toward her in great agitation.

"Miss Trafford! Your mama informed me, when

I returned to London from Malburn yesterday, that your beloved companion is dying. I lost no time in coming here to be at your side in your bereavement."

As Keniston bent over Miranda's hand, she exchanged a helpless glance with Mrs. Shelburne.

"I am happy to tell you that the illness Mama spoke of was not as bad as we feared. Mrs. Shelburne has made a miraculous recovery, thanks in part to the prayers of our good vicar. Shelly, may I present Lord Keniston? And this is Mr. Purvis."

An exchange of polite civilities helped only a little to bridge over a dangerous awkwardness. Keniston moved away from Mrs. Shelburne, now and then casting fearful looks at her as if she had lately risen from the grave and might carry unpleasant tidings from another world.

He told Miranda in a depressed voice that he had taken rooms at the Happy Angler.

"I'm very much afraid that it is not as clean as it might be," he confided with an air of reproach. "I should have had my servants pack a basket, for the food is bound to be ill cooked in such a place."

"Mrs. Curry is poaching pheasants for our midday meal. They are sure to be edible," Miranda assured him. "Sit down and let me send for wine. You look tired."

Lord Keniston sank into a chair gratefully. "I was served a most unappetizing breakfast at an inn this morning and have been feeling unwell ever since. Miss Trafford, I wish to speak to you alone whenever you are free, before I return to the horrors of the Happy Angler."

"I am sorry that I can't invite you to stay here, as I am only a visitor myself, but I hope you will take your meals with us."

"I would ask you to stay, Lord Keniston," a sweet voice said from just outside the door to the terrace, "if I thought you would be comfortable here. Wendover would wish me to offer you his hospitality."

"Lady Trent! I did not know you were here." Keniston got to his feet hastily.

Lady Annabel, who had been walking on the terrace inspecting her domain, stood framed in the doorway looking like an angelic vision in a fluttering white gown. She held out both hands to Keniston.

"It was good of you to overlook the scandal and hurry to Miss Trafford's rescue, Lord Keniston. It is no wonder you are known for your goodness. I have come for Wendover's sake. Between us we shall make everything come right."

Keniston looked confused. "Scandal? Oh, you refer to that nonsense about Miss Trafford being snowbound last winter. I pay no attention to idle gossip, Lady Trent."

"Nor do I. I am speaking of the night they spent together at Wendover House."

"Miss Trafford would never do such a thing. Who says she did?"

"Lady Wendover and Sir Egbert Dartleigh, I believe."

"They are beneath contempt. The story cannot be true. I stake my honor on Miss Trafford's word. You have never set foot inside that evil place, have you, Miss Trafford?"

They were all looking at Miranda through the smoke and gloom, Shelly pale and frightened, Mr. Purvis worriedly, Lady Trent with curiosity, and Keniston with perfect faith.

"I am afraid I did go there, and was forced to spend the night. If you'll give me a chance to explain—"

The door flew open just as she spoke and two young men burst in tempestuously.

"You don't have to explain anything to these people, Miranda! Anyone here who doesn't believe you're the best, most decent person alive will have to answer to us. Oh, hello, Shelly," said young Edgar Trafford. "Charles and I have come to take Miranda home."

"Charles, Edgar! You should both be in school!"

"Not when you're in trouble. We heard it from Barker's brother—we took care of him before we left—and now we're ready to meet anyone who maligns our sister's good name."

While Edgar spoke grandly, Miranda ran to shy Charles and hugged him. He blushed but hugged her back so hard she gasped. Edgar, handsome and charming as his papa, put his arm around Miranda and kissed her lightly before he turned around and directed a frightful glare at Keniston.

"Lord Wendover, I am ready to meet you at your convenience. The choice of weapons is of course yours."

"You are mistaken. I am not Wendover. I am here on the same errand, to protect your sister's good name. From what I have heard in this room, I begin to believe that Wendover attempted to wed your sister by force. If he did, it will be my duty and my pleasure to call him out."

The door opened again, this time to admit Wibberly.

"Lord Wendover," the valet announced loudly in order to make himself heard over the hubbub. Wendover sauntered in looking very composed and dashing in well-cut riding clothes and cast an interested gaze around at the assembled company.

"Tomorrow morning will suit me admirably, Keniston," he drawled.

Lady Trent ran toward Wendover. "No, I forbid you! For my sake, Wendover, control your temper. If you kill him, you will have to leave England and I could never bear to live abroad."

"Where you wish to live is no longer my concern, madam." He turned to Edgar and Charles, who stood side by side looking belligerent. "I am past the age of dueling with lads. Suppose we schedule a mill for this afternoon if you still wish satisfaction, although I should prefer to have time to get acquainted with you first. If you are as charming as your sister, we should be friends."

"We're not taken in by fine words, sir. If you have ruined our sister, you will suffer."

"Ruined is hardly the word I would choose. She looks as pretty as ever to me. Don't you think so, Keniston?"

Miranda stood watching in helpless confusion, thinking that if extremely red cheeks were interpreted as a sign of health and good character, she should pass muster.

"Yes, Miss Trafford looks well," Keniston agreed wretchedly. He pulled himself together with an obvious effort. Miranda guessed that he was wishing he had his mama present to guide him. "But I believe you owe us all an explanation, Wendover."

"I don't owe you anything, but if an explanation will make matters easier for Miss Trafford, you shall have it. Miss Trafford and I were captured and imprisoned by my dear lady mother and Sir Egbert, with the aid of their hired thug, who was known as the Monster in his boxing days. Because we were both somewhat damaged after an encounter with the Monster, we were forced to share the bed and comforter in our small prison. As you can understand, I am in honor bound to marry Miss Trafford, and I propose to do so as soon as I can arrange it."

Keniston's lean face lengthened in horror and disbelief. Lady Trent sank into the best chair in the room, a deep armchair across the hearth from Lord

Keniston. Charles and Edgar looked at each other uncertainly and then toward Miranda for advice.

Before Miranda could speak, Mag bounced in, hot with excitement. "As Mr. Wibberly is setting more places on the table and Ebbets is stirring the pudding, I been sent by Dr. Purvis to say he wants to speak with Lord Wendover right away."

"Ask him to come in," Wendover ordered genially, stripping off his gloves. "Bring wine and tell Wibberly not to count his place settings before they hatch. I suggest that you all be seated."

Miranda started across toward the shabby sofa, but Wendover caught her by the hand and led her to the chair in front of his desk, behind which he took his own stand. Keniston sank back with a murmur of apology to Lady Trent. Shelly and the two boys occupied the sofa while Mr. Purvis hovered behind them like an anxious guardian angel.

Dr. Purvis entered at his usual trot. He took in the scene with an inward smile, although his pleasant square face expressed no more than polite surprise at sight of the odd company gathered there.

"I am just down from London with messages for some among you. Miss Trafford, Sir Henry and your mama will arrive tomorrow to take you home to Templeton. And Mrs. Shelburne, too."

"Mrs. Shelburne is not leaving here," his father said firmly. "You may as well know now that she and I plan to marry as soon as arrangements can be made, Robert."

Dr. Purvis' controlled face broke into a broad smile. "I wish you both happy! I hoped you might come down out of your cloud world long enough to notice that Mrs. Shelburne is an excellent woman, Papa. It will give me pleasure to attend you at your wedding."

"And I," Wendover put in, "intend to serve as usher if no other niche can be found for me. In return I shall expect you to officiate at my wedding to Miss Trafford."

"I refuse to marry you simply to ease your conscience, sir!" Miranda burst out hotly. "Lord Keniston has already spoken to my father, so you may consider yourself free of any obligation toward me."

"You are so wise and sensible," Lady Trent sighed. "Alas, my heart rules my head. And Wendover is already promised to me, so he is in no position to offer for anyone else."

"The terms of my offer to you were that you were to come to me three months ago. While you delayed, my offer expired. Did you not notice that I haven't called on you for some weeks?"

"I thought you were busy preparing the manor for my arrival."

"And meanwhile you were free to carry on your flirtation with Howarth? Keniston, let us hear from you. Do you intend to marry Miss Trafford or to place her in your home for Unfortunate Females?"

Lord Keniston raised a harassed face toward his host. The poor man was suffering the pangs of severe indigestion, Miranda thought sympathetically, and would need a soothing potion or be prostrated very soon.

"It is true that I asked Sir Henry's permission to address Miss Trafford, but then I had to take Mama home to Malburn and did not actually make Miss Trafford an offer. I want to do what is right, but I feel I must have a private word with Miss Trafford before we make any decision. I regret, I deeply regret what has happened. If I had known—"

A wild scream from Lady Trent cut off his halting speech. They all turned to see Mudd crossing the room in his rough work clothes and muddy boots. A skinned rabbit hung from one of his large hands and a pheasant from the other, the bird's wrung neck hanging limply over his bloody wrist. His wooden face split in an adoring grin, he held out his offerings toward the cowering Lady Annabel.

". . . for the pretty . . ." he struggled to say. Lady Trent, her eyes wide with horror as a drop of blood stained her white flounce, shrieked again and again. Mudd turned and ran, a great confusion in his muddled brain.

Lady Annabel fell into a strong fit of hysterics, crying out that she would not stay a moment longer in this dreadful house, which was overrun with madmen, mice and bats.

Dr. Purvis and Shelly converged upon her, the doctor to offer spirits of ammonia and Shelly to fan her, but nothing they did had any effect. Presently Dr. Purvis gave her a sharp slap. She only shrieked louder while Charles and Edgar watched in fascinated horror. Mr. Purvis knelt at the lady's side and began to pray softly, and Keniston sat in his chair as one paralyzed.

Wendover looked across the scarred mahogany of his desk at Miranda with raised eyebrows.

"Mice, perhaps, and even a madman, but—bats?"

"There are generally bats to be found in old houses," Miranda asserted, blushing slightly.

"In the attics, I imagine," he agreed blandly. "No doubt ours are infested with them."

She did not answer, but he was satisfied to see a suppressed smile nibble at the corners of her lips.

CHAPTER 18

In the end it was Mrs. Curry who put a stop to the hysterics. She marched in and applied a cold, wet towel to Lady Trent's forehead.

"How dare you!" Lady Annabel cried. "Take that filthy rag off me this minute. See what you have done to my gown! Wendover, order my carriage brought around. I would rather stay in the meanest inn than in such a degraded place as this."

"As you wish," Wendover agreed. "Shall I send for your carriage at the same time, Keniston?"

That gentleman now rose, looking pale and unhappy, and went toward Miranda. "I must have a word with you alone, Miss Trafford, before I leave."

Miranda held out her hand to him.

"It's no use. I am grateful that you came all this way to offer your help, Lord Keniston. You have done everything that is honorable and I now release you from any obligation you may feel toward me."

"But I do not wish to be released."

"Remember your mother, my lord. She would be devastated if you were to marry a woman of my reputation."

"I don't care what she thinks! I'll marry you if I choose!"

"Bravo, Keniston," Wendover remarked softly. "I

didn't dream you had it in you, but you're too late, you know. Miss Trafford is behaving with suitable reluctance for one in her position, but we all realize that she has no choice but to marry me."

Lady Trent, looking beautiful in spite of her swimming eyes, came across to Wendover and stood before him in an attitude of penitence.

"Forgive me for the way I have behaved. I have been deeply hurt, my dear. I cannot believe that you wish me to go, after all we have been to each other."

"To be frank, Lady Trent, all that ended when you failed to come to me after I was injured."

"But it was snowing. I might have been injured myself."

"You could have made the journey the next week or the week after, when the roads were clear."

"It would not have been proper for me to stay here. I have more regard for my good name than Miss Trafford."

"Then perhaps you had better not linger any longer than is necessary to repack your boxes. You would not want it known that you are on friendly terms with either Miss Trafford or me."

Lady Annabel's perfectly shaped mouth tightened. "Indeed I would not, now that I see you as you really are. Both of you! I have never known two persons better fitted to live in such a pigsty!"

She turned and tried to sweep out of the room. Unfortunately, the vicar got in her way in his efforts to go ahead and open the door for her.

"Kindly move aside, whoever you are," she said as she surged past him, leaving the vicar trembling and humiliated.

"I shall follow her to make sure she leaves none of her belongings behind," Mrs. Shelburne announced crisply. "And to expedite her departure.

Lord Keniston, come with me. You will need a glass of wine before you go."

When the door closed behind them, Dr. Purvis put his bag aside and settled himself in the chair Lady Trent had vacated, grinning widely.

"Well, Anthony, I've come to report, as I agreed to do. I called at Wendover House and treated Dartleigh for his wounds."

"Oh no!" Miranda cast a stricken look at Wendover. "Not a duel?"

"Dartleigh wouldn't put up his fists. I had no choice but to give him the sort of caning Charles and Edgar get at school when they misbehave." Both boys were watching Wendover with the beginning of hero worship in their eyes. "What of Roach, Rob?"

"I think we can help him at the hospital where I took him, although you were anything but gentle when you used his own sapper on him. Dr. Grayson believes that if we can relieve the pressure on his brain caused by those knockdowns in the ring, we may change him into a gentle giant. If that happens, we can use him to help care for our intractable patients."

"And my dear mother?"

Dr. Purvis rubbed his jaw with a crooked smile.

"Clawed me like a tigress until I got her calmed. Bettinger arrived on schedule with the coach you hired and promised to ride with them all the way to Dover and see them aboard the first vessel bound for the Continent. By the way, Anthony, how will they live over there?"

"Decently, though not in the style to which they were accustomed. They'll have the same ten percent of the income from my estate that they've been giving me, while I shall enjoy the ninety percent that should have been mine these past ten years."

"How could you let them hoodwink you, Anthony? Did you never examine the books?"

"Of course I did, and saw only fudged accounts. They paid my steward and their solicitor generous sums to make up false accounts. It didn't occur to me to doubt those men. I've been rather naive, I will admit."

"I agree," Dr. Purvis said lazily. "However, I begin to see signs of increasing maturity. All it needed was a broken leg to set your mind to work again. That and the arrival of Miss Trafford on your doorstep." He rose and picked up his bag. "I wish I could stay to sample the poached pheasant, but I've got a child with quinsy and old Mr. Gumble with a growth to be removed. After that I am expected to attend the accouchement of Farmer Griggs' best mare. Wish me luck, Miss Trafford, and remember that if Anthony doesn't suit you, I'm still available."

"Too late, Rob," Wendover called after his friend before the door closed behind him. "The business is already settled."

"It is far from settled," Miranda declared. "I don't want or need your pity. I shall simply go back to Templeton, and in a short while some new scandal will arise and I'll be forgotten. Charles, I expect you and Edgar to escort me home."

"You won't live it down that easily," Wendover argued.

"She will or we'll bash some heads," Edgar said with a show of truculence.

Charles, the quiet, thoughtful one, gave his sister a long look. "That is, unless you want to marry him, Miranda. It wouldn't surprise me if he's just the right person for you."

"Well said, young Charles!" Wendover drummed on the desk impatiently. "Sir," he said to Mr. Purvis, whose lips were moving though no sound came forth, "will you be so kind as to stop praying and remove these young men to the garden or some such place while Miss Trafford and I resolve our difficulties between us? Perhaps they can help carry out Lady Trent's luggage for her."

Miranda began to edge toward the door as soon as the vicar and her brothers had departed through the French door to pay a visit to the gardens. Wendover cut her off with a quick feint and seized her hands in his.

"This is no time to be shy, Miranda. After all, we're hardly strangers. In view of our approaching nuptials, an embrace would not be improper."

"They are not approaching—nuptials, I mean. How often do I have to remind you that I do not need your sympathy! If I should find that I can't live down the scandal at Templeton, I shall go out to the States. Perhaps I shall take to drink, like that disreputable uncle of yours you told me about."

"It wasn't sympathy I offered. It was my love." She raised incredulous eyes and caught him smiling down at her. "How can you doubt me after having spent a night in my arms?"

"I did no such thing! In the same bed, of necessity, but not—"

"While you slept I took the opportunity I had hoped for ever since you left me alone here. Though I must admit that to kiss the top of your head while you slept was not completely satisfactory." He slipped his arm around her waist. "I hope we can do better than that. If you will cooperate . . . ?"

The fight was gone out of Miranda. She had just begun to cooperate when the door was flung wide. Lady Trent stood on the threshold staring in at them.

"Oh, you are disgusting!" she cried and whirled away in a flurry of muslin and satin ribbons.

"Tiresome creature," Wendover remarked as he

endeavored to recapture Miranda. "Don't hang back, my love. I can't endure simpering females."

A knock at the door heralded Wibberly with word that Mrs. Curry could not hold the pheasants back any longer. One glance at his master's baleful face made him bow out hurriedly.

"Take those birds and go to the devil, Wibberly!"

As he hastened back to the kitchen with word that matters in the library were proceeding as well as could be expected, Wibberly reflected that even if the birds were tough, no one would notice.

Meanwhile Wendover, thwarted and frowning, directed a searching look toward Miranda. "Are you sure, after all, that you are willing to give up the grandeur of Malburn to live in this pigsty with me? It was never my intention to force you into a marriage you may not desire."

"I *was* looking forward to becoming mistress of the finest greenhouses in England, but . . ."

"Then do not let me detain you! If you hurry you may catch Keniston before he leaves."

"But, as I was saying, I had hoped to build them on the manor grounds, unless it does not suit you? When we have restored the manor I expect it to outshine Malburn in every particular. After you become minister for Foreign Affairs, we shall probably have to entertain a great deal."

"You are the most impertinent female I have ever known! I suppose that even should I attain that pinnacle, you will still try to order me about."

"Only for your own good," she agreed with an impudent grin, "except in the case of Edgar. I shall persuade you to send him to our legation in Paris when the time is right. I have always longed to visit Paris."

"My poor country mouse! I promise to take you to Paris myself whenever it pleases you."

"Soon?"

"As soon as the wedding is over." He was laughing down at her. "Though first I shall have to rid the manor of bats."

A loud Ahem! from the terrace startled both of them. "If I may interrupt." The vicar's mild long face appeared at the door. "There never have been any bats at the manor, my boy, although I am bothered with them in my bell tower from time to time."

"Thank you, sir. Now if you will excuse me, I would like to embrace my future wife."

"Oh, of course, of course."

Blushing, Mr. Purvis closed the door. He stood on the terrace lost in thought. Presently, with a resolute air, he went in search of his own promised bride. It was amazing what new tricks the young had to teach an old dog like himself, he thought, hurrying a little in anticipation.